# The Guardians Of Newburn

## By Neal A. Johnson

Copyright © 2008 by Neal A. Johnson

ISBN  0-7414-4769-X

*Author photo by Chloe M. Johnson*

*Published by:*

PUBLISHING.COM

*1094 New DeHaven Street, Suite 100*
*West Conshohocken, PA 19428-2713*
*Info@buybooksontheweb.com*
*www.buybooksontheweb.com*
*Toll-free  (877) BUY BOOK*
*Local Phone (610) 941-9999*
*Fax  (610) 941-9959*

*Printed in the United States of America*

*Printed on Recycled Paper*

*Published  April 2008*

# *Acknowledgments*

I would like to thank first of all my wife, Melissa, who has borne for some years a great understanding of the needs of the writer in me, and somehow hasn't had me killed.

Also, I am grateful to the following, without whom the publication of this book would not have been possible: Miriam Scheulen, Brad Berhorst, Jon Robertson, Lucas Branson, Levi Maxwell, Kenneth Lein, JoEllen Hicks, Rich and Kim Becker, Doris Voss, Linn State Technical College Library, Missouri River Regional Library (Jan Crow and George Dillard), Melanie Peters, Vern and Carol Branson, Patti Dudenhoeffer, Kerry Jenkins, Amanda Grellner, Jeremy McKague, Laurie Kleffner, Judy Verhoff, Larry and Elaine Hunt, Steve and Patti Schnieders, Christa Rhoads, Joe and Margie Bunch, Chris and Denise Boeckmann, Tom Allen, Steve and Julie Siegler, Heritage Bank, Chamois, Cindy Hoffman, Ryan Robertson, Gloria Jett-Gehlert, Linn Subway, Mid America Bank, and Dennis and Terry Bryant, for their unending support and willingness to serve as sounding boards.

Special thanks are also in order for my newfound friend, Mary Veltrop, who has inspired me in many ways, and who always has a kind word.

Thank you all so much.

# *Prologue*

It was hot.

Air conditioning had yet to be something taken for granted on those sultry days of summer, when it was much too hot and humid to do much outside. Ronnie Baxter and Walter Grantz stood side by side, waiting their turn in line as their friends and neighbors passed their subsidy checks through the vertical bars of the teller windows, counting the cash that came back through for accuracy.

The pair exchanged a sour glance as Homer Willoughby lost count and had to start over. Walter thought seriously about telling Newburn's answer to the village idiot to step aside and use the table by the door, but held his tongue. It was hot, after all, and his temper was already flaring as he considered the size of the check he was waiting to cash. Picking a fight with a man who wouldn't understand it would only make it worse.

Instead, he sighed as his best friend Ronnie rolled his eyes.

The first of the month was always like this, though not always this warm; mid-summer in Missouri is a giant sauna and even a lifetime spent walking along the river did not drive it away. You simply did your best to live with it.

Finally, Homer got his count right (or as right as he could make it) and stepped aside, allowing Ronnie to move forward, where Gladys stood impatiently, as aware of the heat and tension in The Newburn Bank as the farmers were themselves.

*When I get out of here, the first thing I'm gonna do is hit Hap's for a root beer and then head for the river,* Walter thought as his friend laid his check on the counter. Even a man of 74 needed a dip once in a while.

As Ronnie made small talk with Gladys, considered a flirt by her contemporaries, though most of the quilting club

1

considered it harmless, Walter was shoved from behind. "Everyone put your hands in the air," a gruff voice demanded, muffled by the handkerchief covering his face. "Do it now or I start shootin'."

Walter couldn't believe his luck. A pair of men, the one who had spoken holding a shotgun and his silent partner scanning the bank with dark brown eyes, looked serious about their endeavor.

Ronnie turned around but raised only one hand, the other holding his cash in a death-grip. His eyes were cold and calculating and Walter returned his gaze with confidence. The two had been friends for a long time, and knew each other very well. The look Walter caught from his friend was full of fury and resolve, feelings shared by both men.

They didn't work their butts off tilling a stubborn field just to have a couple of nitwits come in and take it from them. Besides, the day felt like a preview of Hell, and like it or not, it was a perfect excuse to vent some of his frustration.

Despite his aged appearance, which at first glance made Walter appear thin and insignificant, the 74-year old was tough. Wiry and strong from years of honest labor, he was also as quick as a water moccasin.

Ronnie was a year older and little heavier but not fat by any stretch of the imagination.

The Newburn Bank was the only gig in town, and had been a major improvement to the community. Since its Grand Opening, no one had entered with mischief in mind; and if Walter had anything to do with it, this would be the last time.

In the course of time, there are events which seem insignificant when they are committed to memory. A few stay that way; others grow and are molded by future generations through the passage of recollections, from lips to ears.

Like most events, the original is often much less exhilarating than what becomes of it after years of the telling. And every once in a while, the final result is close to the truth, though almost never in every detail.

Such was the case in the town of Newburn.

*****

It is not accurate to say he knows everything, as if he were some kind of omniscient being, but his old eyes had certainly seen a lot in their day.

He had wanted to become a Guardian more than anything, since the day he heard the story about his great-grandfather standing up to robbers.

And now, as his body is reaching the end of its endurance, he stands alone in that role, save for one other.

He gets up every morning at 5:15, rain or shine, whether he wants to or not, and his life revolves around making sure the streets (and alleys and parks) are free of crime.

He doesn't always succeed, and today will challenge him in ways he'd not considered, but without him, Newburn would be just another small town by the river.

Something told him today would be bizarre, though he couldn't tell you why.

It's in the bones, he might say. What he saw last night on his routine trip through town might have something to do with the way he feels, but even he can't be certain that what his old eyes perceived actually happened.

The old man, known reverentially as Grandpa G to the folks who know him, is a follower of the old-world philosophy that holds freedom is self-responsibility. Since most of the people he knows are lacking in self-discipline, his own family included, Grandpa G stands watch.

That is not to say he goes looking for trouble. As is happens, for good or ill, trouble usually knocks on his door or hails him on the street. Try as he might, Grandpa G simply can't turn a blind eye (which is almost literal) or a deaf ear to criminal acts. He never thought of Newburn as a hotbed of illicit activity, but by the end of day he will concede the point. And if he's very lucky, he'll live to guard the streets another day.

As his great-granddad would say before revival week, "Let the madness begin."

3

# Chapter 1

He was running late for work. Again.

But this did not bother Nick Crawford in the least. Most people in a position of authority, or at least perceived authority, would have cared at least a little that they presented themselves in an orderly fashion. By default, it was their example to which the masses looked for direction.

Ah, but there was the paradox: he hated being shepherd to a bunch of diseased sheep, especially with a splitting headache and cotton-mouth.

*There*, he thought. *I just summed up my troubles.*

Actually, his troubles were widespread and too cumbersome to bear thinking about, at least not without a double-shot of something strong, say anti-freeze or formaldehyde.

Nick was a sergeant with the Newburn Police Department, which meant very little.

He was nominally in charge of three other officers, two of whom were reserve, which meant they only came in when either a) the shit hit the fan, or b) somebody really needed the day off. Of course, he knew that option A would have to be huge, considering they were technically suspended.

This Monday morning was already dipping into the 9 o'clock hour, and Nick had barely had a chance to have a sit-down because of last night's shenanigans.

That was a word his mother loved to use, as in "Don't be starting any shenanigans while I'm gone," and in his position, he could ill-afford any more of those, thank you very much.

*The beauty of hindsight*, he thought, sighing as he dropped his boxers.

Nick took his rightful place upon the throne of his castle and went about his morning business.

One of the three officers under the shadow of leadership cast by Nick was Allen Frye, a likable but vapid veteran of five months. He was the town of Newburn's latest addition, thanks to funding made possible by former President Bill Clinton, although that funding was supposed to have dried up years ago.

Though he didn't make a big deal of it, Allen carried a striking resemblance to Moe of the legendary Three Stooges, and yet he rarely got to knock any heads together. Besides, he secretly thought himself a stand-in for *Law & Order* hunk Chris Noth.

His hair had symmetry that could only have come from a Pyrex storage bowl, and every attempt to create something new was met with a cowlick that existed only to make him look goofy.

His two reservist colleagues stayed away as much as possible, as the result of the incident two months ago, so there was no help for what happened last night.

Allen was still trying to it sort out, and he wished they were here right now so he could poke some eyes and kick some ass.

*Where the hell is Super-Cop?* he wondered, double-checking his report about the "disturbance" last night.

It could really only be called a domestic incident, but Allen was damned if he knew the particular ordinance.

Stretching, checking the wall clock for the fifth time in as many minutes, Allen wished he could just pass this off to anyone, even his two nearly invisible partners. Allen was damn lucky not to be among their number.

But the Chief would be in any minute, and Allen hoped he would have the answer.

*****

High again.

Higher than they had been all week, and that was going some, since the main spectator sport enjoyed by Brian Fennigan and Todd Brown was seeing how much marijuana they could inhale over a given time, and how much food they could ingest without throwing up all over each other.

Brian looked around their messy apartment, one they had shared for about a year.

"You gonna clean up in here or what?" he asked.

"No way, man," Todd replied. "I say let it stay where it lays, man."

"Cool." Brian thought his partner was quite the poet.

A lot of pressure had befallen Brian over the course of his 22 years, most of which came from a domineering mother who believed religion was the cure for whatever ails you. Brian believed religion just got in the way, what with all its rules and regulations.

*Pot? Sure, if you want to go to hell.*

*Fornication? No way, you'll belong to Satan for sure.*

Who needed religion? This was a question he and Todd eventually came back to every night, during one of their self-proclaimed "relaxation sessions," a time in which Todd's entire apartment building appeared to be afire as they toked one joint after another.

"Should we clean up a little at least?"

"Why? Are we expecting anyone? Are you throwing a little cocktail party I don't know about?"

*Good old Todd,* Brian thought. Always able to put things in perspective for him.

What did he care that the apartment was a sty? What did he care that if the neighbors complained, he could end up moving back in with his mother? He'd deal with that if it happened.

Besides, his head still felt a little hazy from last night's session.

\*\*\*\*\*

As Nick was pulling up his boxers and preparing to mow a two-day growth from his face, Chief Brad Kocke was pulling into the station's cracked parking lot, unaware that his day was about to take a turn for the books.

He parked his rusted Subaru next to Allen's abused

Chevy Silverado and wondered for the umpteenth time if he'd ever seen a vehicle that reminded him more of a half-dead dog lying in the sun. He decided (again for the umpteenth time) that he had not, his own poor excuse for a ride never crossing his mind.

The chief was called "Old Chief Kockebreath" by some of the more clever youths in the community, though never to his face. He was given that unfortunate moniker in part because of his last name, but also because he liked to hassle the cross-dressers on Riverfront. Rumor had it he would go easy on public displays of affection if they were turned in his direction, but no one knew for sure.

Regardless of public opinion, he was a pretty good cop and a decent chief of police.

He was not appointed or elected, which meant public opinion held little sway in his daily operation, though he did have to be careful about running off the perverts too often. He had spied an alderman on a few occasions doing things he would never admit to in a campaign speech.

Still, Kocke had a good thing going, with a staff of two in this ordinarily sleepy little town, and he was accustomed to a leisurely pace as the day unfolded. Too bad it wouldn't happen today.

*****

Newburn had seen much in the way of improvement since the day Ronnie and Walter became local legends, mainly in the small strip jokingly referred to as "downtown" since there was no uptown, per se.

Visitors without much experience in rural townships often marveled that the highway could sustain life in Newburn, but the truth was the highway was a means of travel and no more.

The town prospered because of an obsession with banks, and to date, three had been constructed, which merely confused out-of-towners.

When you said "the bank," you meant The Bank of Newburn, but the other two, owned by a group out of St.

Louis, were always named in full, as if folks were afraid the FDIC would come down and take their deposits.

On his way to the station, Chief Kocke had seen the lights coming on at the bank, welcoming a new day of debits and credits, and yet he did not see it. There had been nothing of interest in the last few years with the bank, unless you counted the mortgage he'd signed a year ago. The other two, however, seemed to be cursed, he thought with a grimace.

*Can't win 'em all,* he thought, waving to Danielle Stone, who was one of the prettiest girls in town and engaged to his best officer.

Continuing his snail's pace up Route A, Brad needed only a few seconds to see the entrance to the station.

Standing outside Crank's, the store that replaced Hap's twenty-five years ago, was Grandpa G, who gave the chief a brief wave and a dry smile that did not reach his eyes.

*Odd,* the chief thought, then turned his attention to the station.

*****

He was just reaching for a cup of sludge that might have started the day as coffee when Allen accosted him.

"Chief! I have a big problem," the officer began.

Kocke held up his hand to forestall what he was sure would be a rush of babble before it could come spewing from Allen's mouth.

After adding a cup of sugar to his morning shot of caffeine, taking a sip and grimacing as though he'd slurped cat shit, Chief Kocke motioned for Allen to follow him to his office, where his day officially began at 9:37.

Perhaps office is a bit of an exaggeration; Kocke had his own little cubicle set back in the corner with a partition that mostly shielded him from anyone off the street, but it was hardly a secluded shelter.

"Take it easy, son," Kocke said, though he hardly thought of the 21-year old rookie in a familial way. "What's all the hub-bub?"

Steeling himself with a deep breath, Allen related the details of the domestic incident.

*****

Phillip Andrew Thomas was known for his quality, if self-serving writing, above-average photographs, and short temper if anyone tried to stonewall him. He was also known to be something of an enigma, because his position at the newspaper was not based on a degree in journalism or photography. He had gone to college for a year to study beer consumption and discovered an ability to write. Taking pictures came later.

People liked reading his stuff, be it about Newburn's town fathers discussing the pros and cons of septic tank over lagoon systems or his coverage of the local basketball team. The Newburn Crickets had made it all the way to the quarters this past winter, only to be knocked out by the team from the state's deaf academy.

He thought privately (and not so privately if you bought him a drink) that he should have won a Pulitzer for that story or at the very least named Assistant Editor.

"I mean, do you know how hard it was to interview a deaf coach and a bunch of mute kids?" he would say after a couple Jack & Cokes. "They call it sign language but I didn't even take Spanish in high school."

But that was something he would only say in a dark corner booth at Lionel's Lounge, known to everyone as the Double-L, with colleagues who understood where he was coming from, but more importantly, who knew it was just Phillip being Phillip. Besides, who ever took a man with three first names seriously?

This morning he was sitting in his car, across from the police station, hoping that what he'd been told at Jan's over a cup of coffee and four sausage biscuits was true.

Something weird had gone down last night, and he had a hunch that this might be a story he could use to kick Chief Kocke squarely in the testes.

For now, he was reviewing his notes, and reaching the

same bafflement that befell that dipshit stoner Allen Frye, who couldn't solve a kids' jumble, let alone a real case, in Sir Phillip's humble opinion.

He saw Chief Kockeknocker, his own variation on what he'd heard around town, pull into the lot and get out of his rundown Subaru.

*Jesus,* Phillip thought. *An old Subaru and a Silverado ready for the junk heap. These guys need a raise.*

Phillip hadn't always despised old Kockeknocker but he'd never considered him a friend.

The two had clashed on a few stories over the last few years. Phillip Andrew Thomas believed the public had a right to know that the leader of their illustrious police force had a penchant for beating up cross-dressing fruitcakes. Phillip also half-believed the rumors about Kocke, and chalked it up to aggressive behavior masking secret desires.

The journalist shuddered, trying to will away thoughts of such acts and only marginally succeeded.

The final straw had been a subtly-placed line in a budget story which suggested Kocke wouldn't need more officers if he would spend less time cruising Riverfront Park.

Phillip smiled at the reaction that little line had generated, chiefly (*pun intended,* Phillip thought with an even bigger smile), the vein that throbbed in old Kocke's forehead when he screamed at him in the Crank's Convenience store.

The memory of that day was sweet and embedded within his thinning dome.

Phillip's deadline each week was Tuesday at 5 p.m., and woe to the individual who took his time getting something to him, or who chose to avoid returning a phone call.

In such a case, Phillip did one of two things: entered the phrase, ". . . refused comment . . ." or just made something up. It was just as easy to run a correction that nobody would ever see, especially when it was buried on Page 18 amid the Hometown News section.

Newburn's fiscal year ended May 31 every year, and depending on the day of the week, Phillip would work up the story, input the numbers and then get comments.

Last year, Chief Kockebreath had nearly a week to return a call and give him comments on his budget, but chose to ignore Phillip's repeated requests.

So in his typical style, Phillip simply inserted the passage, *Chief Bradley Kocke has requested an additional officer to help police the streets, but the station's traffic journal indicates an inordinate amount of time logged by the chief patrolling Riverfront Park. It is unclear whether the city council is aware of these extra-duty hours and if so, whether that will affect the approval of Chief Kocke's budget request.*

While delivering papers to local businesses, one of the many hats Phillip detested wearing, he was confronted by Kocke at the convenience store, much to the amusement of Old Bally Crank.

"You son of a bitch! You totally made that up."

"What?" Phillip feigned a hurt voice.

"You had no right to just make up stuff about logs you never saw," Kocke said, his vein beginning to bulge. "I come in here for a paper and the first thing I see is this crap. Your day is coming, fat ass."

With that, the chief turned on his heel and stalked out of the store.

Phillip winked at Old Bally and went about his business, happy with the exchange.

*Oh well,* he thought now. *Time to go bust his balls.*

Armed with a page of hastily scribbled notes, Phillip climbed out of his car and crossed the street, unaware that he would be trapped in the most bizarre day Newburn had ever witnessed.

# Chapter 2

Newburn is a small, rural community of about 3,000 souls, plus assorted numbers spread out around the town in rings of farmland. Founded on the Missouri River in 1867, 40 minutes from St. Louis as the buzzard flies, the town began as a village, and moved up with the influx of people looking for a place to raise their kids without fear of being shot by angry bank robbers, who in those days barely got enough for their trouble, even in St. Louis.

Newburn grew (without a bank) for some time before necessity became the watchword.

It was necessary to build a bank, folks said, most of them having forgotten the fears that motivated their ancestors in the eight years since the town was founded. The reason was simple: they were tired of traveling to Waterford, which lay 12 miles to the west, to cash their checks, and local money would help build a school.

Three months after The Newburn Bank officially opened for business, on a boiling day in early June of 1886, legend had it a pair of would-be robbers were beaten nearly to death with oak walking sticks by a pair of senior citizens later called the Guardians.

The town grew, and with it the reputation that the bank was off-limits, but the town fathers had waited too long and the bid to become the county seat was lost to Waterford, which boasted two banks before The Newburn Bank was opened, and already had a school.

A second bank was built in 1941 and the times were dicey, to say the least.

The original cattle-rancher group that built The Newburn Bank was at odds with the man from St. Louis, who came to town and built *The* Bank of Newburn, which the locals took as pretentious, what with the funny-looking word at the front.

By the time Chief Kocke took his post as a Newburn police officer and began patrolling Riverfront in 1985, *The Bank of Newburn* had grown and now owned the *The West Bank of Newburn*; folks still hated that funny-looking word and it had grown to two. *The West* Bank of Newburn had been robbed four times in its history, all in the last three years, and a heist was being planned for later in the week. Apparently, the Guardians weren't as fierce as legend had it.

But today the original bank was the target of such activity.

*****

Brian Fennigan and Todd Brown climbed into the former's Toyota Tercel, losing the battle to get the doors closed all the way and wishing like hell they could just stay home and smoke.

But the situation was rough, and they had places to be and people to see, as Todd the poet had said, so they fought the doors valiantly until they appeared to be closed.

Brian knew the first hard bump they hit would loose the doors like a pair of wings. Todd had nearly fallen out the first time they rode together, and while it was just about the funniest thing Brian had ever seen, the look of pure terror on his friend's face had made him feel bad. For a few minutes anyway.

It all came down to money. Neither had any and both desperately wanted some. And with their limited understanding of economics, they dimly perceived that their now-gone supply of weed would require money to replenish.

Their supplier, Crazy Willy, told them they could smoke tea bags for all he cared, and they had tried, but both experienced only sharp pain and nausea.

Only one place to get money, they knew, and that was the bank. They had been hired on as reservists with the Newburn Police Department as part of the mayor's bid to keep the streets of Newburn clean; he already had Allen Frye's deal in motion, what were two more locals if if meant a victory at the polls?

Neither Brian nor Todd had an account, and their employment history was as checkered as an Italian tablecloth, so they were prepared to engage in some creative financing.

*****

Max Irons, runner-up in the Mr. Newburn body-building competition (there were only two competitors), couldn't believe his ears. Tiny and effeminate, compared to rest of his bulging body, his ears were clogged with hair that crept out in curly sprouts, the result of a childhood ear infection that left him a little slow.

Still, he usually heard what was said to him and understood it. This, however, was not computing.

"What are you saying, Jerry?" Max asked his boss at The Newburn Fitness & Weight Training Center.

"I said I have to let you go," Jerry replied, suddenly finding something very interesting to stare at on his desk. "I'm sorry old buddy."

*Old buddy.* The term struck Max like a fist in the throat. He and Jerry had basically founded this gym together. Jerry had provided the start-up money, some $15,000 he got from his uncle, and Max had provided the picture of perfect health, though his dull gaze left much to be desired.

Together they had built it up from a small leased space next to Crank's to a stand-alone structure in an abandoned warehouse, but which was now located on the south edge of town, two blocks from Lionel's Lounge.

"There's no good way to say it," Jerry said into the deep silence. "Clean out your gear and be out in ten minutes."

As if Max needed confirmation he was real, and this was indeed happening, Jerry Fillabag checked his watch once more, noting another two minutes had ticked off while his former "best builder" recovered from the news, or tried to. It was 9:48.

"Why?" Max managed at last.

"You know our policy," Jerry replied, feeling at a loss in this situation. On the one hand, his business would not have been nearly as successful without the efforts of Max Irons; however, the perception of "natural enhancement strategy and technique" was what set The Newburn Fitness & Weight Training Center aside from the other workout havens. "I'm sorry, Max, I really am," was all he could say now. "You're a good man, better than most. You didn't need to do it, you know."

Max had found himself unable to keep the pace, and subsequently, the image, which had been the foundation of this business.

In short, he was getting old; bodybuilders measured time akin to dogs, so he was nearly 210, and his body was starting to rebel at the constant punishment Max delivered to keep his perfect look. After hurting his calf for the fourth time in as many weeks and possibly tearing his medial meniscus this time, he decided to get a little help from behind the counter.

"Our paying customers need to feel confident that they can actually do the exercises you can do, that they can build muscle and become supermen who can juggle pianos in their off time," Jerry said, not unkindly. "And they come here because we're not a bunch of 'roiders who need a boost to work out. People are finicky about where they work out and you know it. People get wind of this, that the great Max Irons is a junkie who takes steroids to maintain his physique, well old buddy, that's when they start filling out applications to Gold's Gym or Bally's."

Max knew this was bullshit; The Newburn Fitness & Weight Training Center was the only of its kind in town, unless you counted Weight Minders, which was only frequented by women and men who wanted to be. The fact was there were no alternatives, unless you wanted to drive to Waterford, so who gave a shit if the biggest lifter in town dipped into a bottle once in a while?

But Max figured it had been more frequent than that, or he wouldn't have been caught.

He was careful not to take the drugs engineered for cows in front of others but he had lost count of the number of bottles that had gone missing.

Not Jerry. He was as much a stickler for his drugs as he was his own workout status, which earned him the bodybuilding title ahead of Max. "You owe me four for the cow-roids, old buddy," he said now as the duo neared the front door of The Newburn Fitness & Weight Training Center. "I want it this time next week."

Jerry knew he was on shaky ground, considering Max actually had a piece of the gym for tax purposes; he was just too stupid to know it.

Max shuffled out the front door, his belongings stuffed into an old duffel bag that began life beige but now had achieved a vague shade of snot.

His ear hair vibrated with the silent hitches coming from his massive chest.

*****

Nick Crawford climbed into his car, a nondescript sedan with no clear point of origin. He had bought it at a government surplus auction cheap and it served his purposes well, especially when he went on stakeouts, which was every other day.

His one true love in life was spying on people, or was until two weeks ago, when he saw something he really didn't want to. It had altered his view on things and led him to last night's trouble.

Nick checked his watch, noticed it was 10:04 and backed out of the driveway, on his way to meet destiny, which had never much cared for him.

His one holdover from his parents was the house in which he lived. A cute (Danielle's word) little two bedroom nestled beneath pecan trees in a subdivision three blocks from the highway, it had been built in 1953 and it was where Nick and his brother, Billy, were raised.

Sharing a room for so many years had driven them to distraction, another of their mother's pet sayings, and Nick believed it was a deep-seeded need for space that finally drove Billy to the state of California.

His parents were both dead and on some days, just

looking at the house with its yellow trim over a brown (ecru, Danielle had corrected) base, with a dark brown front door, he felt the pang of regret over his brother's departure.

*Don't add that to the list this morning,* he advised himself silently. *You have enough to worry about after last night.*

He continued the short drive to work, his mood a little darker.

# Chapter 3

Chief Brad Kocke, formerly a deputy sheriff who lost his bid for top job in the election of 1984, took his seat in the only swivel chair at the station. He had left the sheriff's office a couple weeks after being trounced by William "Big Jim" Cadbury, a 63-year old country boy who enjoyed the full support of the Knights of Columbus and Waterford Downs, the bar within the race track.

Brad simply couldn't stand to work with the man any more. "He couldn't pick his own mother out of a line-up," he'd been known to say of the perpetually confused lawman.

Chief Kocke went to work with the Newburn PD shortly thereafter, many said as a result of nepotism, since his uncle had served as City Clerk and basically told the board of aldermen what to do.

He'd been the Man In Charge since he was promoted nine years ago, in 1995. Days like today made him glad he lost the election.

Allen Frye looked like a kid trying to explain to his parents that he thought curfew was midnight, even though it was after midnight and he knew full well curfew was 11 o'clock.

Kocke sighed, not wanting to hear this and knowing he would anyway. He wondered where Nick was hiding; this is something he should deal with.

Allen held his tongue for the moment, waiting for the details of his report to gel in his superior's mind before asking him what the hell he should do.

At last the chief spoke.

"So you're telling me that a man went to his girlfriend's house late last night, found her with his brother, and that the first man proceeded to take after the second man with a chainsaw, is that right?"

"Yes sir."

"So what's the problem? I mean, it seems pretty cut and dried to me," Kocke said.

Allen shifted his stance, ready to run if Chief Kocke looked ready to slap him. "Well, sir, the perp was drunk and went to the wrong house, which means it wasn't his girlfriend and it wasn't his brother nailing the woman."

*Perp*, Chief Kocke thought. *Jesus, this kid needs to quit watching Law & Order.* He twirled his finger in a motion of impatience.

"So you see, sir, he attacked who he thought was his brother with a chainsaw he found in the garage, and it wasn't even the right house."

Allen did not add that technically, the couple was merely standing by the sink, with no actual sex taking place.

"How the hell do you mistake your own brother?"

"That's what I'm saying sir, I don't know."

Allen's need to vacate the station now that the Man In Charge was here narrowly beat out his need to hit a joint. It was close though.

Kocke rubbed his forehead, which had darkened a few degrees closer to maroon, caressing his bulging vein without even knowing it.

"So who is the perp, I mean the guy with the chainsaw?" he asked a moment later, deciding he was going to cruise Riverfront all night.

"I don't know. All I have is a description, but that could fit a lot of guys," Allen began, halting when he noticed the fat man standing at the makeshift counter that served the station as the reception area.

*****

The clock seemed to stand still, mocking her rumbling stomach.

Danielle Stone rubbed absently at her firm midriff, quite toned and shapely, wondering if lunch-time would ever arrive.

A loan officer at The Newburn Bank for the last three years, Danielle had to schedule an early appointment to accommodate a building contractor who couldn't come in at lunch time. Fortunately for her, she and her fiance were now she and her *ex*-fiance, so getting there early had not been an issue.

The whole day had gone wrong from there.

An on-the-run breakfast, if you could call it that, provided the basic sustenance she needed, but Danielle spent the first ten minutes of the appointment tonguing flecks of petrified oats from between her teeth. She firmly believed these "breakfast" bars included a little gravel thrown in for texture.

Every few minutes she'd feel another piece as it pierced her gums and cursed the choice yet again.

After the bank opened, Dorf Walkenhorst called to say he would be late, on account of an ill-measured dose of laxative.

"My routine has been off-kilter for a week," he had explained, "I must've ate too many of those goddam muffins Mrs. Kettler was selling for 4-H last week. Anyway, I was all backed up and I thought I was supposed to drink the whole bottle of blue stuff but I guess not and I've been up all night . . ."

Danielle could tell he was prepared to give her the play-by-play of his explosive dysentery so she thanked him for the call and hung up.

Dorf had migrated to Newburn, after having spent most of his life in Oklahoma. He applied for and was quickly rejected for a position with the Newburn Police Department; his pro-Rodney-King-beating views were not welcome. "I'd have kicked him some more," he had said *during* the interview.

But he was determined to be someone who could carry a gun and legally shoot someone with it, should the situation ever arise.

Dorf was a likeable guy if you could tolerate his bluster about how the world would be a better place with legalized cockfighting. But he was also relatively smart. Not book smart; more like Dr. Phil smart, and much of what he spouted had come from such propaganda, which he recorded faithfully every day, thanks his 9-year-old grandson's efforts with the TiVO, and watched every evening with his four cats.

But he was smart enough to keep his mouth shut, except at home, where he complained to his cats, and eventually he got a position as a security guard with The Newburn Bank.

And now he would be at least a half-hour late, if his bowels had anything to say about it.

The wall clock changed from 10:16 to 10:17 with a click and Danielle sighed, wishing she had thought to bring an extra granola bar, to hell with lacerated gums.

Still no Dorf, who must by now be trying to put his insides back inside, Danielle decided.

*****

At the time Danielle Stone was wishing for a snack and Dorf was lecturing his cats on the virtues of regularity from his perch on the john, Brian and Todd were making their way through Newburn's main drag, which consisted of two-lane Route A, which began at the south end of town and met up with a four-lane job (I-41) two miles past Jan's Country Griddle & Bait Shop. They were discussing the fine art of finance.

"So you think they'll give us a loan?"

Todd considered the question for a full minute and replied just before Brian began to repeat it.

"Dunno. Could be, since we got connections at the police station," Todd said. "I think there's a law says they have to, like, give police a break."

"But we ain't really cops no more," Brian said.

"They don't know that."

Todd, who was marginally smarter than his partner, the way a cockroach is marginally smarter than an eggplant, considered telling him he had heard they run things through a computer, which might have their background, but at that moment, Brian hit a pothole and several things happened at once:

22

* Brian reflexively slammed on the brakes and uttered a curse word.

* Todd, who was not buckled in and was not paying attention, flew forward, narrowly avoiding smashing his head in the windshield by hitting the dashboard with his chest. He too uttered a curse that sort of whooshed out.

Both doors swung open with full force.

* Max Irons, alone in his little world, still sobbing through his chest and ear hair, was struck by the passenger door in his left leg, the site of his trouble and subsequent unemployment, which crumpled and sent him sprawling. He was too stunned to offer a word either way.

"Holy shit!" Brian said. "I think we just hit somebody."

Todd, trying to sit back in his seat and failing to find purchase, thanks to a collage of greasy cheeseburger wrappers, simply stared at his partner in disbelief as he rubbed the sore spot on his chest.

"Oh, man."

Brian was more shaken than he would admit. He's been involved in a lot of crazy stuff, but never anything this unsettling.

"Oh, man," he said again. He pulled the car to the curb, shaking, and wishing once more he was home hitting a fattie.

*****

Nick couldn't believe his eyes. The car could only belong to Brian Fennigan, and the mop of greasy blond hair beside him could only belong to Todd Brown. And it had just wiped out a man that looked like he bench-pressed Volkswagen Beetles in his free time.

*Shit*, he thought, pulling up the curb near where Max Irons had achieved a sitting position.

*Time to go to work,* Nick thought, wishing he had taken something for his headache.

# Chapter 4

*This is going to be easier than I thought,* Phillip mused as he neared the completely deserted "reception area" of the Newburg Police Department.

Phillip was not averse to using any and all means to get information for a story, including what he had dubbed "clandestine observation" and everyone else called eavesdropping. He'd even tried casing the deaf team's locker room but found to his chagrin he didn't understand sign language.

His large frame was eerily fluid and his steps as light as he wanted them to be.

The little stoner Frye was unloading the story about last night in fits and bursts.

Phillip consulted his notes as well as his memory, finding that, for a miracle, everything to this point was in agreement.

He would have stood there completely unseen and waited for all of it to come out, but he heard an engine in the parking lot ticking as its owner shut it down.

Phillip took a few loud steps forward and placed his meaty (but gifted) arms on the counter.

"What the hell do you want?" Kocke said, rising quickly with a sudden impulse to start his violence early on one fat weekly newspaper writer.

"Just to talk, that's all," Phillip answered, his eyes automatically scanning the room for details.

"We have nothing to talk about," Kocke snarled. "Get out."

Phillip Andrew Thomas was accustomed to this reaction among small-town officers who believed they were directing the CIA. He simply offered his best smile, which would drive even the most friendly dog into a tail-biting frenzy.

"Oh, but I think we do," Phillip replied. "Beat up any homosexuals lately?" He pronounced it as *homa-sekshulls,* drawing out the end of the word in a weird drawl. Phillip knew it was unfair, since he really didn't *know* their sexual orientation, but he did love to push the chief's buttons.

All Phillip knew for sure was that Kocke was rumored to beat up men at the park; why was anybody's guess, but he hoped that one day he'd find a way to break the story open without losing his job.

Kocke's forehead was now almost black and the vein that resided there took on the verucose appearance which plagued old women in the beauty shop.

"GET THE HELL OUT RIGHT NOW!"

"But I need to make a report," a thin, reedy voice uttered.

Phillip spun around to see what appeared to be a breathing relic. *Man, this guy is old,* he thought, and on the heels of that, wondered if it could be this scrawny man with his belt around his nipples that had driven the car up to the station.

Chief Kocke took in the old man, whose white hair was so thin you could see every capillary on his skull. "I'm sorry for the outburst, Grandpa G," he said, though Phillip didn't think he looked sorry at all. "Officer Frye will assist you with your report."

He motioned for the pothead, whom Phillip would never consider a real officer, to help Methuselah and then turned his glinty stare back on his meaty visitor.

Kocke had not cooled, precisely, but he had calmed down a shade, thanks to the intruding little Gandalf. He eyed Phillip Andrew Thomas with a species of disgust, but made no more demands that he leave.

Instead, Kocke drew a deep sigh, tried on a smile of his own and invited Phillip to sit down.

*Keep your friends close and your enemies closer,* Brad thought.

*****

Max Irons had been thinking about how he was going to raise funds for the 'roids, and what might happen if he didn't get it together. In a fair fight, mano a mano, he had no doubt

25

he could snap Jerry Fillabag's neck like kindling. But Jerry had not risen to the position of gym guru and cowroid kingpin by being nice; he also had plenty of connections.

Max remembered once, when a client had fallen behind on his monthly payments, the Orc convinced him that payment was the only way to avoid having his spleen removed by hand.

Jerry had smiled as this client explained the first lapse as a misunderstanding with the bank. The next month, now in arrears a whopping $44, he had blamed it on oversight, and Jerry simply nodded. But by the third month, Jerry hadn't even waited for an explanation. He simply sent the Orc, so named by Jerry because of his ferocity and tiny brain and the fact he didn't know his real name.

The Orc hadn't said an intelligible word, which must have made the experience even scarier. He grunted a lot and clenched his hands, drool dripping from the corners of his mouth.

The client had come in the next day with $66 in cash to settle the account.

Max thought it was likely he could outsmart the Orc, but his balance was a lot more than three months worth of exercise, and the Orc would not come alone.

All of that was swept away as the already dented door of Brian's Tercel slammed him to the sidewalk.

Now, sitting up, his ear hair vibrating in outrage, Max rubbed his calf as a police officer approached.

"Are you okay?" *Super-Cop* asked in his best "Police Are Your Friends" voice.

"I guess, but I'll be limping for a long time," Max replied, suddenly wondering if there was any way to get money from the police. That car should have been impounded long ago, judging by the bucket of rust that had flaked to the curb beside him.

"Yeah, well I'm going to talk to the guys in the car," Nick said. "I'll be right back."

Brian glanced in his rear-view as *Super-Cop* began walking toward the car. Without much thought, he slammed his foot on the gas pedal and peeled away. Todd, who had just negotiated a tricky compromise with the greasy wrappers, slipped once more and then flew out the door where his shoulder hit the pavement with a dull thud, adding another piece to the already strumming melody of pain.

*****

Officer Allen Frye didn't know what the geezer's problem was, but he was glad to be out of the pissing contest between the chief and the guy from the paper. Allen thought he probably dressed up in women's clothes late at night and pranced around to the theme music from *Golden Girls*.

While Allen was trying to get Grandpa G to outline his problem, Dorf had finally begun to feel steady enough to pull on his security uniform. He had just tied his Always-Glo brand security-guard shoes when a sharp pain sent him scurrying for the bathroom.

The outcome of that race was very close.

# Chapter 5

"They got drugs there like you wouldn't believe," said the old geezer, whose Christian name was Bartholomew Grantz, Grandpa G to just about everyone.

"What kind of drugs, sir?" Officer Allen Frye couldn't believe the turn in his luck. With a little more, he could take care of all sorts of problems.

"You know, pills and powder, I don't know what they're called," Bartie replied, holding himself erect with great effort. "Most of it's legal, I s'pose, but you need a 'scription and they keep it locked up in the back. But I seen three guys go in there with some stuff that I know they don't write 'scriptions for."

Allen was very interested now. "What kind of stuff?"

"I ain't saying I know for sure, you understand, on account of my eyesight's going to hell, but I think them fellas was sellin' mary-wanna," Bartie said carefully, with growing conviction. "They went inside for a few minutes and when they went in they was all holdin' a bag of what looked like grass clippings. They didn't have 'em when they came out."

"Where was this, sir?"

"Over to Esther's." Allen felt his heart rate speed up a bit, wondering who Esther was. Then it hit him the old man was talking about Esther's Warehouse of Drugs & Teabag Emporium.

E's was a place he knew well, had frequented like everyone else in town when you needed a prescription filled or some of that "stuffy-head so you can sleep" medicine they always advertised. To think that was a den of illicit drug traffic was almost laughable but what better cover could you get? *The name drugs is right there in the marquee*, Allen thought.

"All right, sir, I'd like you to tell me exactly when you

saw these men."

Allen was trying like hell to stay focused, but his mind kept wandering to what might be the solution to his problems.

*****

Brian didn't know why he mashed the gas pedal down. He didn't know why he kept going when Todd fell out, but he knew it was too late now to go back and say he was sorry.

So he kept driving.

*Super-Cop*, Nick the occasional private-eye, had mixed feelings about what to do next. On the one hand, Todd was lying in a heap just ten yards from the beefy Volkswagen lifter, and Brian was getting away. In a town this size, though, there really was nowhere Brian could go that Nick could not find. And he was a reserve police officer to boot.

That's what really got under Nick's skin and ate at him. Even technically suspended, Brian should know better than to leave the scene of an accident.

Todd rolled onto his back and let out a sob, tears already drying on his dirty face.

"You okay there Todd?" Nick asked, reaching gingerly under the other's neck to help him up. He'd heard somewhere, a CPR class he was obliged to take as a matter of fact, that you should never move a crash victim unless absolutely necessary, but he figured if Todd could roll over, he could sit up.

"What the hell's wrong with Brian?" he asked now.

"Mmfh nnet shurr," Todd said, pausing to spit out blood and grime collected during his ungraceful exit from the car.

"He should know better than this," Nick said, who understood Todd to say, "I'm not sure," before turning to see how Captain Biceps was doing. He was on his feet and limping toward where the other two were camped.

"He all right?" Max Irons asked as he approached.

"I think so," *Super-Cop* said, introducing himself to Newburn's answer to Arnold Schwarzenegger, who he'd seen around town but never met. "What's your name?"

"Max Irons," the other replied, bending over to rub his calf.

"Where's Brian?" Todd asked, a little more clearly, unsure whether his partner realized he had dumped him like a sack of trash when he peeled out.

"Dunno," Nick replied. "We'll find him soon enough. Max, this is Todd Brown. He and his partner, Brian Fennigan are reserve police officers, though they've been suspended for a while."

"You mean a cop ran me down?"

Max had visions of the city writing him a check for what he needed and them doubling it; he was, after all, unemployed.

It was 10:43.

*****

Phillip Andrew Thomas, author of such weekly newspaper articles as *Newburn Sewer Hits The Fan,* and *Fans Struck Dumb By Loss To Deaf Squad,* sat with his ballpoint pen poised above his writer's notebook, waiting for Chief Kockespew to speak.

Chief Kocke was fully aware that his obese counterpart was hoping to use last night's episode as a means to scare Newburnians. But the Chief knew if he didn't say something official, the fat prick would print whatever he wanted to anyway.

"Tell me what you know," he said unhappily.

Phillip smiled, showing very large (and very fake) teeth caps, which he had sent off for a year ago in an effort to improve his image. It didn't help.

"I know that an unknown, allegedly inebriated assailant entered a private residence on Oak Street, found some guy schlepping his girlfriend, and pursued him briefly with a chainsaw," Phillip leaned forward. "Who is it?"

*What a windbag,* Brad thought before asking, "Where did you hear this?"

"At Jan's this morning," Phillip replied honestly. "A neighbor was in there, said she heard the commotion and talked to the woman this morning. Takes a lot to make a guy mistake his own girlfriend, don't you think?"

Calculated silence greeted this question, which when combined with the lean, made it seem somehow conspiratorial and definitely gross because Phillip emitted a foul smell from his fake teeth.

*Like we're two colleagues hoping a comparison of notes will lead to a break in a case,* Brad thought.

Phillip finally took a seat nearby.

"The guy's name is being withheld pending our investigation," Chief Kocke said, hoping Mr. Three Names didn't realize the NPD simply didn't know. "And don't think you're going to bully Allen into telling you either."

Unfazed, Phillip continued. "But it's a given fact that this man entered a house in the dead of night (9:30 p.m. was hardly the dead of night, but Kocke let this go) and attacked the rightful owner with his own chainsaw, right?"

"Pretty much, though he wasn't the owner, just a visitor, but you're not getting his name."

"Oh, I'll find out who it is soon enough," Phillip said slyly.

The two sat staring at one another for a few minutes, neither speaking, before Phillip closed his notebook and stood, his sweaty pants pulling away from the plasti-form chair with a sound very much like ripping paper.

Brad Kocke didn't much like this situation, knowing that Phillip Andrew Thomas had a way of getting things out of people.

# Chapter 6

Jerry Fillabag sat in his office overlooking the gym floor, mentally calculating how much firing Max Irons might hurt the business. He shook his head, sighing, wishing he could have brought Max into it, knowing he could not.

Never. No one but him could know the depths to which he had traveled. His tastes had always been on the bizarre side, including a phase in his life when he was into midget hookers, but that was before he came to Newburn with Uncle Stan's $15,000, and here, such delicacies were not to be found.

This didn't bother him; he still had some homemade videos that kept him running when the urges struck.

*It's really ironic, firing Max for using cowroids,* Jerry thought.

That was because his rise to kingpin status was based on the sale of steroids to most of the members in the joint. But he was man who believed in keeping up appearances, even at the cost of a longtime association.

If people *knew* he was selling 'roids, and that said 'roids were actually designed for cows, he really would have trouble keeping a straight face when he promised success through a regimen of physical exercise.

It wasn't morals or ethics, but business.

Yes, it was definitely ironic. If Max Irons had only known that a lot of the people he helped every week were taking the same drugs he had helped himself to . . .

Jerry allowed the thought to float away. The truth was he didn't know how Max would have reacted, and that is why he let him go.

Sticking him with a bill for the pilfered cowroids was only fair, Jerry believed, knowing he would likely have to send the Orc to collect.

It was fifteen minutes to 11 and the lunch losers would

start to drift in, depending on their allotted feeding times. Yes, they really were like cattle, and how fitting many used his bovine treatments to create the illusion of fitness without even knowing it.

*****

Sometimes a voice spoke to Brian, offering suggestions or criticisms. Most of the time the voice reminded him of his Bible-thumping mother, and he ignored it. This time, however, he listened as he sped down County Road 201, with part of his mind freaked out over hitting some poor bastard on the side of the road, another part worried about the consequences, and most of it centered on how he could score a joint.

Only by association had he thought about Todd, who he now realized might really be hurt back there. But it was distant, like the sound of a chainsaw in the night four blocks away.

There was something weird about that deal, but he didn't have the focus to consider it for long. He had to get off the road, find some serious weed and get his act together.

*****

Allen Frye thanked Bartie Grantz and practically pushed him out the door, planning to stop in long enough to tell Chief Kocke of his plan to investigate Esther's Warehouse of Drugs & Teabag Emporium. But the chief was not there, nor was the fat paper guy.

Allen frowned, not knowing what else to do. He figured the two would be sitting there killing each other with hard stares or maybe doing the real thing with a couple of chairs. He hadn't even heard them leave.

*Damn*, he thought. *How am I supposed to check out E's with no one to man the desk?*

The clock on the wall read 10:49 and Allen let slip another curse; he was due for lunch in almost ten minutes. He could only tell time in increments of about ten, a product of many afternoons sliding through his classes after a lunch-time doobie in the men's room, most of the time with Brian and Todd. It was a bummer he couldn't pal around with them, not since the investigation.

A light bulb went off over his head, an idea of such simplicity he should have thought of it right away. Allen decided he would leave a note saying he was out checking a drug-bust lead and that he had left at eleven. Since this was also his lunch time, he could reasonably be expected to combine the two errands. And what are the odds of anyone coming in here in the next ten minutes? he reasoned. *I'll just say I was taking a crap.*

And so Allen scrawled out his note, leaving it on the front door with masking tape.

*Gone to the drug store for a lead and lunch. Be back. Allen Frye.*

*****

Seeing no viable option outside calling an ambulance from Waterford, some 12 miles away, Nick thought his best bet was to load up Max Irons and Todd Brown in his nondescript sedan and take them to the clinic, where Dr. Hemphill could look them over.

Because of his enormity, Max sat in the middle of the back seat, where he could stretch out most comfortably. This created a problem for Nick, who couldn't see through Captain Biceps' muscular skull.

He wondered what exercise built muscles in your head and then decided he didn't want to know.

Todd was the worse of the two, what with a blow to the chest and another to his shoulder, but he kept saying "I don't need no doctor," like some weird mantra.

Instead, Nick drove toward the police station, where the duo could file a report with Allen Frye while he went looking Brian. He had a very good idea of where to start.

*****

Danielle Stone usually spent Monday's lunch hour working out, but with an early appointment, and only a bit of gravel-subsidized granola in her system, she decided her energy would be better spent eating something solid. And despite the fact that Dorf had called back to say he he lost a close race of some kind and would not be in until after noon, Danielle decided to take an early lunch at Jan's Country Griddle & Bait Shop, where you could get greasy chicken at all hours.

She stepped out the front door of The Newburn Bank at 10:52, just in time to see a brown car crawl sedately by with what appeared to be two adult men in the front seat and a bear in the back. Danielle knew the driver, Nick Crawford, and the blond guy was Todd Brown, but she had no clue about the zoo exhibit in the back seat. And she most certainly cared nothing for anyone in the car except Nick, who had ended their relationship two weeks ago with a brusque phone call.

"I know what you've been doing and I won't stand for it," he had said. "We're through."

Click. The hum of an open line prevented any response she could have made. For a woman who had graduated in the top 55 percent of her class, she was dumfounded.

Danielle had tried to call him back, find out what in hell's name he was talking about, but he refused to answer the phone. And even when she saw him about town in the police cruiser (the town had two one for Chief Kocke and another for the officer on duty; unsurprisingly, both were in for repairs today), she got the runaround about how he wasn't on duty when she called the station. That little guy Allen Frye was covering for him, and she hated him for it.

Refusing to be bullied by two weeks of cold-shoulder treatment, Danielle offered a wave to Nick as the car trundled past the bank, but he apparently ignored her entreaty.

At this, she abruptly changed her lunch plans (greasy chicken with an aroma of nightcrawlers had lost its appeal anyway), heading for her car and planning to confront Nick at the station.

# Chapter 7

As much as Dorf Walkenhorst was a fool for his daily dose of Dr. Phil, Evvie Fennigan was a fool for her morning soaps, ever since Joe rolled his John Deere into the pond. Thankfully his insurance was up to date, which meant $435 a month to her and the place was paid in full.

Evvie didn't like just one soap, but all of them. She didn't understand how anyone could put one above the rest, since they were all pretty much the same, only with different names.

She could keep up with *General Hospital, Young and the Restless, All My Children, Days of Our Lives,* and was equally at home with the *Bold and the Beautiful and Guiding Light*; it was simply a matter of knowing who was who.

The biggest reason she could keep everyone's affairs and double-crossing in check was that no one bothered her more than once. Anyone stupid enough to interrupt her during her special morning time was in for a world of hurt.

She had sat contentedly, as she did every day during the week, a bowl of oatmeal with a slice of toast giving way to a bowl of mixed fruit and then to popcorn. She ate exactly one selection per show, and only got up during the commercials to stretch. The first show today had been rather dull and predictable, but Evvie ate her oatmeal and toast with relish anyway. During the break between the end of the next show (Carmen's Hysterectomy) and the next (Sex With Everybody), she put her slime-coated bowl in the sink and went to the bathroom.

This was a custom dating back at least two years, she couldn't remember exactly when Joe died and she quit her job at Jan's, and it was as sacred to her as slinging Holy Water was to the Pope.

There was always a news brief foretelling the noon report, and as much as it galled her that her next show started a couple minutes late, she used the extra time to put on that day's pair of nylons.

Evvie Fennigan had won the Newburn "Best Legs" contest 16 years ago, and while they were no longer likely to get notice from anyone but the postmaster, she still loved the feel of nylons, especially when everyone on the soaps wore them. It seemed to Evvie nylons equaled sex, and though she was a devout Christian, she was not without her fantasies, especially with the supercharged actresses on the set.

Besides, she was sure God understood.

After she flushed, Evvie heard the theme music starting up, a very hip diddy that made you want to have sex with all your in-laws, co-workers and basically everyone on the set.

She settled into her recliner, pulled the handle for the foot rest and prepared to enjoy an hour of back-stabbing and misguided passion.

Instead, her heathen son burst into the living room.

"Mom, I need help," Brian said, panting like a dog. He noted she was wearing her black nylons today and wondered briefly what exotic name they were called.

Faced with the choice between seeing whether Olivia would get breast implants and listening to her wayward son, Evvie turned up the volume.

*****

Nick piloted his car into an empty police lot, noting the paper taped to the front door, knowing it was put there by Allen and wondering where he had run off to.

*No telling with him,* Nick thought, killing the engine in one of three spaces marked "Reserved" and opening his door. It had never occurred to Allen to simply call someone.

Todd was still muttering "I don't need no doctor," and Max Irons rubbed his ear hair absently yet lovingly as the two got out of the car.

"I guess I'll have to take your report," Nick said as they approached the awkward note left by Allen. "Looks like Officer Frye skipped out."

Using his cockroach-level smarts, Todd had a

brainstorm. "I could write it up for you and you could sign it," he told his one-time fellow officer.

Nick considered it as they entered the empty station, which smelled vaguely of nursing home.

It wasn't the first time one officer helped another out, but this was a little different. Todd was an officer *non gratis*, which is a phrase Nick had heard that jerk Phillip Andrew Thomas say after the investigation. Nick really didn't know what it meant, but he knew enough to realize that if Chief Kocke found out, he'd be pissed.

Maybe not Riverfront-pissed but still not happy.

And yet there was Brian to consider. And this was really Allen's fault for not being here.

Which is how it came to be that Nick left a suspended reserve police officer at the deserted Newburn Police Department with Max Irons.

The rest of the day's events might have been different had Nick stayed with them.

*****

Allen Frye stood at the pharmacy counter at Esther's Warehouse of Drugs & Teabag Emporium, hating the fact that he, a five-month veteran of the police department, had to look up at Esther Pickering while conducting his official interview.

"So you're saying you don't sell drugs?"

"Of course I sell drugs, didn't you see the big sign out front?"

"I mean special drugs."

"Like what? Anti-Biotics? Viagra?" She said this last with arched eyebrows, knowing full well how the young folks liked to use it for their wild sex parties.

"No, the other kind of special drugs."

Patience and Esther hardly knew each other, and what little she had begun with today was gone as this little stoner of a police officer asked questions that made no sense.

Besides, it was going on eleven-fifteen and she had been on her feet for half an hour.

"Son, you're going to have to start making sense," Esther said. "There's a line waiting."

"I mean, do you ever sell drugs not prescribed by a doctor?"

"Oh, you must mean over-the-counter stuff," Esther said. "What's troubling you? You got the jock itch?"

Several elderly customers in line snickered like winded mules at this query, asked in Esther's typically loud voice, which always sounded like a flock of geese.

"No, it's just that . . . ." Allen was in way over his head. He knew it, but couldn't figure a way out of the box he was in. He didn't want to say he was looking for marijuana because he knew his reputation as a stoner was already bad enough and would only grow more solid, what with half a dozen fogies here to spread it around that he was asking about drugs.

Esther, meanwhile, had exhausted her supply of patience. "Look son, I'm kinda busy here," she said. "You just head over to aisle four. That's where I put all the jock itch cream, the hemorrhoid cream and every other cream for when stuff below the belt starts itching. Who's next?"

Red-faced with equal parts embarrassment and anger, Allen withdrew for the moment before heading to Aisle 4. Then he had an idea maybe it was a code.

*****

At first, Todd Brown took the part he had volunteered for seriously, but as the minutes ticked off and the silence of the police station continued, he decided to do what he had always done as an officer: blow it off.

The only thing missing was the fragrant smell of smoke as it wafted from the end of a monster joint. And Brian.

Ah, Brian, his best friend who had peeled out and left him lying in a heap on the sidewalk. Todd wanted to be angry with him, but found he couldn't hold it.

The pair had been all but inseparable since grade school, long before they shared their first special cigarette behind Newburn Junior High, which for them was an appropriately named school. The truth of the matter was that Todd lived in awe of Brian, precisely because of stunts like today's. It wasn't the first time Todd had wound up on the wrong side of such a play, and eventually, they would drift back together and keep on as they had always done.

Todd was the epitome of awkwardness as a kid. His feet were too big, he had no balance and his attention wandered in time with his lazy eye. Always picked near last for the team, he eventually gave it up as a bad idea.

His depth of field wasn't very good anyway, so it really didn't matter.

Todd and Brian had met in the fifth grade, appropriately enough in detention. Todd had refused to read from the board and Brian had been caught defacing a teacher's car with a permanent marker.

It was like love at first sight, except they were both guys and would never admit emotions that deep.

Todd saw in Brian someone who was fun (writing on Ms. Brick's car!), while Brian saw Todd as someone who would hang on his every word.

Over the next two years, they spent a lot of time in detention together and were together most of the day, parting only a few hours when they had different classes.

By the time they hit junior high, they were something of a local legend among students hoping to learn how to be a delinquent. They had moved from marking up cars to experimenting with fireworks and finally they found marijuana.

Again, it was love at first sight, or smell if you prefer.

Attending college had never been on their to-do list, and to be honest, neither was graduating high school. Somehow they managed to get through, though neither could remember much beyond the haze of reefer and the dull walls of the detention room.

Todd smile once more as he thought of his oldest friend.

Max Irons had been very quiet, taking in the scenery, so to speak, and wondering if it would even be worth his time to demand money from the police. Clearly the department was hurting, and he had serious doubts.

"What do we do now?" he finally asked Todd, who looked about as intelligent as a box of hammers.

"I dunno, but I ain't gonna fill out no damn report," the other said. "I wish I had some pot."

"I wish I had some . . . pills," Max finished lamely.

The two exchanged a look that told the other he knew exactly what it was they were feeling, and then shared a short laugh. Max liked the kid, even if he would never answer in the form of a question on *Jeopardy!*.

"Do you think the police will pay me for what happened today?" Max asked.

"Nah, they ain't got shit," said Todd. "Me and Brian don't even get a paycheck anymore."

The implication was clear, but there was more to it than Todd would admit. "We were on the way to the bank to get a loan when we hit you."

"Why would you do that?" Max was genuinely curious.

"Because we need money for, um, things," Todd replied.

"You ran me over because you need money for things?" Now Max was mystified. Had Jerry hired Todd and whatshisname to run him down?

"No, we were going to get a loan," Todd said, his off-center eyes rolling in their sockets.

"Somebody was going to give you a loan to run me over?"

Now Todd was mystified, wondering if he wasn't still on the floor of his apartment, a laced joint burning away as he hallucinated.

"The bank was going to give us a loan," he said. "It had nothing to do with you."

"Then why did you run me over?" Though Max Irons looked a little miffed, he still bore the face of a man trying to understand the Python Theory or whatever it was called; his grasp of math, especially geometry, was non-existent.

Since Todd felt no anger from the man who looked big enough to eat an entire cow at one sitting, he explained about how the doors would never close all the way, and how Brian hit that pothole.

He threw up his hands in a gesture as if to say fate had hit him, not Brian and Todd, and Max seemed to accept this.

In his heart, though, Max was even more convinced that he would have to face the Orc.

And then both seized upon one word: bank.

*****

When the phone rang, Brian, who had briefly considered strangling his mother with an extension cord, picked up the kitchen handset instead. He listened for a few moments, a smile breaking on his haggard face.

When he replaced the phone and headed for the front door, Evvie didn't notice.

Olivia had decided on the double-D implants and was negotiating for them with the very handsome Dr. Bryce Cornol. This was going to a be a great day on YTR, Evvie decided.

# Chapter 8

As Brian Fennigan was pulling out of his mother's driveway and heading back to town, Nick had approached Newburn's one blinker, a monotonous yellow flasher warning motorists of potential danger, namely that a cow might traipse across the road; a handmade yellow sign depicting a bovine and her calves was mounted on the side of the road.

Nick Crawford was sore all over, beginning with his head and working its way down through his arms. At this moment, he had virtually no idea why his arms hurt, but he clearly remembered dousing his brain cells in grain alcohol. Not much else, but at least the cause of the headache was clear.

He was still fuming over Brian's complete lack of responsibility and was on his way to Evvie Fennigan's pond-front trailer on County Road 201, where he was pretty sure he'd find the object of his pursuit. Brian was probably cringing in the back bedroom, or maybe just sitting there watching the Young and the Restless with good old mom.

Either way, Nick was sure he'd be bringing Brian back to town.

A quarter-mile before the blinker he signaled to the cows his intention to turn left, and then did so, his mind running on auto-pilot for the three-mile jaunt down CR 201.

He didn't notice the Chevy Caprice turning behind him.

*****

Danielle Stone had driven to the police station, which was only two blocks from the bank, but before she reached the lot's only entrance, she saw Nick pulling out. Her first irrational instinct was to ram his car and demand an explanation. Instead, she slowed and let her former fiance gain a little distance.

His head barely turned before the car did, and Danielle found herself infuriated with him all over again.

How dare he call me up and tell me it's over without so much as a word of explanation?

She honestly believed they'd been through too much together for it to end that way.

Couples fight all the time. It's a reality of life. But this wasn't fighting, to her mind. Instead, she felt like he had sucker-punched her with the phone call.

Newburn had a small populus and people from bigger places like St. Louis often joked about the gene pool being shallow. But as far as Danielle could tell, she and Nick were not related.

*A lot of high-school sweethearts get married,* she thought defensively.

Theirs was a relationship built on mutual respect, but Nick's behavior of late had led her to wonder if he respected her at all.

This was a burning question she needed to answer before moving any further. He had wounded her with his words and then his silence.

The wedding wasn't until the fall, some three months away, but Danielle pondered whether it would take place at all. Her mother was pushing, wanting grandchildren before she grew too old to spoil them.

The way things were going, her mother might never hold a grandchild.

Danielle's bitterness was understandable, and her impulsive decision to follow him no matter where he went was fueled by the hurt beneath her tough exterior.

*****

It was nearly 11:20 and Dorf was still sitting on the only throne he would ever own, wishing to God he had read the directions more carefully or at all. His previously attentive quartet had fled the bathroom for less offensive regions, like their litter box.

At Jan's Country Griddle & Bait Shop, meanwhile, Chief

44

Brad Kocke and Phillip Andrew Thomas of the Newburn News, had just settled in for the lunch special, namely greasy chicken. The former was trying his best to be a good public servant, while Phillip was simply content to eat as much chicken as his elastic waistband could handle.

Brad still hadn't gotten over the poke he took from Phillip, but the council had given him approval to hire another officer, and then came Allen Frye and the morons. Not exactly the combination that would make him Chief of the Year in Missouri, but until recently, he had made it work.

Bartie Grantz, meanwhile, was watching another case of drug trafficking as he stood in the post office, this time only attempted, as three fellas approached the locked door of the Double-L. Each was carrying a bag of grass clippings, which he thought had to be mary-wanna. From his vantage right across the street, he could see another man sitting behind the wheel of an old truck, and knew for sure he was same guy from Esther's. He wished Mrs. Kettler would get off her 4-H high-horse and peddle her muffins somewhere else, so he could get back to the police station.

*****

Nick Crawford was less than a mile from Evvie Fennigan's place, a rundown trailer on about an eighth of an acre she inherited after her husband drowned, including the pond, which was really a lagoon. By now he had noted the car behind him, but not its driver.

He rounded a corner, saw a cow in the middle of the road, and slammed on the brakes, thinking absently that this is where the blinker should be. Danielle, reacted to his maneuver and also slammed on the brakes, feeling her car skew to the right as the gravel shifted.

On the other side of the cow, which had wandered through an open area in Jeb Stuart's fence, came Brian Fennigan. He was far more accustomed to roaming cows from the Stuart place, and his reaction was less panicked, especially considering the string of events that had put him on this road.

So instead of meeting head-on, the two former colleagues passed by one another without a confrontation. Nick was worried about hitting a two-ton side of beef and didn't see the battered Tercel; Brian, who had avoided the collision, now worried about threading his sometimes airplane along the ditch without falling into it.

Danielle, meanwhile, had regained some measure of control but not enough as her Caprice clipped Nick's bumper, sending both cars to rest in the ditch on east side of the road.

Brian made it through the slim section of road and continued on his merry way, oblivious to his would-be captor's situation.

His wing-like doors stayed shut for a miracle.

Another cow emerged from the hole in the fence to investigate.

# Chapter 9

Nick felt the impact as the Caprice clipped him, and he realized there was no way to avoid the ditch.

The cow merely lowered its head to crop, saw there was no grass, and began moving toward Nick's car, hoping to find some there.

Danielle was momentarily stunned but chagrin was what she felt most. It was completely unlike her to lose control so rapidly.

And yet there was a cow in the road. *What else could I do?* she thought.

Still, she was granted her wish to see Nick, albeit under odd circumstances.

Danielle pushed open the door and climbed out, seeing Nick do the same. She had endured several sleepless nights since his enigmatic phone call, and many of those were spent wondering what she would say when she finally caught up with him.

"Hello, Nick," she said now, her voice quavering only slightly.

"You hit my car," he replied, giving his rear bumper a once-over.

"That's all you have to say?"

Nick paused in his inspection to consider what, if anything, he still felt for the woman he'd caught cheating on him.

*****

As 11:30 came and went, Jerry Fillabag was speaking with the Orc, whose real name he never knew or cared to know. All Jerry cared about was making sure he got paid for the cow-roids Max Irons had stolen, and the more he had thought about it, the more certain he was that a little push would be necessary in this case.

"So you understand I want him to pay me, right?"

"Uh-huh," Orc replied.

"I don't want you to hurt him," said Jerry, who paused, then added, "not too much anyway. He's an old friend, but he's also pissed off and I don't know what he might do. Just be careful and make sure he understands what happens to people who cheat me."

"Ugh-kay," Orc replied, a banner day for him in terms of understandable lingo.

He and Jerry went back to the days of the midgets, when the Orc was in the public-relations department of a pimp name Alphonse, Alfie to everyone but the cops. He'd always liked Jerry, and when he left to start his gym, the Orc had stayed in touch, how, even he wasn't sure.

All the Orc knew was that Jerry paid pretty well and sometimes he let him gnaw on some of the people he went to see.

"Just so we're clear," Jerry said.

He looked out over his gym empire, surprised to not see Danielle Stone among those breathing hard on the equipment he had financed with his sale of cow-roids. She wasn't one of *those* customers, but she was easy to look at; and Danielle gave the place some credibility, unlike that Sheila Fowler, who was always leaving slime on the machines.

The Orc made no sound as he left the office.

*****

Chief Kocke just barely found the tolerance to watch his lunch-time counterpart burrow into his food like a hog at a trough, including slurping the grease from his pudgy fingers. Kocke reached for the ketchup, inadvertently knocking a dead fly to the floor.

"What am I supposed to do here?" he asked Phillip with a glance at the buzzing neon Nightcrawlers For Sale sign and clock, which read 11:40.

"All (slurp) I want (slurp) is a chance to write a good story about (slurpppp) what went down last night," Phillip answered.

"Stop that!" Kocke cried finally, earning the attention of several nearby diners. "Jesus, that's why they invented pants, so you could wipe your hands off." This time Kocke's voice was more controlled. Barely.

Phillip regarded the chief with a blank stare, one that said, *I always do what I want and you can't stop me*.

But he did stop the slurpfest, digging into his cold mashed potatoes topped with gelled gravy instead.

"You know that what happened is under investigation and that until we charge somebody, I don't have to tell you anything," Kocke said.

"Yeah, I also know that you'd like to keep what you do at Riverfront to yourself."

Phillip enjoyed the slight intake of breath and the light color that filled Kockesucker's forehead.

"That's none of your business," Kocke said.

"I know, believe me, and I'd really like to help you keep it that way," Phillip replied easily, reaching for his nearly empty glass of iced tea. "Call it one hand washing the other."

Chief Kocke considered this carefully. On the one hand, he'd like nothing better than to run Mr. Three Names into the ground, preferably at Riverfront; on the other, he couldn't do that without serious repercussions, namely the shit sandwich the mayor would give him to eat if anything happened to his wife's fourth cousin twice-removed. And given Alderman Eric Engram's own peculiarities, not to mention his relation by marriage to the mayor, Chief Kocke thought things could go very bad indeed, even if he couldn't stand Lard-Ass himself.

He sighed, thinking that all he really wanted was a nine-to-five office job and his evenings free to engage in a little fruit-smacking.

"I'll take that as a yes," Phillip Andrew Thomas said with another of those freakish smiles.

# Chapter 10

Allen Frye was seriously pissed.

He was tired and hungry, his lunch time now nearly gone, and he still had no viable lead. He was sure that old bat Esther was sending him to Aisle 4 for a reason; he had no idea that she actually believed he was suffering from a bad case of crotch-rot.

So here he was scanning the shelves for a clue or perhaps a sign reading "For marijuana and other drugs, go to Aisle 6," where there would be another sign leading him to another aisle, and so on, until he found the source of the drug trade.

Allen thought maybe Esther had sent him on a wild-goose chase and it was starting to aggravate him.

*****

Dorf felt better than he had all morning. He had changed his shorts for the third time by the end of the weather report in the noon news.

But now he felt that maybe the last of the poison he had inadvertently taken was out of his works, and he laced up the second Always-Glo brand security-guard shoe and was ready to take on the day, what was left of it. *Carpadeem*, he thought.

His cats sat by the door, waiting for their stinky roommate to leave so they could wallow in their litter box without being lectured.

Dorf thought he'd grab a quick sandwich at Jan's and then head into the bank. But first he had a stop to make at the post office.

*****

Mrs. Anita Kettler, whose years of service to the Newburn 4-H had always included baking homemade oat-bran muffins, continued her suggestive conversation with Postmaster Herbert Mays. The 61-year old David Spade look-alike (if David Spade was 61 and looked like death warmed-over) had always been something of a flirt, even with a senile wife at home.

Most thought he was harmless, but Mrs. Kettler, who really believed his comments were sincere and directed only at her, always left the post office a little flushed. It was the only thing more exciting than selling her homemade muffins, which nobody except Dorf ever ate.

No one had the heart to tell her they were something of a joke around town.

"How many teeth you break this time?" was a common jocular greeting. Danielle Stone would have noted a close resemblance to her granola bars.

And so, like most mornings, she found an excuse to visit the local post office, even if only to buy a single stamp. This fine Monday morning, she wanted to get a letter out to the county extension office, requesting booth-space at the next year's county fair.

Behind her, Bartie was convinced beyond all doubt that every minute he stood here listening to Herbert doing everything but sticking his tongue down Mrs. Kettler's throat was one more drug deal going down in his home town.

In his lineage was a man named Walter Grantz, one of the Guardians that had a hand in beating up two would-be robbers and scaring off plenty of others.

Now it was Bartie's watch, although unofficially and very quietly, and he had seen suspicious behavior which surrounded drugs, and while he didn't carry an oak walking stick, he was sure he could find something else just as useful.

"I love licking stamps in my free time," Herbert crooned, licking his liver-spotted lips. "How 'bout you darling?"

At last Bartie could stand no more; he crumpled the electric bill in his hand, fully addressed and needing only a stamp, and shuffle-stalked toward the door.

Mrs. Kettler asked Herbert Mays what else he liked to lick.

\*\*\*\*\*

As lunch came to a close, and the spectacularly annoying finger-licker was done eating, Chief Brad Kocke pulled a battered pack of Camels from his breast pocket and lit up. Phillip Andrew Thomas declined to join him, a bit piously, Kocke thought.

With just a few minutes before the noon crowd piled in, Kocke nodded to several of Newburn's residents seated round the room before returning his attention to Phillip.

"One hand washes the other, huh?" Kocke said. "Okay, I'll tell you what. You leave me and my personal stuff alone and let me read this story before you print it, and you got a deal."

Phillip, who could have told him that no one ever read his stuff prior to seeing it in the Newburn News, nodded his head instead. He could change anything he wanted after Kockeknocker perused it; all he said was "let me read this story."

They flipped for the check, and Phillip was mildly annoyed that he lost, but the paper would cover it, and he had gotten an inside track on the story in the bargain.

He had no idea that this story would pale by comparison to the rest of the day.

# Chapter 11

A hand the size of a television seemed to clench around Dorf's middle as he pulled into the diagonal parking space in front of the post office. He cursed, thinking he had rid himself of the trots.

Barely pausing to put the old Jeep in park, he lunged from the vehicle and bounded toward the door, not sure if Uncle Sam had equipped its postal centers with restrooms, not caring.

He only knew he was about to change his shorts for the fourth time in one day.

As he reached for he handle, the door opened and Dorf collided with a very angry Bartie Grantz, who was about 40 pounds lighter than the security guard.

Fortunately, the door remained open through the exchange, and both men stumbled back through it, landing in a heap, Bartie underneath with his fine white hair pressed to the tile floor (though not pinned enough to avoid an unabridged view of what passed for Mrs. Kettler's underwear).

Both Mrs. Kettler and Postmaster Hays were stunned to silence, the discussion of what he liked to lick in addition to stamps temporarily forgotten.

The elderly 4-H muffin saleswoman started toward her most loyal customer but cringed as the smell hit her.

Dorf had lost yet another race.

*****

Allen Frye was almost positive there was something here, but his mind had begun to drift, for he had neither eaten nor had his post-lunch hit of Crazy Willy's best. As he was preparing to re-interview old lady Esther, he saw a man come out of a door marked "Teabag Emporium" near the back of the store, which sold organic foods and Pakistani teas for all occasions.

In his hand was a small bag of what appeared to be grass clippings, just as Bartie had reported; of his partners there was no sign.

Allen was just about to approach him when that flock of geese erupted behind him.

"Find the cream for your jock itch?" Esther asked.

The officer spun, nearly pulling his police-issue automatic and shooting her in the face. "Jesus, don't do that," he said.

"Do what?"

"Sneak up on people."

"I've never snuck up on anyone in my life." Esther was clearly enjoying his surprise. "I was only trying to help."

Allen turned back to locate the bag-carrier but he was gone. *Shit*, he thought.

"Well, did you?" Esther intruded.

"Did I what?"

"Find the cream for your jock itch?"

"Oh, that. No, I didn't."

"Well I was on the way to the office for m'lunch," Esther said, rubbing the small of her back to indicate how lunch would be a relief after standing for 40 minutes straight. "C'mon, I'll help you get it."

Allen tried to tell her he did not have crotch-rot, but she was already moving, so he followed her to a huge display of jock-itch creams with an equally large sign, which proclaimed "The itch stops HERE!"

Allen decided that for a drug dealer, Esther was pretty clever.

*****

"Well?" Danielle prompted. "What's going on?"

The two had remained by the car, Danielle staring holes through him, Nick trying to count the individual grains of dirt as he crafted an answer.

One of the many aspects of Danielle's personality which had attracted him was her forthright attitude; he decided the least he could do was respond in kind.

"I saw you cheating on me, that's what's going on," he said.

"What on earth are you talking about?"

Danielle was as mystified over this claim as Max Irons had been in his conversation with Todd.

"I mean, I went to your house two weeks ago and I saw you with another man," Nick said, not looking at her.

"That's just crazy," Danielle said. "You know I love you, or I did anyway."

"What does that mean?"

"Leave it. How could you believe that about me?"

"I know what I saw."

"Who was I supposedly with?"

"I don't know, but I think I'd know him if I saw him," Nick said. He was drifting into territory laced with ambiguity.

Danielle threw up her arms in a gesture of incredulity. "You don't know but you're sure I was screwing around on you."

Nick started to feel less sure of himself as the conversation continued. After all, he and Danielle had been together for more than two years and were engaged.

"Were you drunk when you saw this guy?"

A glimmer of memory, not much more than a pulse of double-insight, struck him. Overlaid like double-exposed film, he saw himself leaving the Double-L two weeks ago (and last night) very drunk and deciding he would surprise Danielle with a late-night visit. The rest was hazy, but he remembered seeing her through the kitchen window, a man with his arms around her waist and moving north.

*Didn't he?*

Danielle saw the confusion on his face, and with no clear understanding, related his claim with the weirdness that went down last night.

\*\*\*\*\*

Brian smiled all the way to town, pushing the Tercel for all it was worth, which wasn't much.

He turned beneath the blinker as Dorf and Bartie became intimately close, and wasted no time on watching the speed limit because his car, technically, did not travel fast enough to warrant such consideration.

As he passed Jan's Country Griddle & Bait Shop, he saw Chief Kocke and the fat guy from the paper emerge. Both saw the dusty, trailworn Tercel with its shimmying doors but thought nothing of it.

For Brian, the chance of a lifetime had just been granted him, his phone call creating an emotion he had not felt for some time: hope. Greed was mixed in with good measure, but for now, he only knew he had to get to the police station, where his long-time friend and partner had devised a plan with someone named Maxine, whoever that was.

The clock on *The West* Bank of Newburn read 12:35.

# Chapter 12

Lionel Leanman, proprietor of Lionel's Lounge, often joked his place should be called the Triple-L, but no one ever got it. Some customers would look at him as if he'd just pissed on their best shoes, but most chuckled dutifully, as drunkards do whenever there's the possibility of a free drink.

Lionel did occasionally pour freely, but only if he'd done well at the track in Waterford (though he didn't know it, this was another reason Waterford earned county-seat status).

Today, as he prepared to flip the switch proclaiming the Double-L open for business, he scanned the dim room with mixture of resignation and disgust.

Thanks to a change in the liquor laws a few years back, he could open on Sunday, provided at least half of his receipts were food, which was easy when you were a creative guy like Lionel. He introduced a reverse cover charge, collecting $5 each at the door for food, then put out mixed nuts and a crock pot filled with barbecue sauce and recycled Vienna sausage, calling it the Double-L buffet.

Nick Crawford, called *Super-Cop* by most everyone behind his back, had complained about the healthy constitution of this buffet; most others stayed away from it altogether. But they *were* willing to pay for the privilege of drinking on Sunday.

That name rang a bell with Lionel as he collected dirty plates, scraping their contents into the crock, but he couldn't connect it with anything but his threat to report him to the county health department, not that Lionel was worried; that palm was as greased as one of Jan's skillets.

No, wait, it was something to do with last night. Nick had been even more boisterous than usual, killing one beer after another, occasionally stepping out to what Lionel called his Hawaii 5-0 car for a shot of grain alcohol.

"He said something about proving that bitch was

cheating on him," Lionel muttered to himself as he poured the old glasses into a bucket, which he would sell as "Mystery Shots" to anyone brave or stupid enough to pay. Aside from recycling food and drink, muttering was Lionel Leanman's favorite activity.

A tap on the door jarred him from his prep work and he pulled aside the curtain for a look.

Standing bent at the waist with his hands over the glass was the last person Lionel Leanman expected to see this early in the afternoon.

*****

Dorf tried to push up off of old Bartie but the effort produced another fragrant grunt and suddenly the old man did not appear very old, scrambling backwards to escape.

Mrs. Kettler put a hand to her face and scurried out the door, to hell with what Herbert Mays liked to lick on his off time. Mays, who had done a hitch in Vietnam and had seen his fair share of atrocities done to and by the human body, knew immediately what had happened, but this in no way made him sympathetic. He reached up and pulled down the shade, announcing the staff was at lunch, though Herbert Mays didn't feel especially hungry.

"Sorry about that," Dorf said as Bartie fetched up against the counter and stopped, his eyes wide and one hand over his mouth.

"You just crapped on me," Bartie said in an astonished voice.

"Technically, I crapped myself, and for the fourth time today," Dorf said, trying to maintain a bow-legged stance as he stood. "It's all Mrs. Kettler's fault."

Bartie didn't ask and Dorf didn't elaborate. All Dorf wanted to do was find a restroom, where he could strip, dump (no pun intended) his soiled underwear and then get home. All Bartie wanted to do was find some fresh air and then put the hurt on a few drug dealers.

Turning like a man on ice, Dorf was so focused on his balance he almost missed what Bartie said.

"What?" he asked, reversing his turn in the same cautious fashion.

"I said is that a gun?"

Dorf felt like telling the old man he was a fool, of course it was a gun, what was he, blind? But he reminded himself that he had just shared a shitty embrace with the old guy, and that was an experience no one deserved.

"Yeah it's a gun," he said instead. "I run security up at the bank."

"*The* Bank or *The West* Bank?"

"The Bank," Dorf repeated, rolling his eyes, feeling an unpleasant wetness creeping down his leg.

"Oh." Bartie was chagrin; he knew that but the incident had temporarily left him befuddled. He had hoped to get Dorf to help him track down the drug dealers, but he doubted there would be any druggies opening an account at the bank any time soon.

"If you don't mind, I need to get cleaned up," Dorf said into the silence, duck-walking toward the door.

Bartie most certainly did not mind.

*****

Brian pulled into the deserted parking lot and rushed to the front door of the police station, where he saw Allen's note fluttering in a slight breeze. Inside, he found Todd and whom he presumed was Maxine, but Maxine was a guy, and a huge one at that.

"Todd, my man," Brian said with a cheerful grin.

"Hey bud," the other replied. "This is Max."

"Good to meet you Maxine," Brian said.

"I'm not Maxine," Max replied.

"But Todd just said you were," Brian, now a little uneasy, what with his comparatively tiny hand wrapped by Maxine's.

"My name is Max, not Maxine," Max said. He noticed he still held Brian's hand and quickly dropped it. "Max Irons."

"Okay, Maxirons, whatever you say." Turning to Todd once more, Brian asked him what the plan was.

"We're going to get some money from the bank," Todd said.

"We were gonna do that anyway when we hit that guy," Brian offered.

"I'm the guy," Max said.

"I know you're a guy and I'm sorry I called you Maxine," Brian said.

"No, I mean I'm the guy you hit," Max explained.

Todd had stepped away during this exchange and had now returned with a pair of shotguns from the gun tree in Chief Kocke's cubicle.

"What are those for?"

"To get some money," said Todd, rolling his good eye almost in sync with the other.

"I thought we were gonna get a loan," Brian countered.

"This is better," Max interjected. "This way we don't have to pay it back."

Brian, whose cat-litter-level IQ led him to the conclusion they would sell the guns as part of the loan, simply shrugged and followed his new partners toward the door.

*****

Now that her daily routine had been satisfied, which always included the news at noon, followed by a big bowl of rice pudding, Evvie Fennigan dressed for her afternoon trip to the post office (to hear how much Herbert Mays loved to lick large envelopes), followed by a trip to Esther's to check out the latest nylons in Aisle 7. She vaguely remembered Brian stopping by but she had ignored him; he of all people should know not to interrupt her morning routine.

She slid into her 1978 Dodge Duster, which had been paid off with Joe's untimely death, and headed for town.

*****

Nick Crawford and Danielle Stone both came to a similar conclusion, though Danielle's was the more lucid of the two. She understood now what had happened, and in time, she thought Nick could be led to the same insight. She also decided she still loved him.

Now all they had to do was get their cars out of the ditch before they were overrun by Jeb Stuart's bovines.

# Chapter 13

It was almost 12:45 when Lionel, owner of Triple-L (to himself at least) opened the door and admitted Jerry Fillabag.

"What are you doing here?"

"I got a message you wouldn't receive my associates," Jerry replied, wincing as he took in the macabre operation before him, then shrugging it off as not his concern.

"What associates?"

The gym guru sighed. Dealing with people like this was so tiring. "My associates, the amigos I sent here this morning."

"I didn't see anyone this morning, but I didn't get up and around until about noon," Lionel replied.

He lived in a small apartment above the bar, on account of not having any family and no desire to pay for a big, empty house.

After a moment's study, Jerry decided Lionel was telling the truth and moved on to the gist of what the hombres were sent to offer.

"I wanted to bring you in on a special deal I have brewing," he said with a smile; Jerry loved turning phrases, even if only he understood them.

Lionel had no idea what kind of deal was in the works, but only a fool believed first that Jerry Fillabag ever "offered" anything, and second that you could actually refuse. Like every other businessman in town, Lionel had heard about the Orc.

"What's the deal?"

Jerry paced the bar, weaving through dirty tables but careful not to touch them, as he outlined his objectives.

***** 

Dorf squelched with every movement, which was a lot since the Jeep had a standard transmission. His first thought of finding a bathroom was set aside as he suddenly realized the magnitude of his situation. Simply throwing soiled underwear in the trash would not do, and who in his right mind would carry them outside?

So he had two choices: drive all the way home to change, or find another place that offered at least some privacy. The bank popped into his mind. He had a key to the back door, where no customers would see him, and the employees' bathroom was just inside that door. He could be in, changed, and back out the door before anyone knew he was there, and his little problem could be dealt with.

An added benefit, he just realized, was that he had a back-up uniform in the security closet. It was old and only used in emergencies, but if this didn't qualify, he didn't know what did.

He'd just have to go raw the rest of the day, as his grandson was wont to say.

*****

Allen Frye, now the proud owner of a 64-ounce value-size jar of Rot-Be-Gone brand jock itch cream, decided that no further clues were forthcoming from Esther Pickering, who had retired to an office with a sign reading "Private." He was going to have to proceed alone.

He tentatively pushed open the door marked "Teabag Emporium" and was immediately accosted by an odor that made him think of goats and licorice.

Tempted to shut the door and walk away, Allen reminded himself that somewhere behind that door could be a very large supply of weed, and with his badge and gun, he could soon come into possession of most if not all of it. Which would clear up his name at the station as well as with Brian and Todd, who had blamed him for their expulsion.

He entered the organic food and Pakistani teabag store, unaware he was breathing through his mouth.

"Help you?"

Allen was surprised for the second time while in this store, and this time he pulled not his pistol but his jar of itch cream, trying to pull a trigger that wasn't there.

"Sorry." The tiny woman squeaked a little at the sight of the giant jar of cream, then took in the gun on Allen's hip and squeaked some more.

*Like a fucking rat,* Allen thought, putting the jar back in standby mode.

"You people love to sneak around," he said.

"I'm sorry, sir, I was only trying to help," the woman, Roseanne said.

"All right. I'm a police officer and I'm looking for drugs." Allen couldn't help stating the obvious, despite being in uniform.

"The drug store is back there," she said, pointing helpfully. "This is the Teabag Emporium."

"I know that, but I had a report of drugs being sold in here," Allen said, noting the smell again as he switched back to nasal breathing, a big mistake.

"No sir, just tea and organic foods is all we sell back here," Roseanne countered.

"Mind if I look around?"

Roseanne, whose name tag declared her a *Super Associate*, gestured to the room in silent acquiescence.

Allen began his search, though he was still hungry and now needing a hit very bad.

*****

Evvie Fennigan passed by the two cars crowding the ditch, recognized *Super-Cop* but did not stop to offer assistance. She simply steered around two cows in the road, which had moved considerably closer to Nick's car, and continued her afternoon excursion.

Nylon Mountain, as she called the display at Esther's, was beckoning her to come and browse. With her monthly check safely in her large purse, Evvie decided she might do a little more than just look.

Especially if there was a nice pair of Oriental or Latina. They were not her favorite, but they were exotic, and she was intrigued after seeing the Chinese nurse on General Hospital.

The two bovine investigating the crash watched her pass. They were joined shortly by three more, the small herd patiently looking for grass.

# Chapter 14

A few minutes before the three newest cows emerged, Nick and Danielle had managed to get her car back on the road. It hadn't traveled as far into the ditch, and with a little manly grunting, Nick was flushed but satisfied.

At 1:15 the couple, which was now officially a couple en route to marriage again, drove back toward town.

"I'm sorry I believed the worst about you," Nick said.

"I'm sorry too."

He almost blurted, "For what?" before caution stilled his tongue.

Nick Crawford, AKA *Super-Cop*, AKA *Private-Eye*, glanced over at her but said nothing. In his experience with women, which was limited to be sure, he had learned two valuable lessons: if a woman apologizes, don't ask her why, and if she asks your opinion on an outfit, especially whether or not it makes her look fat, remain silent. It was a core right, after all.

"It must have been difficult, thinking I was having an affair," Danielle said into the silence.

*Back on safe ground,* he thought.

"Yeah, but that's okay. I won't believe that again."

"Are you going to apologize to my neighbor's boyfriend?"

"Who?"

"The guy you chased with a chainsaw. You scared Brenda half to death."

Nick was having difficulty following this line of conversation. "What guy? What chainsaw? What about Brenda?"

Danielle made the turn onto Highway A, which ran the length of town, and then moved her attention to her reinstated fiancee. "You don't remember, do you?"

"I guess not." Definitely not. Nick knew he'd been drunk

both times he's watched her house, and that his arms were very sore today, but that couldn't be from chasing some guy with a chainsaw, could it?

"It all made sense after you admitted to spying on me while you were drunk," Danielle said. "You really don't know what I'm talking about?"

"No."

She put aside her astonishment for a second, thanking God yet again she was not a male of this species. "Okay, first, you said you saw me at the sink with a man, right?"

He nodded, not really sure anymore, and she continued. "My kitchen doesn't have a window over the sink."

*Some private eye,* he thought bitterly.

"But the kitchen in Brenda's house does, and she's been seeing this new guy, Dalton," Danielle said. "I've seen them standing there myself."

Silence as deep as thoughts of last night's drunken shenanigans filled the car.

It was 1:25 as Danielle theorized his activities.

*****

Phillip Andrew Thomas and Chief Kocke were crammed into the chief's Subaru, since his official unit was having the brakes repaired; they pulled into traffic directly behind Nick and Danielle, but both were too occupied with their conversation to notice.

"Where do we start?"

Kocke didn't like the sound of that. "First, we're going to the station, where you and I will part company," he said. "Then, I'm going to have a meeting with my officers and try to get to the bottom of this."

Phillip Andrew Thomas was aggravated but not discouraged. He thought the day would be spent traveling with the chief, taking notes and pictures as the case unfolded. Call it a hands-on story.

"Don't worry," Chief Kocke said. "I'll call you the minute we get a suspect."

"You know I have a deadline one day hence," Phillip

said with flair. "I think it best for my readers, especially those who would just love to find out how you spend your off-time, if I just tagged along with you today."

Kocke wondered briefly how this guy slept at night. Like a baby, most likely, he decided.

Disgusted, even a bit angry, but with no real choice, the chief agreed to let Lard-Ass stick with him for the day, but added a warning. "You don't interfere, you got it? And don't hassle my officers."

"Agreed."

And with that, they were joined for the remainder of the day, the irony of which was not lost on either as the odd shenanigans, as Nick Crawford would say, began to unfold.

Dorf entered the back door at 1:30, seeing no one as he first grabbed his spare uniform and then made for the bathroom, still duckwalking, as if that would help.

Bartie, meanwhile, was nearly run over by Evvie Fennigan as she pulled into the diagonal parking space recently vacated by The Bank of Newburn's funky security guard.

And while Bartie was collecting himself, Danielle piloted her Caprice past the post office with hardly a glance, the chief behind her doing the same.

The cows, two of which were likely smarter than Allen Frye, sauntered up to Route A and aimed their freight toward town, still searching for grass.

# Chapter 15

"So you want me to sell your product here in my bar?"

"First I want you to try it for yourself and then if you like it, yes, I'd like you to sell it here."

*Translation: Try it all you want but you're going to sell it regardless*, Lionel thought.

"Okay, how's it packaged?"

"You can dress it up anyway you want," Jerry Fillabag replied. "Put it sandwich bags for all I care, but the point is, you have to sell it, not just put it out there for these morons to try."

Jerry was thinking of the disease-on-a-plate buffet, which sat here rarely touched every Sunday, regardless of how hungry the clientele might be. "Once they get a little taste, this will rival beer in terms of sales."

"Jesus," Lionel muttered, wondering how he had been chosen for this little enterprise.

Jerry produced a gallon-sized Ziploc bag, which appeared to hold about two pounds of grass clippings. "You'll have to pick out the hair but other than that, it's easy," Jerry explained. "One serving is four ounces, don't forget that. And don't give them any more than that at a time or you'll have guys running around puking. This stuff is very good and very potent."

"Do I have to cut it, mix it with anything?" Lionel had been around long enough to know that grass was usually cut down, so as to extend the life and up the price.

"Nope. Just measure out four ounces and serve."

"What about the cops?"

"What about them? The amigos will be by later with a shipment and to collect."

Lionel was already 30 minutes late opening the door for business, not that he usually had a line waiting to crawl in here. But if Jerry Fillabag was right, there just might be.

*****

Chief Brad Kocke and his unwanted passenger pulled into the station's parking lot, still cracked, but without any other vehicles.

*Where the hell is everybody?* he wondered, then noticed the note on the door.

*Gone to the drug store for a lead and lunch. Be back. Allen Frye.*

Kocke checked his watch, noted it was almost 1:20, and grunted. Leave it to Allen to leave the station unattended for more than two hours.

"That guy's a bonehead," Phillip said after reading the note over Kocke's shoulder.

"I know, but don't hassle him when he gets back," Brad warned again, wondering privately if that would be today.

The unlikely allies entered the station, Phillip heading for the men's room, Kocke making his way to the cubicle and his Man In Charge swivel chair. He didn't notice the gun tree, which was actually an umbrella stand, was short a pair of 12-guage shotguns as he sat down.

*****

"Are you crazy?" Bartie shouted at Evvie as she slowly exited her Duster.

"Are you blind?" she countered before offering a haughty sniff and walking to the post office door.

Bartie supposed that yes, technically, he was blind enough to have been denied a driver's license last month in Waterford, but that didn't stop him from driving. He gave Evvie a dirty look and then got into his own car, an Oldsmobile Delta 88, which was a lot of car for such a small man.

Still armed with a boatload of suspicion, Bartie decided he'd head back to the police station and try to make another report, preferably with someone smarter than Allen Frye.

*****

Todd and Max had devised a simple plan, one that even

Brian understood - after it had been explained half a dozen times, much to the annoyance of Max Irons.

They would enter the bank just before closing (at 3 p.m.) with their stolen shotguns. With any luck, they could do this with only employees to worry about. Plus, Todd had heard about "Next Day's Business" and figured that meant they would get tomorrow's money as well.

"So when do we give them the guns?" Brian was stuck on trading the guns for money.

"We don't give them the guns, bro," Todd replied. "We're going to aim the guns at the teller and she'll give us the money."

"Do we have to pay it back?"

"Pay what back?" Max asked.

"The money."

Todd and Max exchanged a look that suggested it would probably be easier to just shoot Brian right now and be done with it. After what seemed to be a choreographed sigh, the two began the explanation a second time; and so it had gone, until just before the trio turned onto County Road 201, when Brian finally got it. His whole face lit up.

"Man, that's freakin' brilliant!" He reminded Max of a teenager who finally understands fractions.

Now they were heading to Evvie's place, where Brian knew they'd find a good selection of panty-hose with which to cover their faces.

*****

Bartie Grantz, traveling at the same speed as the cows marching up Route A, turned into the Newburn Police Department lot just behind Danielle Stone and Nick Crawford. He was happy to see the chief's Subaru parked there as well, because that meant most likely he wouldn't have to deal with Allen Frye.

"Hello officer," Bartie said in greeting to Nick, who had his arm protectively around Danielle's shoulder.

"Hello, sir."

"Can you help me?"

71

Nick, who was planning to stop in long enough to tell Chief Kocke (whose Subaru he had also noted with relief) about the morning's episode with Beevis, then check on Butthead's report before heading again to look for Brian. Somewhere in the mix he and Danielle were planning to stop for lunch at Jan's.

"What's the trouble, sir?"

"I saw some more of those drug dealers while I was at the post office."

"What drug dealers?" Nick did not connect Allen's fragmented note with this conversation.

"I told Officer Frye about it this morning," Bartie replied. "He said he would look into it, but then I saw those same fellas at the Double-L and they were carrying big bags of mary-wanna."

"Are you sure it was marijuana," asked Nick, pronouncing it correctly for the benefit of Bartie, who missed it completely.

"Not a hunnert percent, that's what I told Officer Frye, but I'm almost sure."

Nick and Danielle shared a glance which only long-time couples telepathically understand: *This guy is a fruit.*

"Well, let's go inside, see if maybe Allen left something."

Danielle didn't want to impose on Nick's official duty, so she told she'd be back for him shortly, and left him with a smile and a light kiss on the corner of his mouth.

Nick and Grandpa G entered the police station.

*****

Allen Frye, after a 10-minute search provided nothing more than a headache, returned to the counter where *Super Associate* Roseanne was leafing through a catalog which featured the latest in Middle-Eastern tea accessories. He had no idea such things were possible.

"Find anything?" she asked, closing her magazine but leaving her index finger between pages 34 and 35.

"No, but that doesn't mean anything," Allen replied

cryptically. "You'd have had plenty of warning to hide it while Esther had me tied up in the itch-cream aisle."

"We have nothing to hide, sir," Roseanne replied in her squeaky voice, which set Allen's teeth on edge.

"What's in all those bags back there?"

"What bags?"

"The big black garbage bags in the corner there."

"Trash?" Roseanne offered.

"I doubt it. I'm going to look in those bags."

For Roseanne, who watched *Law & Order* as regularly as Allen, but who also watched all 16 episodes of Dateline each week, an alarm went off in her head.

"You need a warrant."

"You already told me I could look around," Allen pointed out, making what he hoped was his best Chris Noth face. To Allen, Noth had being a cop down to an art and it was a shame he left the show, and all he would watch now were re-runs. "That means I can look without a warrant."

"It won't hold up in court," Roseanne, whose favorite *L&O* character was the assistant D.A. played by Jill Hennessy. "They'll tear you up on cross."

Her voice was not so bad, the more he thought about it.

"We'll get a slam-dunk confession and it will never go to trial," Allen said, taking a step closer to Roseanne.

"No judge would let evidence obtained without a warrant stand," Roseanne (Jill) breathed.

"Fruit of the tree of knowledge," Allen (Noth) replied. "Besides, he would with a confession."

"I've got a confession of my own," Roseanne (Jill) said in a breathless voice.

"You can tell me, I'm a cop," Allen (Noth) said.

Roseanne (Jill) lost her place in the catalog as her hand went to Allen's (Noth's) chest.

Both heard the *Law & Order* theme music at their lips met; Allen dropped his giant jar of itch cream.

*****

The Orc, whose real name was Branford Rollins, was

having no luck whatsoever finding Max Irons. He'd checked Jan's Country Griddle & Bait Shop and he was fresh out of ideas, so he plodded back to The Newburn Fitness & Weight Training Center.

# Chapter 16

Chief Brad Kocke sat in the MIC chair, a little slanted since one of the casters was chipped, reviewing the report turned in by Allen Frye. How a dimwit the likes of Allen ever got a job he couldn't rightly say, despite the fact Kocke had hired him.

Nick had vouched for him, and the two reservist deadbeats were part of the package, though Kocke's condition had been they remain on reserve unless the town was a) invaded by thugs so many in number that sacrificing Brian and Todd was necessary or b) someone really needed the day off.

The fact that Brad Kocke himself really needed an afternoon off for personal business when Nick was at Waterford for CPR training had led to the missing evidence and subsequent investigation.

While it appeared that Brian and Todd had helped themselves to the marijuana stored in the evidence locker, it was Allen Frye who had been on duty and in charge, which made it his responsibility. No proof existed that the Moronic Duo had actually done it, but they were the odds-on favorite. Chief Kocke had ordered an investigation, which turned up very little.

The marijuana, about four pounds of it, was missing. Allen Frye swore on on a Bible that he did not take it, nor did he witness Brian or Todd hanging around after their three-hour contribution to Kocke's afternoon off. Nick surmised that during one of Allen's habitual jaunts in which the station was unattended, an unknown perpetrator entered and stole the evidence.

Phillip Andrew Thomas had loved that angle, Brad remembered.

In bigger cities, the evidence locker would have been padlocked, but this was Newburn, where umbrella stands doubled as gun trees and a cardboard box labeled "EVIDENCE" with a permanent marker served as the "locker" for said evidence.

Since it was easier to slap Brian and Todd with suspension, Kocke had done that, rather than jeopardize federal funding for Allen's position. Young Mr. Frye did get a stern lecture about leaving the station empty, which kept him from wandering for about a week.

Both Chief Kocke and Phillip Andrew Thomas looked up as two figures walked around the "reception area" and headed their way. Both recognized Gandalf from earlier in the day, and wondered why he was trailing Nick.

"Chief, this man wants to report a drug deal of some kind, and I have to find Brian Fennigan, can you talk to him?"

Nick saw the report in Kocke's hand but dismissed it. He had no idea it concerned him.

*****

Phillip Andrew Thomas was bored. Simply put, he began to wonder if there were better things to do with his afternoon than sitting here watching some old man claim there were drug dealers afoot. He said nothing, but Chief Brad Kocke picked up the vibe nonetheless.

"So you saw some guys at the Double-L with bags of marijuana?" Kocke addressed Grandpa G aka Bartie in the same way Nick had; again he missed the point.

"That's right chief," Bartie said. "They were carrying bags of mary-wanna and another one was sittin' in the truck."

"And these are the same guys you saw earlier coming out of Esther's, you're sure about that?"

"Yes sir. I'd just had my pills filled when I seen 'em."

Kocke thought about what to do. With Nick out hunting for Brian, and Allen presumably at Esther's, he would have to leave the station unattended again. He then thought it probably wouldn't make much difference, so he scooped up the paperwork, noticing finally that the gun tree was a little lighter than it should be.

"What is it chief?" Phillip asked, following his gaze but not making a connection.

"We're missing a couple of shotguns."

For the first time that day, Chief Brad Kocke had a bad feeling in his gut. The three left the station, heading for Esther's Warehouse of Drugs & Teabag Emporium to get some answers from Allen Frye.

\*\*\*\*\*

Evvie Fennigan, whose planned visit with Herbert Mays didn't materialize due to the pervasive odor Dorf had left behind, had spent the next 40 minutes in Aisle 7 at Esther's Warehouse of Drugs & Teabag Emporium, checking out the mountain of nylons now available.

There were midnight-black, peach, nude (her favorite), Latina, and a host of others, in styles ranging from knee-highs to full-body with built-in girdle. When Joe was alive, he would moan and groan about her meanderings through Aisle 7, which made afternoon idling even more enjoyable.

There, she said to herself. Exotic Oriental, the package proclaimed. Evvie pulled the egg-shaped carton from the mountain, nearly disrupting the entire structure, and headed for the counter.

With her purchase tucked into her purse, she thought about checking out the Pakistani tea room at the back of the store, but opted instead to head for The Newburn Bank to cash her insurance check.

\*\*\*\*\*

Danielle entered the bank at 1:44, just in time to see Dorf emerge from the bathroom. She wondered if his condition was better and decided it must be for him to have come to work.

Smiling at the tellers, who stood together chewing gum with great vapidity, Danielle went to her desk and checked for messages. None.

With no one scheduled for this afternoon, she thought it

perfectly reasonable to take the rest of the day off. But she had to clear it with bank president Edward Von Waterman III, who reminded Danielle of Mr. Whipple from those old toilet-paper commercials. He was always trying to look down the front of her blouse.

"What happened?" Von Waterman III asked, sneaking a peak at her bust, which unfortunately, was covered today by a business suit.

"I was in a car accident and I need to leave a little early," Danielle answered, resisting the urge to cover her chest.

"And what if we get a customer who wants a loan this afternoon?"

*Then you can deal with it,* she thought bitterly. *It is your bank, after all.*

Instead she did what any professional woman with an obvious tool would do she leaned over and let him look at her collar bone. "It's only an hour or so."

Little beads of sweat had formed at Waterman's temples, and slowly began their course down his face. Danielle shuddered at the thought of him ogling her, but she was in no mood to sit here at the bank.

After another minute of this perversity, Waterman churlishly agreed to let her go, and Danielle retreated to her desk, pointedly ignoring the look she got from the tellers, whose gum-chewing had reached enough speed to power a small motorboat.

Dorf approached as she hastily gathered her personal items and tucked them into her purse.

"I'm sorry about earlier," he said.

"That's okay, Dorf," Danielle said absently. "I hope it all came out all right."

She did not intend to make light of his problem, and his chuckle indicated he was not put out by her choice of words.

"You could say that, though I bet old Grandpa G wishes he had skipped the post office."

This cryptic comment went past Danielle, who was logging out of her computer.

"Anyway, I should be okay now," Dorf said. He glanced

down and noticed a splotch of what might be gravy on his Always-Glo brand security-guard shoe but probably wasn't. "I have to go to the bathroom."

He departed, leaving a distant Danielle to her end-of-the-day routine. She heard the bell announce a visitor, but didn't look up.

She wouldn't have recognized Evvie Fennigan anyway.

# Chapter 17

Jerry Fillabag was pleased. He had managed to place his product in four of the most heavily-trafficked businesses in town, the Double-L being the last. He now had Crank's, Jan's and the bar, and of course, Esther's, where the product was delivered initially.

His three amigos, who doubled as back-up for the Orc, were very persuasive, and aside from his one trip to see Lionel, it was going well.

But now the Orc was sitting in his office, looking around nervously and not making much sense.

"You can't find Max?"

"Uhn."

Knowing it would be a fruitless enterprise to discuss the situation any further, Jerry dismissed the Orc. It wasn't his fault; the Orc had to be given explicit directions and the gym owner had forgotten that.

He returned his gaze to the workout floor, ignoring the Orc's departure. Mentally, he'd already moved on to his next project, which basically involved using the money from his latest investment to buy a lot more cow-roids, which he would sell to the basketball team. It was just not right, losing to a bunch of deaf kids.

*****

For the few minutes it took to walk to The Newburn Bank, Nick was trying to force his head (which still hurt, though not as bad) to recall for himself what he did last night. Bits of memory, like the occasional M&M in a bag of trail mix, were floating through his consciousness, but all were as rounded as the hard-shelled candy. Despite being told what he'd supposedly done, he still could not reconcile the events in his own mind.

Maybe someday he'd remember exactly what happened,

but for now, he let it go as he walked into the bank.

He went straight to Danielle's desk, where she was waiting for the day's files to be saved to 14 different locations before the computer authorized shutdown. He knew she was not ready, and decided he would go to Evvie's place and then come back for her. She agreed, saying she was a little worried about Dorf.

He shrugged, departed and climbed into Danielle's Caprice, unaware that The Newburn Bank was about to become a hot spot.

*****

Nick was traveling up Route A as Brian was approaching from the other side, his Tercel in rare form with both doors securely shut. With him were Todd and Max, and in the back seat next to Captain Biceps was a plastic bag containing their masks. They had tried to call Allen at the station but no one answered, so they figured he was on his own, unless he offered a peace pipe filled with some of Crazy Willy's finest.

Brian had been the mastermind (a scary thought in itself) behind raiding the evidence "locker," and Todd had gone along willingly enough, as had Allen. The marijuana had been seized from Crazy Willy's place, though the dealer himself was not home at the time.

Nick had made the grab after an anonymous phone tip, and Brian thought he looked happier than a dog with two dicks.

There was no complicated plan; Brian just walked in and took the marijuana while Allen was on the crapper. Then he and Todd returned to their apartment and smoked until they passed out.

They kept a bag for themselves and gave Allen a taste, since he was the one on duty when it went down, then tried to sell the rest of it back to Crazy Willy at a discount.

Crazy Willy, known for his psychotic tendencies (hence the nickname) as well as his street smarts, told them he was taking it back for free, and neither Brian nor Todd thought to argue, since Crazy Willy was by then holding the pot.

A few days later he sold them some of the marijuana they had given to him at a twice the regular price, explaining that he had to figure inflation into the equation. Then he cut them off.

Now, as Brian pulled the Tercel into The Newburn Bank's parking lot, Todd thought surely there would be enough loot to convince Crazy Willy to sell to them again and wondered why they gave his marijuana back to him in the first place. Max was thinking in terms of not only paying Jerry before the Orc and his buddies found him, but also buying more cowroids. Brian, meanwhile, was still worried about the guns.

*****

Chief Brad Kocke and Phillip Andrew Thomas were quite surprised when they opened the door marked "Teabag Emporium" to find Allen Frye and a young woman rolling around on the floor. Brad was thankful he had ordered Bartie to remain with the car. He might have keeled over from such a sight.

She was saying "Faster Chris!" and he was mumbling about how he didn't need a warrant. It was really quite disgusting.

Both were covered in some kind of cream, the origin of which neither Brad nor Phillip wanted to guess, but otherwise the two were naked. Evvie would have appreciated the YTR-esque scene immediately, but she was in line waiting to cash her insurance check.

"Allen!" Chief Kocke shouted. He noticed the smell of goats and wondered if it was connected to the cream the couple was lathered in.

"Allen!" he repeated, finally getting the other's attention. "What in the hell are you doing?"

The woman threw her hands up over her tiny bosoms, and while it was unnecessary because of the jock-itch cream, it was natural reaction when confronted by two strange men who happened to barge into a place of business to find the Super Associate writhing on the floor in a compromising situation.

"Well?" He knew what they were doing, but not why they were doing it. "I thought you were here checking on a lead in a drug case."

Allen at least had the decency to look embarrassed, but Phillip was hardly looking at him. His attention, like that of most fat men who spend their Saturday nights watching adult cinema, was riveted on the petite woman trying vainly to cover herself.

"Sorry chief," Allen said at last. "I was following a series of clues, which led me here, and well, you see, we both love *Law & Order*."

Chief Kocke didn't even want an explanation to that. "Tell me what's going on here right now or I'll see you on the street by the end of the day," Kocke said.

"I took a report from a man this morning," Allen began. "He said there were drugs being sold at Esther's so I came out here."

"I know. I just talked to him, but you do know this is a drug store, right? I mean, the word drugs is on the marquee."

"I was told they were selling mary-wanna out here, chief," Allen replied, unaware he had used Bartie's dialect.

"Did you find any?"

"Not yet."

Roseanne, who no longer felt like Jill Hennessy but was still "in the mood" as Esther liked to say, covered a grin as she remembered how this little escapade had begun.

Kocke turned to Phillip with a look that asked, *See what I have to put up with?*

Phillip offered a very brief but sympathetic glance before once more storing the image before him for later use, berating himself for leaving the camera in the car.

"Are you done here?"

Allen wasn't sure if the chief was referring to his investigation or sex with Roseanne, but said no in order to cover both bases.

"Well finish up," Kocke said. "I want a report by the end of the day.

"About the drugs," he added a second later.

With that, he and a very reluctant Phillip left the tea room to talk to Esther.

But before he had traveled halfway up Aisle 4, where "The Itch Stops HERE!", he saw two men with bags of grass clippings. They took one look at the chief and reversed direction quickly, heading for the exit.

Brad pulled Phillip's arm and headed for the front door, reaching it just in time to see the two men cram into a pick-up truck, which already had two men in the cab.

Phillip could tell old Bartie was excited but with the windows rolled up, he couldn't technically hear him. Chief Kocke opened his door and Bartie nearly escaped in his zeal.

"That's them! That's the guys I saw earlier," as Brad grabbed his frail arm.

Kocke had already surmised as much, and shoved Bartie back into the car. A moment later the unlikely trio was in pursuit.

Allen and Roseanne resumed their private investigation.

*****

Dorf couldn't believe he was still cramping. He had entered the bathroom, bent over to check on the stain on his shoe, and felt the now-familiar clenching that told him he was in trouble. Fortunately, he was in the right place this time, and avoided fouling his fresh uniform.

# Chapter 18

It was 1:54, about an hour earlier than originally planned when Brian, Todd and Max pulled into the parking lot which served The Newburn Bank. Pulling on their masks was a little difficult.

At Evvie's place, the search for something to hide their identities was quickly over, as Brian found his mother's trunk full of nylons. It was actually tougher to get into than the evidence carton, but they managed eventually.

Brian and Todd argued over one particular pair, but Max settled that dispute by taking it for himself. The other two scooped their own "masks" and then they headed for town.

Now, as they climbed out of the Tercel, Todd thought maybe they should have spent a little more time picking out their facial coverings.

"I can't see a thing," he complained.

"Me neither," Brian said, and Max's comment was oddly muffled.

Brian and Todd squinted at him but couldn't make out more than a large shape. Their nylons were knee-highs, each having one leg worth on their head. It made viewing nearly impossible and with their noses turned at severe angles, it was hard to breathe as well.

Disgusted, Todd removed his nylon. "This is never going to work."

Brian pulled off his knee-high and both he and Todd stared at Max, who was struggling to breathe through the girdle portion of Evvie's full-body nylons.

*****

The Orc and the amigos passed in front of The Newburn Bank as two small men were trying to pull something off a bigger man.

"Ughh ehhhr."

Amigo numero uno took this to mean "Look there" and so he did, a smile pushing his bushy mustache up noticeably. "Tres Stooges," the man in the middle said.

The truck continued on Route A, headed for the Double-L, where they would try again to deliver a shipment of Jerry's product.

*****

Nick saw the empty driveway and wondered if Brian was actually stupid enough to have gone back to Todd's apartment. Knowing the answer to that, he used the driveway to turn around, and headed back to town, passing his brown car, still in the ditch, and still serving Jeb Stuart's growing escapees as a sort of shrine.

Max cursed, his eyes watering as Brian and Todd pulled against one another in their effort to free him, instead of working together. The result was that Max's hair was being ripped from his ears. He reached out with his giant hands and grabbed a handful of shirt, one from each, and pulled. Brian and Todd seemed to embrace and both let go of the legs on Evvie's nylons.

The only good thing to come of it was a small tear, which provided Max a line of sight on the left side. "Stop it both of you," Max said, releasing them after they quit struggling.

"We were only trying to help," Todd said.

"Give me your nylons," Max said. He used a thumb to poke through the fabric, enough to give his partners an eyehole and then gave them back. "Put them on before we get inside."

Brian put his on backwards and got help turning it around by an unhappy (and ungentle) Max Irons, who was ready to break the moron's neck with his huge bare hands.

## 1:56 P.M.

Jerry Fillabag sometimes did things on the spur of the moment; this business strategy had sometimes hurt, but there were good results as well, such as the cowroids, which were selling quite well.

He had sat pondering how to establish the pipeline to the basketball team when his cell phone rang. Jerry answered, listened to for a minute and then hung up.

His amigos were in trouble.

Jerry grabbed his Colt Widowmaker and ran out the back door to his Dodge Ram 2500; he would have preferred a Cadillac, but this was cow country.

Max Irons carried one of the NPD's shotguns and Todd had the other; neither had to discuss the stupidity of allowing Brian a firearm.

Evvie Fennigan was thinking of what color nylons to buy for Wednesday's Bingo! Nite at at the Knights of Columbus, and was debating between her favorite, nude, and evocative Latino-brown.

Danielle, who considered herself a tough person, did not feel tough as she pressed the OFF button on her computer and started to rise. The doors were just swinging shut as three men, one of them very large and all of them wearing nylons on their heads, took a few steps into The Newburn Bank with shotguns. She couldn't stop the scream that boomed from her throat.

Dorf heard the scream and thought one of the tellers must have seen a mouse; that or Mr. Edward Von Waterman III had finally crossed the line from ogling to touching. Either way, he was in no position to care.

The cow quintet, meanwhile, had just passed Jan's Country Griddle & Bait Shop, drawing curious looks from several greasy-chicken diners.

# Chapter 19

## 1:59 P.M.

Danielle didn't know the giant man with the firm-support nylons on his head, though one of his eyes was visible, and she noted the color as hazel, which she would report later. She reached beneath her desk and pressed the panic button, which sent an alarm to the police station. Her brief loss of control and subsequent scream had been replaced with almost relief as she realized her attackers were young men she knew used to work with Nick. The bear might be a problem.

## 2:01 P.M.

Allen Frye and his new girlfriend, Roseanne Perkins, were all used up. Their private investigation had been very fruitful, but now Allen was starving. Roseanne offered him the last of her oat-bran muffin, which had been processed in an organic setting and had nothing to do with Mrs. Kettler.

It helped, but his belly was still gnawing at him for something solid. His eyes happened on the black bags in the corner and suspicion returned.

"What is in those bags?"

"Grass clippings."

"As in marijuana?"

"No, as in special tea from Pakistan."

Allen was, for about the hundredth time that day, confused. "Tea?"

"Yeah. That's what we sell here, specialty tea."

"What about the marijuana?"

"We don't sell that here."

"Where do you sell it?"

"We don't sell it anywhere."

Allen was disappointed, but he didn't consider the day a complete loss.

Sensing her new boyfriend's dismay, Roseanne took his hand and led him behind the counter, where she had him sit. They were still naked, which should have been a problem but was not, since hardly anyone visited the tea room. As he sat waiting, she turned and pulled out a cigar box from beneath a stack of catalogs.

He had finally found some quality pot, and his concerns floated away.

### 2:02 P.M.

The teller forgot all about chewing her gum, which stuck in her braces. She also forgot about Evvie Fennigan, who had pushed her insurance check across the counter.

Britni Chambers was staring at Brian, Todd and Max, who seemed to be arguing. Though she couldn't hear them clearly, it was obvious the blond guy was urging his partners to wait.

*****

"We have to wait until they're on 'Next Day's Business' so we get tomorrow's money," Todd said, his knee-high still pressing his nose into his cheek, but at least he could see a little.

"What time is that?"

"I think it's at three o'clock."

"They close the bank at three," Max said. "If we wait until then, they'll put all the money in the safe. We need to get it now."

"But there might be a lot more money with tomorrow's business," Todd replied.

"Somebody already screamed," Max said. "They know we're here."

"Yeah but they don't know what we want."

Both Todd and Max ignored Brian's interjection, and both wondered again why they didn't shoot him earlier.

"Well we can't just stand here," Max continued. "They

89

know we're up to something."

"Okay, but tell them we want tomorrow's money," Todd countered.

Brian locked the inner doors of The Newburn Bank.

# Chapter 20

**2:05 P.M.**

Newburn's Chief of Police pulled his rundown Subaru to a stop in front of the Double-L and left it idling (wheezing) behind the truck parked in the diagonal parking space on the street. It contained one of the four men he had seen leaving Esther's, and he was anxious to make a bust.

"What's the plan, Chief?" Phillip asked.

"Gonna take down some drug dealers," Kocke replied, secretly hoping Phillip would include it in the story.

Bartie was once more left in the car as Kocke and Phillip got out and approached the truck, also idling.

"Afternoon sir," Kocke said pleasantly enough.

"No habla *Espanol*," said the driver, who was very nervous.

"Save it Pablo," Kocke said and pointed to a gallon-sized Ziploc on the dash. "Give me that bag."

The driver tried the same line but Chief Kocke, who was long overdue, slapped him. "Give me the fuckin' bag right now!"

One hand rubbing the suddenly-red splotch on his face, his eyes filled with disbelief, the driver handed the bag over.

"What have we here?"

The driver, wisely in Phillip's opinion, remained silent. He continued to rub his cheek.

"Looks like grass," Phillip said. "Marijuana?"

After a moment of pinching, rubbing and sniffing, Chief Kocke placed it; the grass smelled like the tea room at Esther's minus the jock-itch cream. Kocke didn't know what to make of it.

\*\*\*\*\*

91

Phillip Andrew Thomas was excited, though not nearly as wound up as he had been in the tea room as *Star Associate* Roseanne sat naked in a heap. The old man had been right. The veteran weekly paper writer made a mental note to interview Bartie Grantz when this was over, but for now, he wanted a picture for the front page of the Newburn News.

"Chief, do you mind standing beside the cab?"

"Not at all."

Kocke's handprint was still a reddening welt on the driver's face, but it wouldn't show up in the picture, and if it did, well, that's why they invented PhotoJob, right?

Chief Brad Kocke put on a big smile, leaned in slightly while holding the bag of grass clippings just below the window, so the thug could be seen clearly.

He still didn't know what the stuff in the bag was, but he was pretty sure it wasn't marijuana; still he was convinced it was something illegal and that Esther's was offering a front for it. She had some 'splaining to do, as Desi Arnaz used to say.

Teabag Emporium indeed.

After Phillip took half a dozen shots and proclaimed them good, the chief put the bag of grass clippings in his Subaru.

### 2:09 P.M.

Nick returned to The Newburn Bank, noticing the Tercel sitting there looking somehow disheveled, its doors closed loosely. There was no sign of the Moronic Duo so he assumed they were inside.

Inside, Evvie Fennigan stood a foot in front of her wayward son, though she didn't know it at first. She had finally realized that Britni was actually looking at something and turned around, her face two inches from the business end of a shotgun.

"Those are my best nylons," she shrieked before caution could still her voice. "I'd recognize that stain anywhere."

Max, whose face was on the other side of the stain, had

no idea what the old woman was talking about. He raised the gun to stroke her upside the head but Brian grabbed his arm.

"Don't hit her man," he said.

"Brian? Is that you?" Evvie discovered he was wearing one of her best knee-highs, though it couldn't be called that anymore, what with the rip down the middle. She noticed Todd had its mate.

"Don't use my name, mom," Brian said.

"Why not?"

"Nobody's supposed to know who I am." Brian didn't realize that secrecy was moot by this point.

"I always knew you'd wind up in trouble, doing something stupid like this," Evvie nearly screamed. "My precious little boy, always too smart for his own good."

Max and Todd rolled the three good eyes between them and stepped around the Evvie and Brian reunion to talk to Britni, who had resumed chewing her gum in all the excitement.

"Help you?"

"Yeah, we want all the money, including tomorrow's," Max said, brandishing the shotgun at the recent high-school graduate.

"How can I give you tomorrow's money? It's not here yet."

"What's not here?"

"Tomorrow."

Max looked at Todd, who had a pretty good idea of what was going on. "Don't mess with us," he told Britni. "We know all about 'next day's business' and we want that money too."

### 2:14 P.M.

Unaware his former co-workers were robbing The Newburn Bank, Nick walked through the outer door but nearly ripped his arm out of the socket when he yanked on the inner door. Alarm bells immediately went off in his head and a few seconds later his suspicions were confirmed.

On the other side of the glass, he could see Todd and Max pointing shotguns at the tellers while Brian stood with his mother, who was really letting him have it. Beyond them, Nick saw Danielle, who was pressing the panic button repeatedly.

*Max? he thought. How did he get involved with these two?*

Nick had thought him a decent enough guy on the sidewalk after he'd been run down by Brian, and to see him with a pair of full-figure nylons on his head was weird. The stain didn't help.

He thought about forcing his way in, but soon dismissed that idea. Anything could set off these morons, and Nick did not want innocent civilians shot by accident.

Thirty seconds later, Dorf, now pulling up his pants sans boxers, heard a tapping on the back door and wondered who could be trying to get in. The scream had not been repeated, so either the mouse had been found or a teller had been fired.

He had no time to mess with air freshener.

All Jerry wanted to do was get his amigos out of harm's way, and get back to the gym. He had work to do with his new project. He neared the Double-L and saw that fat-ass from the paper talking with Chief Kocke, who was rooting around the back of Miguel's truck.

*****

"Well I'll be damned," Kocke proclaimed as he uncovered four large black bags, each filled with more of the mystery grass. He wasted no time in having Phillip take his picture, visions of grandeur filling his mind.

Lionel Leanman watched Chief Kocke tossing bags of grass from the back of the truck, and wondered what else could go wrong with this deal. First he had inadvertently pissed off Jerry Fillabag (never a good idea, he thought) by not answering a knock on the door by his hired thugs. Then he had to sit through a lecture about the town's business community working together to succeed together. Christ, he thought for a minute he was being harangued by Tony Robbins. Then, no sooner than these guys come tromping into the bar, which was still devoid of customers and only recently restored to buffet status (which he kept "fresh" daily as a lark), the Newburn chief of police comes pulling up and starts throwing bags of grass over the side like extra rations on a sinking ship.

Well, it does appear to be sinking, he thought of his investment, the payment for which was still in Scott's dirty fingers. Lionel wondered if there was a way to get that back, for surely Jerry Fillabag wouldn't charge him for product that wasn't delivered. Right?

*Yeah, right,* he thought. *We're talking about Jerry Fillabag, who once charged his own mother a late fee on her monthly account.*

Lionel didn't know exactly what the product was despite Jerry's assurances it was Pakistani tea, but he was convinced it would earn him a ride to prison. The bright side is that it was outside, and not technically in his possession. Surely he could turn that to his advantage.

*****

Dorf heard a muffled "Police, open up" and decided he would do it even though he knew Edward Von Waterman III would have a hissy-fit. Nick entered, offering not a word of explanation, so Dorf did what any security guard who loathed the police would do: he ordered him to halt.

Nick recognized Dorf not just from around town but from the interview in which he learned of Dorf's contention that beating people with police-issue batons wasn't enough. Considering Kocke's sideline activities, some might be surprised at the lack of comradeship, but the chief didn't want competition.

"There's a robbery in progress," Nick said. "Get out of my way."

"I ain't heard nothing," said Dorf, discounting the scream as some silly feminine reaction.

"I saw them," Nick said, brushing past Dorf, who considered briefly pulling out his gun but thought better of it, opting instead to follow *Super-Cop.*

## 2:16 P.M.

Perplexed, Britni looked for help from Danielle, who had not moved from her desk; all she offered was a minute shrug.

Dalton Fisk stood completely ignored at the other teller's window. He was being ignored even before the guys with the shotguns came in, but now was no time to be picky.

The bear had glanced at him with one eye, which was creepy, but said nothing; so far, the other two, one of whom was being derided by a fifty-something woman who was apparently his mother, hadn't noticed him at all. His one goal was to finish his transaction and walk out of here with his money, preferably unwounded.

His teller, Gina, had ducked down behind the counter, his check lying forgotten on the counter, beneath which she was pushing her station's panic button with no idea that the police department was deserted.

## 2:17 P.M.

Jerry Fillabag couldn't believe his eyes. Chief Kockebreath was pitching his product over the side, where it was spilling onto Route A.

At The Newburn Bank, Todd leaned in close to Max and told him to hurry up. "Just get whatever she has and let's get out of here."

Max couldn't agree more. He turned back to Britni, and demanded that all of the money she could get be put in a bag. Quickly.

Jerry thought very hard about putting a couple of slugs into Kocke's head, but that would be troublesome. Instead, he parked at the curb and watched for a while.

## 2:19 P.M.

Nick was about ready to storm out when Dorf slammed into him from behind. Both went to the marble and Dorf's gun clambered loudly across the floor. Dalton forgot all about his money as he saw Nick, convinced the crazy bastard had come in to torment him some more.

He turned and raced for the door, expecting it to open when he hit it. He rebounded when it didn't, falling to the marble floor, his head connecting solidly enough to knock him out.

Max and Todd turned and followed Dalton's progress, then turned back to Britni, who had a piece of paper in front of her.

The cows had made it to the Double-L, where they discovered the big bags of grass on the pavement.

# Chapter 21

## 2:22 P.M.

Jerry Fillabag, self-made gym guru and cowroid kingpin, sat in plain view of both Phillip Andrew Thomas and Chief Brad Kocke, but both were so caught up in their "drug" bust neither noticed him.

He sighed, marveling at the buffoons now taking notice of Lionel, who had come out of the bar with two of the amigos and the Orc. One of the amigos, Scott, was holding a wad of greasy bills, which Jerry knew was payment for the first shipment of product, now lying on the street while a group of cows - Jerry counted four but a fifth was hidden by its larger mates - approached the pile of Pakistani tea. He knew what they were going to do; this was cow country after all, and Jerry couldn't allow it.

He sprung from his truck, leaving the gun behind, and began slapping his hands and stomping his feet to get the attention of the foraging bovines.

*****

Dorf's one dream in life was to shoot somebody in the line of duty, so he could be declared a hero and not have to deal with the hassle of being charged.

But now that dream faded as his Smith & Wesson .38 slid across the polished floor, coming to a stop at Danielle's desk.

None of the robbers turned to look at them, which took some of the sting out of being bowled over by this idiot in Always-Go brand security-guard shoes who smelled very bad.

"What they hell were you thinking?" Nick demanded.

"I was just trying to help."

*That seemed to be everyone's line,* Nick thought. "Listen,

I don't need any help. We can't move on them while they have those shotguns. Now stay back here out of my way and I'll yell for you if I need help."

He did not wait for an answer. Nick slithered his way across an open space in the direction of Danielle, who was still pressing the button like a madwoman.

### 2:22.34 P.M.

"What's the trouble Chief?" Like most everyone in town, Lionel knew Brad Kocke from way back, when his rumored nightly adventures might have cost him his bid for sheriff.

"Drug deal."

"Here, in Newburn?" Lionel couldn't have sounded more skeptical if he tried; it was a bar thing. But he knew full well there was some deal going down, and he saw the product he'd just paid for being chewed on by a group of cows. The roll of bills was in full view of the chief.

The entire group spun to look at the other side of the truck, where the sound of clapping and stomping was getting louder. "Yah! Get out of that!" Jerry screamed.

The cows, ignoring him, continued to eat his product.

### 2:24 P.M.

Danielle nearly screamed again as Nick touched her hand, stopping its automated poking of the panic button. "No one's hearing that alarm," he said.

Once she saw his face, she felt a million times better.

"What are we going to do?" she whispered.

"I don't know yet," Nick admitted. He thought perhaps the best thing to do would be to let them go, alert the chief and then grab them outside, away from people. "What's with the guy at the door?"

"Oh, him. That's Dalton Fisk, the guy Brenda's been seeing."

"The guy I chased with a chainsaw?"

"Yeah."

Nick was not sure he would ever live that down.

## 2:27 P.M.

"Stop that!"

Jerry was screaming now, panting a little but determined to stop the cows from eating his profits. He reached the first to have wandered into freedom, and punched her in the flank. The cow merely stared at him.

"What's the problem here?" Chief Brad Kocke asked.

"These cows are eating my stuff."

"This is your grass, sir?"

"Yes, yes! And these goddam cows are eating it."

A soft snick sound interrupted that of chewing, and Jerry Fillabag looked down, astonished to find a handcuff bracelet firmly around his wrist. "What are you doing?"

"You're under arrest, sir," Kocke replied.

Phillip Andrew Thomas snapped another picture, temporarily blinding both men with his powerful flash.

"What's the charge?"

"Possession of a controlled substance with intent to distribute," Kocke said, and then with a smirk added, "and assault."

"Assault? That's crazy." Jerry was getting a little pissed now.

"You hit a cow." Kocke said, as if that should have been obvious.

While the chief was joining Jerry Fillabag's hands behind him, the amigos turned and fled up the street, while the Orc issued a warning growl and the remaining thug sat dejected in the truck.

Lionel just stood there, wondering again how he had gotten into this.

## 2:31 P.M.

Back at The Newburn Bank, Max Irons was about to lose it as Britni pushed an application form across the counter, where Todd snatched it up.

"What's this?" Max demanded. "I told you to give me money."

"I know, sir, but I need you to fill this out first."

Todd, whose major economic education came from pricing marijuana and snack food, had actually passed geometry, and so thought the form was simply a way for the bank to protect itself. "It just means they gave us money because we told them to," he told Max.

Captain Biceps, who was not much better at economics than Todd, turned to verify this with Britni, whose gum could be seen between vicious chomps. It was enough to make a Big-League player proud.

"That true?"

"Yes, sir. It also allows me to give you tomorrow's money."

Nick and Danielle shared a glance, wondering if the ruse would work.

"Okay then."

Max and Todd bent over the document, which was just a standard loan application, which normally would be signed and then delivered to Danielle for inspection. Thinking this, Danielle sketched a plan. She quickly laid it out for Nick.

Evvie, meanwhile, had moved on to Lecture #48, which basically let Brian know he was going to hell and nothing could save him now.

### 2:39 P.M.

*Shit*, Chief Kocke thought. The punks were getting away, and they had a wad of bills, most surely payment for this shipment; in other words, the other half of the deal.

"Who are they?" he asked Jerry.

"Just some guys who stopped in for a beer," Lionel said.

"Bullshit, they were . . .," Kocke broke off as he realized he couldn't see the other one, the one who was now purring in his ear, which the Orc promptly sank his grimy teeth into.

"Owwww!"

*He's chewing on him*, thought Phillip, who lined his camera up for the bizarre shot.

"Jesus H. Christ," Lionel muttered as he noticed blood

coming from the chief's neck. "What is he, a vampire?"

Chief Brad Kocke still had hold of Jerry by the arm with one hand, the other holding his mahogany night stick, which he'd dubbed Fruit-Smacker. Kocke flailed about, whipping Fruit-Smacker up in an effort to dislodge the Orc, but the wiry little guy was well-seated.

Jerry yanked free of Kocke's grip, still handcuffed, and wove his way toward his truck, with no idea how he was going to get away with his hands behind his back.

### 2:44 P.M.

"We close in about 15 minutes, so you might want to hurry, sir," Britni suggested in her pseudo-professional voice. She had come up with the same plan Danielle had, once she had seen Nick by Danielle's desk. Britni didn't believe it would work, but these two were actually filling out the form she'd provided.

"Home address," Todd said. "Should that be mine and Brian's or yours?"

Max thought about it, then decided it should be theirs, since they would have most of the money. He did suggest using his cell phone number to keep it fair. Neither spared a glance at poor Brian, whose mother had pulled out her Bible and was reading him the parable of the Prodigal Son.

*****

Jerry Fillabag stood bent over the door of his truck, trying unsuccessfully to open it with his mouth. Phillip Andrew Thomas, who couldn't miss such an obvious, stationary target, slammed into him with all his bulk, driving his face into the window and narrowly avoiding snapping off Jerry's four front teeth on the door handle.

"Mmmphh!" was all Jerry could utter before pain overloaded his circuits.

Looking back, Phillip noted that the little guy had nearly chewed through Kocke's ear and showed no signs of stopping. Kocke, meanwhile, was offering a shrill shriek as his blows to the Orc's head were ineffectual at best.

*****

Finished with their application, and feeling quite satisfied, Max and Todd watched as Britni examined it, nodding and chewing her gum. Finally, she pronounced it good and told them to follow her.

"Where?" Todd asked, his cockroach-level instincts jumping forward.

"To this desk over here," Britni said. "Danielle has to approve me giving you tomorrow's money, but in your case, it's just a formality."

Todd was puzzling over the word "formality" but followed her, with Max at his side, and Brian wishing he could melt into the marble floor and thus escape his mother's tirade. Everyone involved, except the unconscious Dalton Fisk, was glad Brian didn't have a shotgun.

# Chapter 22

## 2:49 P.M.

Lionel wasn't stupid; perhaps not the brightest candle in the window, but he was a long way from the likes of Brian, Todd and Max. With the amigos gone with his money, another that couldn't speak English, and ringleader Jerry Fillabag a limp form on the street, his solution to the problem was to jump the chief.

Actually, it was the Orc, who had taken up residence on the chief's back, upon whom Lionel leaped, though the result was the same.

All three crashed to the pavement, right beside the cows, who had stopped their grazing for a moment to watch the festivities.

The chief hit first, the air pushing out of his chest and cutting off that God-awful shrieking; the Orc, still snapping like an alligator turtle, fell to the side, finishing the job of gnawing off a half-inch of Kocke's ear. Last came Lionel, muttering about his damn back being too old for this shit.

Phillip, ever the opportunist, took a picture.

*****

Near silence had descended over the bank, the only sounds being collective gum-smacking and the ticking of the giant clock on the wall. Danielle played the part very well, offering a warm smile and a handshake to both Todd and Max, offering them a seat before her desk as though they were the owners of a new textile mill hoping to open up shop here in Newburn.

Seated, Danielle took the form from Britni, who fled to the relative safety of her teller's booth.

"I need to ask a couple of questions," Danielle said, seeing Nick make his way through the teller's area to the far side, where he would double back behind the Moronic Duo. "What is the purpose of this, um, loan?"

"We're not paying it back," Todd said petulantly.

"I know that," Danielle replied with another charming smile. "I know technically you're not borrowing this money, but I still have to fill out the form, okay? So what will you do with the money?"

Todd and Max hadn't talked about this yet. Their aim was to rob the bank, split the money and then, well, Todd didn't know what.

"We haven't decided yet," he said finally, knowing somehow that telling her they were going to buy pot was not an acceptable answer.

"I see. Well, let's just make something up, so the bank examiners have something."

Max, despite his ear-infection-induced dullness, nonetheless began to smell something funky. Before he could answer, he felt something pressing behind his right ear.

"Afternoon, scumbag," Dorf said in what he thought was a fair Dirty Harry voice.

Danielle wanted to kill Dorf.

## 2:51 P.M.

Miguel watched the scene unfold, and *Espanol* or no, he knew he was in deep shit. He clambered over to the passenger door and fled to parts unknown.

Phillip, meanwhile, had heard Jerry Fillabag mumbling and kicked him in the back. He was starting to gain an appreciation for Chief Kocke's ambitions.

Apparently satisfied, the Orc sat gnawing on the chief's piece of ear as Lionel helped Kocke to his feet.

To Chief Brad Kocke, his visions of grandeur, not to mention a little action at Riverfront, were blown away. His drug bust was falling down around his ears, well, one and a half of them anyway.

He pulled back Fruit-Smacker and hit the Orc as hard as he could, right in the temple. The Orc dropped to the pavement like a sack of grass, the absconded part of the chief's ear flipping a few feet away, where the cow on that side took notice.

Chief Kocke bent and picked it up even as the cow started to lick it.

Feeling like the cop in *Reservoir Dogs*, sans gasoline, Kocke uttered a short hiccupping bark and then leaned against his Subaru, where he saw Bartie slumped against the seat.

He appeared to be asleep.

*****

Meanwhile, at The Newburn Bank, Dorf had what he believed to be the upper hand, what with his nightstick shoved under Captain Biceps' jaw, and the blond too confused to move.

"Dorf what are you doing?" Danielle's anger came through loud and clear.

"I'm stopping a bank robbery, what's it look like?"

"I have the situation under control."

Max sat with his ear-hair quivering, Todd looked ready to puke, and Brian approached unseen by the would-be hero. His contribution to the robbery had been minimal, but he thought it was time to earn his keep.

The problem was he didn't have a gun. Using countless hours of TV as a reference, he formed a gun with his forefinger and thumb, and poked Dorf in the back. "Drop it, punk."

His Dirty Harry was a little better.

### 2:54 P.M.

"What the hell's going on Lionel?" Chief Kocke asked as he lit a Camel, now holding an old t-shirt against the side of his head.

"It all started when Jerry Fillabag asked me to sell that grass over there," Lionel Leanman said. "I don't know anything about this guy who was trying to eat your ear. And those other fellas worked for Jerry."

106

"So you agreed to sell this grass for him?"

"Yeah," Lionel said. "Didn't have a lot of choice. You can't say no to Jerry."

Phillip was hastily scrawling notes for what he believed would be the story of the year. He already had a clever headline picked out *Crazy Drug Deal Played By Ear* or maybe *Chief Loses Ear In The War On Drugs*.

"What the hell is it?"

"I have no idea," and Chief Kocke believed the aging tavern owner when he said it. Lionel was a very convincing liar.

"I guess we better get the cows away from it or there won't be much of a case."

*If there was one at all*, Phillip mused, not that it would in any way hinder his ability to craft a good story.

# Chapter 23

Edward Von Waterman III was a self-centered little pig of a man whose net worth was beyond measure, at least by the numbskulls he tolerated in Newburn. Why his family had chosen to settle here was beyond him, but like any good shepherd, he didn't complain about the fleece. It was consistent, and that's all that mattered.

Of course there were fringe benefits, such as ogling his employees, and Danielle had damn near given him a stroke when she leaned over his desk.

But even more than that, he loved to count money, roll in money, rub money all over his naked body while taking care of personal business, which he frequently did after eye-humping his female employees.

He was doing this as The Newburn Bank readied for the close of another day, and that's where he was, naked from the waist down, when a group led by Danielle burst into the vault.

"Ohmygod!" Danielle let out in a rush. Her sudden outburst was coupled with a sudden stop and attempted moonwalk, but her rearward progress was halted by the push of bodies against her as Brian, Todd and Max herded them into the chamber.

"Move it," Max said. He brandished the shotgun for full effect.

Nick took Danielle by the arm, embarrassed at having been caught from behind, but how was he to know that Evvie Fennigan would choose that moment to loose a blood-curdling scream in warning to the son she had just sentenced to hell?

This was definitely a crazy day, he reflected as the Moronic Trio was now on the same page, albeit a page from *The Dimwit's Guide To Bank Robbery*. Nick had to give

Britni credit; the ruse would have worked had Evvie not brought the house down. He'd been closing on Brian steadily, like a cat about to pounce on a very stupid mouse, when the shriek alarmed everyone, including Dorf, who crapped his pants again.

Everyone spun toward the sound, and just like that, Max and Todd had their weapons aimed at Nick, pinning him like a deer in the headlights; but instead of threatening him, they did the one thing guaranteed to make him toss his gun over: Max pointed his shotgun at Danielle.

"Don't be no hero today." Though Max showed no signs of stopping the madness, Nick could see the look of recognition in his eyes as the big lifter recalled his accident. "I don't want to shoot this pretty lady. She's been very helpful, but I will if I have to."

Dorf looked ready to say something, or at least aim his gun back in the general direction of the robbers, but a pained expression crossed his face, and he doubled over.

Now that they were in very close proximity once more, Nick could definitely smell crap. Nick thought initially the old dude had just let one go in the heat of the moment, but the longer he stood next to him, the more convinced he became that old Dorf was not as punctual with the adult diapers as he ought to be.

"Jesus, what is that smell?" Todd went to each of his hostages in turn, sniffing them like some deranged dog seeking an appropriate fire hydrant, and finally shoved them the rest of the way into the vault.

Edward Von Waterman III had been all but forgotten in the search for the rank smell, but now his semi-nakedness became the topic of conversation.

"Pull your pants up you dirty old man," said Danielle, squeezing as far to the opposite corner as possible, then turned to her captors. "I don't want to stay in here with him."

Brian and Todd shared a glance, the former vaguely worried about his mother thinking him a pervert on top of everything else, and Todd just happy that things were going their way for once today.

Ever the gentleman, Max stepped in partway and aimed his gun at the bank president. "Get yourself together and stay decent while there's a lady in here with you," he said. "I'll come back and shoot you in the face if I hear different."

Nick thought a man that big needn't threaten anyone with a firearm; it seemed like overkill for a giant that could do a lot of damage with his bare hands, but Waterman complied at once, shaking himself out of the paralysis that had stolen over him when the door opened.

"Please don't shoot me," he said pleadingly. "I'm the president and you can have whatever you want, just don't shoot me."

Danielle had a moment of clarity just then. She understood that *Mr. I Have Millions Of Dollars So Don't Shoot Me* would happily secure the blindfold on his employees if it meant his ass could get away in one piece. And why not? The bank was insured for just such an occasion.

### 3:05 P.M.

Allen Frye hadn't been this medicated in a while. Not since before the incident that drove a wedge between him and his two companions.

It wasn't that Allen begrudged them the score, but they could have at least warned him. He thought they went a little overboard, taking the whole wad, especially since his take was meager.

Not to mention the fact they put him on the hot seat.

Allen was a year younger than Brian and Todd but the three had graduated together because the other two had been held back a year. They'd been friends since junior high but he was never as tight with them as they were with each other.

Over the years he had witnessed some completely ridiculous behavior, and often wondered how they managed to avoid jail.

When he applied for the position with the NPD, he did it as a lark, in part because Brian and Todd had dared him to do it. That they also applied made it impossible to back out.

With funding from the feds to pay for his position, Allen had been hired conditionally. He had a year of college but that had been as half-assed as the rest of his life.

Chief Brad Kocke had told him he was hired to comply with the city council, which was making a big deal of keeping the streets clean. It was an election year, after all.

"But I don't anticipate any serious activity," Chief Kocke continued. "You're basically going to sit in the office and answer the phone. Occasionally you'll go out on patrol, but only after you prove yourself."

The lark had suddenly become a real job. He promised to do whatever it took to improve, including finishing college.

Kocke had smiled, nodded, and then led him to the storage closet, where Allen found a uniform shirt that fit.

"You have to supply your own pants," Kocke said.

A stain clearly caused by spilled coffee bothered Allen at first, but there were no other shirts to be had in his size, so he did his best to clean it up in the bathroom.

"Do you know Brian Fennigan and Todd Brown?" Chief Kocke had regained his MIC chair and shouted to be heard.

"Yeah," Allen replied. "We went to school together."

"Well, they've also been hired as reserve officers," said Kocke.

"When do they start?"

"They'll be here tomorrow," Brad answered. "They're going to work three four-hour days a week, more if the shit hits the fan."

Allen wondered what that meant, but decided he didn't care. He was the one with the uniform shirt, a badge and a battered training pistol that may or may not fire. For once, Allen decided they weren't going to hold him back.

That didn't last. The three were young, immature and completely absorbed in getting high.

Allen fought the urge to join them out back for a toke more times than he could count. It amazed him at the quantity of weed they went through each week.

Since they worked when he did, always while Chief

Kocke and *Super-Cop* were off patrolling the streets, there was little chance of being caught.

Allen Frye thought it odd the two veterans would absent themselves with three new cops at the station, but it always seemed to work out.

Until the crazy report last night. Allen still had no answers, but at the moment, he didn't care.

He'd never had anything as fine as what was now coursing through his entire system like brushfire.

He smiled at Roseanne, who appeared to be as content as an old tabby, and the damn thing was, he would swear in church she was purring.

In all reality, Allen felt he could just lay here for as long as Roseanne would stay with him; he no longer cared about being a cop, especially the part about being the laughing-stock of the entire community, including his colleagues. It just wasn't worth it, he thought.

But what would he do?

As if reading his thoughts, Roseanne spoke up for the first time since they had laid down. "Do you want to work here?"

"I don't think old-lady Esther would go for that," Allen replied, remembering the loud proclamation that his jock-itch could be addressed in Aisle 4.

"She's harmless," Roseanne said. "A little abrasive, I'll give you that, but my aunt can be very nice once she gets to know you."

"Your aunt?"

"Yeah."

"Great. I can just picture her staring at my crotch at a Thanksgiving dinner."

Roseanne couldn't help but laugh. A moment later, he was laughing too.

### 3:10 P.M.

"How much air does one of these rooms hold?"

The question was valid, Max thought, and one he had not

considered in the spur-of-the-moment decision to herd these people in here. But now that it was out in the open, he had to give way to his conscience. He did have one, though it had atrophied.

He only wanted to clear the books with Jerry; murdering a bunch of people by trapping them in a vault with no air was not in the plan. He pulled Brian and Todd a few steps from the door and told them so.

"I heard they keep, like, air masks in there in case somebody gets locked in by accident," Brian said.

"You're such a dipshit," Todd said, not unkindly. "They only keep the air masks for show when the inspectors come around. They don't really work."

"You're both idiots. How I ever agreed to this I'll never know."

"Hey, genius, this was your idea, remember?"

"Yeah, but it was supposed to be clean and easy, and now we've got hostages," Max replied. "Hostages. That means any real cops we run into will shoot first and not bother with questions."

Brian and Todd were shaken at that, neither catching the insult.

"So what do we do?"

"I don't know, but I'm not locking them in there to suffocate, I'll tell you that right now," Max said.

"Let's just close the door and not lock it."

Todd gazed at Brian for a few seconds before saying, "I think the door locks automatically."

"Let's just lock them in the office."

As the three were arguing about how best to secure the four people inside the vault, the automatic timer took the choice from them, the heavy door closing of its own accord, thanks to the latest in security measures. A micro-computer no bigger than a wheat cracker was telling the door that the day's business was now concluded, close up shop for the night.

The soft pneumatic wheeze as the door began to close caught Brian's attention, but he had no idea what it meant

113

and quickly dismissed it. All three had their attention snared when the door shut with a click.

"Well, I guess that answers that question," Max said, satisfied that he had not ordered the door to close, which was as good as absolution in his mind, though he was not Catholic.

Not one of them considered the possibility that the door, though closed, required manual lockdown. Nor did they take note of the pile of cash lying at Waterman's feet, ripe for the taking.

### 3:16 P.M.

A minute (plus two seconds) after the door closed on the Moronic Trio's hostages, Jerry Fillabag opened his eyes cautiously, wary of another kick to the face by that fat bastard from the paper. His cheekbone felt like it was broken and the knot above his right eyebrow throbbed in time with his heart.

He swore he would have that SOB knee-capped if the Orc didn't kill him first.

But first things first.

Jerry surveyed the situation, noticing at once his enforcer prone on the street, a puddle of slobber dripping from his slack lips. No help there.

Phillip had his back to Jerry as he spoke with the chief and that greasy Triple-L; Jerry was one of the few that got the reference, but it did nothing to assuage the fury that was building.

All his product, lying out in the open for any old cow to come along and eat up.

And the chief thought he was selling drugs. What kind of world was it when a steroid kingpin and gym guru couldn't even sell giant bags of Pakistani tea without being hassled?

And where were the amigos? Gone like a bunch of sissies, and with his money, no less.

He didn't even know their full names, for Christ's sake. He knew they were Scott, Eduardo, and Brandon, and that they had come around with the Orc a couple times before he made them his permanent entourage.

"Looks like our friend is awake," Chief Kocke said.

Phillip turned around, his jowls quivering in excitement at the prospect of kicking Jerry again.

"Chief," Jerry tried to say, but it came out "Shf" since his face was numb; it was like trying to talk to the dentist.

"I'm glad you're awake," the chief said. "You have the right to remain silent . . ."

Kocke finished the Miranda rights, making sure he explained them with clarity, then knelt beside the handcuffed gym owner. "Do you have anything to say at this time?"

"Shf," he tried again, but the pain was too much.

"That's what I thought," Kocke said. "You're under arrest for possession of a controlled substance with intent to distribute."

"Shf."

"I've heard enough," the chief said, hauling Jerry unceremoniously to his feet. He stowed him in the back seat of his Subaru, next to the slumped Bartie Grantz.

Next he secured the Orc's hands and squeezed him into the back seat next to Jerry, who was shoved violently into Bartie, whose head lolled over until it was resting on Jerry's shoulder.

It took only a moment for the kingpin to believe he was seated next to a dead man.

Brad's open wound screamed for attention, but he fought it, deciding he would stop by the clinic and have Dr. Hemphill look at it when this was resolved.

### 3:20 P.M.

In all the excitement, with the three robbers completely focused on the people in their immediate vicinity, Britni took the opportunity to help herself to some of the cash. In the darkest corner of her heart she knew it was wrong, but then again, these idiots were going to take it all anyway, and the bank was insured, so what was the harm? Everyone would think they took it; who would blame her for taking a couple thousand?

Evvie Fennigan, that's who. Britni was very careful.

Brian, Todd and Max returned to the lobby and headed straight for Britni's station. She had only been able to pull about $900 from the drawer before they made their appearance, but she figured another few seconds would increase that bundle nicely. She thought they might be upset about the ruse, but she needn't have worried.

"Let's try this again, and I'm not filling out anything else," Todd said. "Put all the money in the bag and do it quickly."

Evvie watched her son, wondering if anything she could say would turn him from this path. Not likely, she decided. Brian belonged to the devil now.

She cried softly into her handkerchief as the money was put into the black bag.

Dalton Fisk began to stir, his head still ringing from the solid connection it made with the marble floor. He thought about getting up, even rolled over a bit, but his guts felt loose and his vision was blurry. Better to just lie here until he felt better.

Todd took the loot, minus the $1,400 bonus Britni awarded herself, and headed out. After a moment's fiddling with the lock, and nearly tripping over Dalton, one large man and two sidekicks, nylons still hugging their mugs, left the bank, where the real fun was about to start.

### 3:30 P.M.

"How much air does this room have?"

Nick directed his query to Danielle but said it loud enough for everyone to hear, just in case the bank president had anything useful to contribute.

"A couple hours I think," Danielle replied, squeezing Nick's hand, both offering and receiving what little comfort there was to be had.

Dorf had straightened up but still looked like a man

116

trying very hard not to fart at a funeral.

Waterman stayed on his side of the vault, wishing he could wash his hands. He didn't trust himself to speak; anger, no, fury, was replacing his embarrassment. He was still fuming over having one of his employees call him a dirty old man. So what if it was true? He was still the top of a very big heap, and he knew right then he would fire Danielle Stone as soon as they got out of this mess.

No one, not his wife, not his mistress, and certainly not some uppity woman who worked for him, could expect to get away with that kind of talk. He'd miss her collarbones, but perhaps he would find someone even better looking.

That thought cheered him up.

### 3:40 P.M.

"Uh, chief, I think we got a problem back there," said Phillip Andrew Thomas, riding shotgun in a severely overcrowded Subaru on its way to the police station.

"What's wrong?"

"I'm not sure, but I think old Bartie's dead."

"What?!" Chief Brad Kocke stopped the car, not far from where Max Irons had been run down by Brian's Tercel. "You sure?"

"I believe I just said I wasn't, but he doesn't appear to be breathing," Phillip answered. "That *usually* is a bad sign."

"Don't get smart with me."

"Whatever man," Phillip said, resisting the urge to add "Kockebreath." It had been a long day already and he had miles to go . . .

Kocke climbed out and pulled the seat forward with a vicious yank. The Orc was still stirring but not fully awake, but the look of disgust on Jerry Fillabag's face said it all, even though he could for the moment utter not a word.

Grimacing, Chief Kocke leaned in and put two fingers to Bartie's throat, hoping for a pulse and finding clammy skin instead. Bartie's head still lolled on Jerry's shoulder, as if he was leaning in for a kiss from the kingpin.

Brad applied pressure, Bartie's body shifted, and a great belch escaped him, right into Jerry's downturned face.

"Holy oher a ga," he said through dead lips. "Shf ge hi off ee."

Jerry did not appreciate the fact he sounded almost exactly like the Orc, who was groaning, and he further did not appreciate his current situation.

"Hold your water," Kocke said, pulling his hand back quickly. "I'll get you out."

Before Chief Kocke could do much more than consider how he was going to accomplish that, Jerry Fillabag, normally cool in most circumstances, vomited all over the Orc, with a little left over finding the chief, who had just leaned into the car.

"Jesus H. Christ," Phillip screamed, a second before blowing up chunks of Jan's finest greasy chicken in his lap and on the dashboard.

A chain reaction set off, with the Chief responding in kind, his evacuation catching the Orc squarely in the face. That got Jerry going again, and within 10 seconds, all three men were coated in slime. The Orc groaned.

### 3:45 P.M.

Allen Frye and his new lady friend, their minds abuzz with what people their age refer to as "love at first sight," but usually only if they get laid in the bargain, had left Esther's Warehouse of Drugs & Teabag Emporium. They had approached Esther with zeal in their hopes of getting Allen a job, and Esther, who could see her niece's feelings clearly, agreed with hardly a hassle, though she did offer a warning.

"You keep your jock itch to yourself," she said. "What happens at home stays at home. I don't want no trouble down here, you understand me?"

Allen, who did not understand at all, agreed anyway. That was the extent of the interview, and Allen was hired on to work with Roseanne selling organic food and exotic teas from the world over, so long as his crotch-rot didn't interfere with his job. His salary was a little less than he made as a cop, but he would be close to Roseanne so that was all right.

Now they were driving to the station, where he would turn in his uniform, gun and assorted equipment, change into his civvies, and then blow that little hot-dog stand.

For the first time in his short life, Allen felt really good.

### 3:51 P.M.

"I don't understand."

Truth be told, Danielle wasn't the only one at a loss. Nick Crawford still had his arm around her, feeling a bit like a caveman protecting his woman, but he was loath to remove it.

And the jackass Waterman was ranting.

"I said I don't care about your collarbones," Waterman repeated, speaking slowly as if to a retarded child. "As soon as we get out of this vault, you're fired."

"Fine. Just for the record, I'll be bringing a sexual-harassment suit against you and the bank."

"What the hell do her collarbones have to do with anything?" Nick still didn't get the reference.

"I'll tell you later," Danielle said, hoping there was a later.

Edward Von Waterman III looked at them with beady, rat-like eyes.

Dorf continued to sit in his own feces, staring glumly at the floor and wishing he could be anywhere else. His dreams of shooting someone in the line of duty were gone, and with it his primary reason for putting on his uniform every day. He had blown it. Dorf thought he should have shot the big guy first and then offered his Clint Eastwood to the other one.

The only thought keeping him from complete depression was that he could watch Dr. Phil when this was all over; his dream of attending that show was still alive.

119

# Chapter 24

## 3:59 P.M.

Allen Frye was enjoying himself. He had a new job, his arm around Roseanne, who had snuggled right up beside him in his old Silverado, and he would shortly be hitting another fabulous fattie.

The new couple had left Esther's Warehouse of Drugs & Teabag Emporium, happy to cruise sedately toward the police station. Such was their progress that when Allen neared the Double-L and found five cows standing in the road, he hardly had to apply the brakes.

"What the hell is that about?"

"I don't know."

Allen had decided to blow off his investigation into the drug trade, but seeing the black bags full of grass brought that back in a hurry. "Is that what I think it is?"

"Looks like grass clippings," Roseanne replied.

"They're eating it!"

With little thought he jumped from the SUV, nearly tripping in his haste to collect what he could of the uneaten grass. He suddenly envisioned himself and Roseanne smoking it for the next month.

## 4:05 P.M.

Reeling like sailors returning from shore leave, Chief Brad Kocke, Phillip Andrew Thomas and Jerry Fillabag entered the station, which was as silent as a church on Super Bowl Sunday. The Orc was left moaning in a car full of sour fluid.

Still no Allen, Chief Kocke noted without surprise or concern; after all, he was covered in vomit and cared only for getting himself cleaned up. He supposed the Subaru was a loss, considering the copious amount of discharge and old Bartie, who would start stinking any time now.

Kocke made the time to call Chipper McGraw, the county coroner, and then headed for the restroom.

Phillip and Jerry eyed each other, feeling something akin to a bond; it's not every day you throw up with a guy who had body-slammed you to the curb and smashed your face.

The sound of the toilet flushing broke the moment and the two went back to eyeing each other distrustfully.

"Shf," Jerry tried and then quit. He took the reporter's notebook from Phillip, who squawked indignantly.

A pen was on the counter and he quickly composed a note.

*I am not selling drugs. It's tea,* he wrote.

"Tea? What kind of crap is that?"

*It's from Pakistan. It is not drugs, I swear.*

Jesus H. Christ, Chief Kocke thought, wondering what the hell he was supposed to do now. He hadn't really believed it was marijuana when he'd first smelled it, but something odd was going on, he was sure of it. And if it wasn't old maryjane, it must be something else; Jerry Fillabag was dirty and Chief Kocke knew it.

"What's this all about, Jerry?"

*Guy I know wanted to sell tea here. Esther Pickering agreed to sell it. That's why she added the Teabag Emporium to the name and opened the back room.*

Feeling left out, Phillip Andrew Thomas asked a question which was surprisingly lucid. "Why didn't you put the tea in bags with Esther's name on them?"

*We were just getting started. I hadn't worked out all the details yet.*

"Well that's just swell," Kocke said. "Bartie's been worked up all day over this and that's probably what gave him a heart attack."

"That and he was as old as Moses," Phillip interjected.

*Sorry. I'm just a business man trying to make a living. I didn't mean to cause any trouble.* A half-truth to be sure, but Jerry Fillabag was gaining confidence that he'd be able to walk out of here and get back to his gym.

"There goes your drug bust story," Kocke said with a glance at the portly pundit.

"That's okay. We still have the guy with the chainsaw, right?"

Jerry chose not to inquire about that particular investigation as Kocke removed the handcuffs, wishing he had a reason to run the gym owner in, knowing he did not.

### 4:10 P.M.

Nick and Danielle were growing desperate to escape the foul-smelling vault but were not sure how to go about that. For his part, Edward Von Waterman III had calmed down after a while, still holding to his original resolve to fire Miss Collarbones, but deciding to forego unpleasantness.

Dorf Walkenhorst, however, could not do anything but live in a state of unpleasantness. His whole day had revolved around trying and failing in the personal hygiene department, and now he was stuck in a confined space where not only he, but three others were privy to the result.

"I have to get out of here," Danielle said quietly. "I can't take much more of this."

She really had no desire to hurt Dorf's feelings, but this was all his fault. If he hadn't tried to play hero, Nick would have brought the situation under control, of that she had no doubt.

Of course she couldn't forget Evvie Fennigan. That pious little woman ought to be horsewhipped for screaming when she did.

None of these thoughts helped alleviate her current situation, and aside from the smell, she was pleased to be close to Nick again. His little tirade had scared Brenda and practically incapacitated her new boyfriend, but Danielle was certain she could smooth it over.

For now, getting out of this vault was the primary goal.

A question suddenly occurred to her. "Mr. Waterman, does the door lock automatically or just close by itself?"

He still eyed her with open lust, regardless of his surroundings, but at least his answer was helpful.

"I think you have to lock it manually," he said.

"So we can get out of here?" Nick was to his feet immediately, searching for a handle.

Finding none, he turned to the bank president. "Well?"

Having been trapped in here more than once with his pants around his ankles, he knew full well the door required manual lockdown, and further how to open it. But the events had temporarily frozen his thinking.

Now, however, the aroma of the situation brought his thoughts more clearly into line.

"Here," he said, pushing a button near the top of the door.

With a gasp, the air-seal disengaged and the door parted from the wide jamb.

A moment later they were standing in Waterman's office and Nick was urging his fiance toward the lobby.

Waterman stared at the view as Danielle left the room, reconsidering his earlier resolve to fire such a beautifully proportioned employee.

Dorf fled to the restroom.

### 4:15 P.M.

Brian, Todd and Max were traveling through town on the way to Brian's house. His mother was still in the bank and would be for some time as police responded and began taking statements.

Max still didn't like the idea of sentencing those people to a slow death in the vault, but hoped help would arrive. He had a bag full of money, more than enough to cover what he owed Jerry, with some left over for more 'roids.

The trio had not discussed in advance where they would split the money but Max's suggestion as they piled into the Tercel had made sense.

Only a fat joint would set this off as the best day ever, and Brian and Todd believed they could acquire that delicacy once the money was divided.

## 4:17 P.M.

Allen Frye shared a look of bliss with his new girlfriend as the two continued their journey to the police station, where he would rid himself of badge and gun, content to play Chris Noth in private and forget all about being a real cop.

Both were still feeling good from the joint they'd shared before leaving Esther's but seeing bags of stuff just going to waste was a bummer. Taking it wouldn't hurt anyone, would it? Besides, cows weren't allowed to get high.

It never crossed Roseanne's mind that she had seen these clippings before.

## 4:20 P.M.

Chief Brad Kocke hated being out of control, which in this case meant being in the passenger seat of Mr. Newsman's filthy car. His own Subaru was full of sickness and Bartie, at least until Chipper got there, and now that he thought about it, the Orc, who he'd left there since he couldn't rouse him and had no desire to touch him. Besides, he didn't appear to be competent, so charging him with assault seemed futile.

"Man this thing stings like a mother," he remarked, touching his torn ear gently.

Phillip Andrew Thomas chose not to comment, though he secretly enjoyed the other's pain; it was about time his baton-wielding days came back to haunt him.

"Where are we going?"

"There's a lady I was told about who might be able to shed some light on our chainsaw guy," Phillip replied.

"What makes you say that?"

"A woman I know is friends with the victim," Phillip said. "Word is he's scared to go out much since he saw the guy two weeks ago, and then after last night. Afraid the guy will finish the job, I guess."

"This day just keeps getting better and better," Chief Kocke said. "Who is she?"

"Sheila Fowler."

"Like I said, better and better," Chief Kocke said, realizing Phillip Andrew Thomas had played him from the get-go, trying to get the name of a man he already had. *Bastard*, he thought.

# Chapter 25

**4:25 P.M.**

Nick and Danielle wasted no time in leaving the bank, taking the latter's car since it was parked out front; Nick's would have been faster but it was still leaning into the ditch on the road to Evvie's trailer.

"We have to get to the police station," Nick told her.

"Why?"

"We need some help on this," he replied. "I'm pretty sure I know where those idiots wound up, but I don't relish the idea of taking them on by myself."

"Okay." Danielle turned the wheel and headed east toward the station.

They turned into the lot to find Allen Frye's Silverado parked near the entrance with both doors wide open.

"This is interesting," Nick muttered as he jumped clear of the car. "Stay here. I'll be right back."

Inside the station, Allen was trying to compose his resignation as Roseanne paced the room. She hated being in the police station; too many bad memories there. She'd much rather be in the hospital awaiting major surgery.

At last he proclaimed it was finished just as Nick Crawford approached the counter.

"Allen! What's going on, man?"

"I'm quitting."

"Why? What's going on around here?" Nick noticed the tall, rail-thin woman standing behind Allen and wondered where he met her. "Did you find anything at Esther's?"

"Yeah," Allen replied, taking Roseanne's hand. "I found love and a job. I'm leaving."

"Okay, but first things first. Brian and Todd robbed The Newburn Bank just a little bit ago and I need to go after them," Nick said. "I'm sure I can find them but I need some back-up."

"Not me, man. Not anymore. No one ever thought of me as a real cop, not even you."

Nick sighed and had the grace to blush. Of course the pothead was right. He was the product of federal funding and nothing more. Then the shit hit the fan with the missing drugs and Allen held onto his job only because there wasn't any evidence pointing to his involvement.

"You're right," he said. "I'm sorry about that, okay? I know we were a little hard on you, but you have to admit having friends like Brian and Todd kind of skewed our thinking."

Allen had to admit at least that much was true, but he was not ready to go after his friends.

"Just do me a favor. Follow me out to Brian's and help me get them under control. After that, you can leave knowing you did your part as a cop." Nick waited for a response, not really hoping but daring to believe it was at least possible.

"Okay. I'll do that much," Allen said. "But no more. And you square it with the chief about the drugs. Brian and Todd took that marijuana and let me hang."

Nick stared at the other, hardly believing his ears. "You realize you'll probably have to testify to that," Nick said. "I don't want any confusion about that."

"Just ask them. They'll probably admit to it."

Nick realized his counterpart was likely right. With a bank robbery looming, they probably would spill anything to save their miserable hides.

*But what about Max?* Nick wondered, as they headed for their cars, what to make of him.

### 4:35 P.M.

Jerry Fillabag turned his Dodge 2500 into the diagonal parking slot in front of the Double-L, noting an absence of cars considering the time of day when most drinking folks got off work.

Despite his purpling cheek and throbbing forehead, he'd left the station in a pleasant mood, although with the crap he'd been forced to endure, fresh air was enough to do that. Jerry wanted little more than a shower and fresh clothes, perhaps a cup of tea.

But first he had to visit Lionel Leanman, who had stood by while the chief got the jump on him. Even the poor Orc, who was too stupid to know better, had tried to hurt the chief in an effort to help his boss, or so Jerry believed, though in truth the wiry man was just hungry.

"Evening, Lionel," he managed in a still slurred manner to the figure whose back was to him behind the bar.

"Uh, hey Jerry," the bar owner stammered. "Glad you got way from Kockebreath."

"Me too, no thanks to you," Jerry said, his voice gaining strength as the Tylenol did its work on his puffy face.

"What was I supposed to do? You didn't tell me the cops was watching for God's sake!"

"They weren't watching, you idiot," the other replied acidly. "They got lucky. All you had to do was keep your mouth shut and everything would have been fine."

"I doubt that, man," Lionel said. "They were gonna run me in, and it wasn't even dope they had there. What happened to you anyway?"

"I was sitting next to a dead man," Jerry said with a shiver. "At least I think he was dead. In the back of the tiny piece of shit the chief drives. Everyone threw up on me."

"I'm sorry to hear that, Jerry," the older man said. "I really am. You want something to drink? On the house, of course."

"Where are the amigos and where is my money?"

"Your amigos took off. I had already given them the money when Kocke and the paper guy showed up."

Jerry knew this was true, having seen Scott with the wad of bills. "Okay. I'll try to track down the amigos, but they better have my money. I'll be back with another shipment tomorrow and we'll try this again."

Lionel Leanman wasn't pleased but as he'd told the

chief, you just can't say no to a guy like Jerry. Not with his amigos and the Orc running around ready to bite parts of your face off. Further, Lionel knew that whether Jerry found his amigos or the money again, he would only be safe if he continued to play along.

Lionel decided it was time to up the Buffet cover to $10.

### 4:45 P.M.

At The Bank of Newburn, the people who'd been ordered to stay inside were still huddled around Evvie Fennigan, who had become something of a leader.

Dalton Fisk was still lying on the floor, unsure whether to get up or stay where he was until the FBI showed up. Surely they would come to the scene of a bank robbery. That's what always happened on TV.

Dorf Walkenhorst had cleaned up once more and was now standing next to Britni, hoping like hell he could control himself until Edward Von Waterman III said they could leave.

Britni continued to chew gum in a manner defying all sense of etiquette, unaware that her chomping had increased proportionately to the guilt she felt for helping herself to $1,400 of the bank heist.

Waterman could only sit and stare at the front door, which was now unlocked but devoid of any new customers, considering the bank was almost two hours past its closing time.

He wondered what would become of the insurance claim, and whether or not he could increase the take due him from the FDIC. All he would have to do is claim the thieves took money from him in the vault and the feds would reimburse him for everything. No way the morons got away with $100,000.

Evvie broke the silence. "I wonder if we're supposed to wait here all night?"

"We have to wait for the police to come and get our statements," Waterman said. "It's standard procedure."

129

"But I'm tired, and hungry, and I don't want to miss my shows."

Dumb sheep, moving through life from one idiotic television show to another, blindly obeying whatever suggestion was put before their vacant faces. Waterman was disgusted with the whole lot of them.

"We have to wait. Britni, give the lady some candy."

*Very generous,* Evvie Fennigan thought bitterly, eyeing the door with longing. Would the dirty old man try to restrain her if she just walked out? Probably not, she decided, but he could have Dorf do it. Although Dorf had been acting strange and Evvie wasn't at all convinced he would react in time to stop her.

Only one way to find out.

### 4:50 P.M.

Allen Frye and his skinny lady followed Nick and Danielle to Evvie's trailer. Of course Allen knew it well, had spent many days there after school watching Brian's dad get drunk and take the tractor out for a spin.

*Damn shame about his accident,* Allen thought, *but it was his own fault.*

No one in their right mind would pull an Evel Knievel stunt over a lagoon on a tractor.

The soon-to-be ex-cop couldn't believe he was on the way to arrest a couple of high-school buddies for robbing a bank. Hell, he could hardly believe they had done the job, and he knew nothing about this Max person, who Nick had warned was a huge man.

How had they connected with someone like that? Did he live here? Allen had never encountered anyone big enough to fit that description, but then, he wasn't the most observant human in existence either.

Roseanne felt like the girl from *Rocky,* watching her man fight just one more time before he called it quits. It was a very romantic view, one that she intended to remind him of when they snuggled beneath the covers from 8 to 11 for *Law*

& *Order* on TNT.

She just hoped her ex-boyfriend didn't find out who she was dating now. He had a mean temper and was a little loopy, if you wanted her opinion. The only good thing about him was his connection to the best dope she'd ever hit.

### 4:51 P.M.

Danielle was not feeling like *Rocky's* girlfriend. She felt more like a woman who was seeing her man off to a war from which he might not return. Those guys had carried shotguns, and one did not walk away from a close-range examination of the business end.

But it was his job, and though it scared her sometimes, she understood the necessity, the drive behind the man. His own father was a convicted felon, a career car thief who had tried once too often.

All his life Nick had tried to play that down, to prove he was better than his old man.

As far as she was concerned, he was the best man she'd ever known and was proud to be engaged to him. If only he'd realized that and not gone off half-cocked with a chainsaw . . .

She allowed the thought to drift away as CR 201 came into view with its perpetually flashing blinker.

Slowing, Nick made the turn with Allen Frye a few seconds behind him. Neither vehicle was equipped with lights or radio, so they were on their own. But at least they could cover their approach by not blaring sirens.

A few moments passed and the trailer came into view. Creeping toward Evvie's place, Nick could see the Toyota Tercel parked in the grass. It's rust-red exterior actually complimented the deep green of the grass and assorted colors in Evvie's garden.

Nick squeezed Danielle's hand and gave her a smile. "It will be all right," he said, "these two aren't very bright, and I think I can handle Max if it comes to that. You just stay out of sight in the car and I'll be back quick as I can."

After delivering a similar assurance to Roseanne, Allen Frye joined Nick for one last job as an officer of the Newburn Police Department.

# Chapter 26

## 4:55 P.M.

"We're a few minutes early but I'd like to get started if we can," said the nominal leader of the Newburn Society For Compulsive Disorders, noting that a regular member was absent. "Who would like to start?"

"My name is Ron and I can't stop licking my hands," said a balding middle-aged man, believing they would cast him out of the group with his pronouncement as he was new to this sort of thing.

When no one jeered at him, Ron relaxed; when the leader of NSFCD gestured for him to go on, he did so with more poise than he'd felt in a long time.

Licking his left palm and then his right, he said, "Since I was a little boy, I've had a need to lick my hands."

Back of the right hand, then the left, each now covered with a thin layer of saliva.

"I just can't stop myself."

He progressed to his fingers, running his tongue over his thumb and then the index, tracing his hand as countless children do in daycare centers with a crayon and sheet of paper.

NSFCD's founder, a compulsive toenail biter, marveled at the feline quality of the act before offering her most stern expression, one which said, *If I can sit here while my toes itch, begging me to chew off their nails and not do it, then you can quit with the tongue-bath.*

She didn't say this aloud, but Ron seemed to catch her drift and forced his hands to intertwine in front of him; he stole lusty glances at them from time to time but did not lick them for at least four minutes.

"Sheila, how are you doing with your problem?" asked Georgina, who preferred to be called GiGi, though no one

133

knew why, while flexing her toes in an effort to still their riotous mood.

As was the custom in NSFCD, each member had to reiterate their compulsive behavior at each meeting, as a way of acknowledging it was a problem.

"I'm doing a little better," Sheila replied in a small voice, not wanting to actually express her compulsion, though she knew the rules.

"What is your problem?" GiGi noted two new attendees and wondered what they wanted.

"Do I have to say it again?"

"Yes."

Steeling herself with a deep breath, Sheila said, "I pop my pimples."

She was a walking acne factory, having been afflicted with her first at the age of two. It had grown out the bridge of her nose and was the cause of childhood cross-eyed vision.

"Where do you pop them?"

Sheila said nothing.

GiGi knew the answer: everywhere. In fact, she had spied Sheila liberating a particularly gruesome zinger at Jan's Country Griddle & Bait Shop, where each was sitting alone with food on their plates. GiGi had approached her and asked quietly if she could avoid doing that while there was food on the table.

Sheila blushed, apologized and dug into her four-egg omelet, unaware of what was running down the side of her nose.

GiGi gave her a business card and invited her to a meeting of the NSFCD, returning to her table, where her disgust was outweighed by hunger as she dipped into her own omelet, into which she had secretly deposited a few clippings from the previous night's harvest.

"Do you pop 'em in church?" Buford asked, drawing a snicker from everyone but Ron, whose need to lick his hands had become almost unbearable.

"That's okay, Sheila," said GiGi. "You just keep working on it and remember to squeeze something else when the need arises. Buford, how are you doing with your problem?"

"The way I see it, most of the time it ain't no problem," Buford said with a grin. "But I got it under control most of the time now."

Buford had, since the time in every adolescent boy's life when seeing she shape of breasts produced an immediate reaction, taken care of the problem just as immediately. His compulsion had followed him through too many jobs to count, and nearly as many sexual harassment complaints. GiGi found herself grateful he didn't lick his hands like Ron.

Instead of calling Buford on his failure to name the problem, she turned to two new faces in the group.

"Gentlemen, what brings you here?"

The two shared a glance and Chief Brad Kocke motioned for his unlikely partner to speak.

"We came by to speak with Sheila," Phillip Andrew Thomas said. "But I had no idea what this group was all about. This is disgusting."

"And you have no impulses?' GiGi asked mildly.

"Well, maybe, but I don't do anything like that," Phillip said, pointing at Sheila. "I mean, at the lunch table?"

"We all have our crosses to bear," GiGi replied, again in that maddeningly serene voice. "Talking about your problems in a friendly environment, with the support of those like you, is how the afflicted in society improve. If you are not here to share in the bond of confession, then I must ask you to leave."

"Fine with me," Phillip said, hauling his beefy frame out of the chair.

Chief Kocke eyed the group thoughtfully and decided to stay. "I'll stick around for a bit and talk to Sheila when this is over," he told Phillip in a hush. "I'll call you when we're through."

"Whatever man. I'm getting out of this freakshow."

The door closed and GiGi turned expectant eyes on the man who had stayed. She, like everyone else in the room, knew who he was, but all were curious as to what he would say.

"My name is Brad Kocke and I beat up perverts with my baton," he said.

Ron licked his hands as Reginald described his need to pick his nose.

*****

With the chief baring his soul, and Nick and Allen working their way toward the rundown trailer, no one was on duty at the police station, violating several city and state regulations.

In the parking lot, the Orc finally shook off the final vestiges of unconsciousness, and came to with a headache, puzzled as to where he was. The last thing he remembered was biting the chief's ear off. Now he was in a small car with another man who did not seem to be breathing.

His analytical skills were so paltry as to be nonexistent, but his instincts were sharp as razor-wire. He had to get out of the car and flee the area immediately, that much he knew.

He put his hand beside him for support and felt it give way in a sticky substance. Having missed the violent retching party, he had no idea what he was lying in, but he found it unpleasant.

Scrambling, he managed to push himself out the car window as fast as he could, landing squarely on his back and neck. Pain lanced up and down his spine, sending out tendrils of pulses as his brain registered what had happened, and then it simply stopped.

When he tried to get up, he suddenly found himself unable to move. His arms and legs would not obey.

The Orc was out of commission.

### 5:01 P.M.

Evvie Fennigan took the proffered *Tootsie Pop* sucker from Britni, marveling again at how messed up this day had become. She hadn't been exaggerating when she said she was hungry, but a lousy little sucker wasn't going to help.

Smiling, she turned to resume her place in the floor, but instead of stopping, she walked straight for the door.

136

Waterman guessed her intention and immediately understood the implications.

"Stop right there, Mrs. Fennigan," he said. "You can't leave yet."

Evvie ignored the order, pushing the door open and walking boldly into the evening air, which had cooled nicely since she entered the bank.

"Dorf, get her back in here," Waterman ordered.

Dorf stood where he was, his eyes on the floor, terrified of moving even a muscle lest he suffer a breach of contract with his body.

Waterman was furious. His years of tolerance were at an end. "You're fired, Dorf!"

"Thank you sir." Dorf had never felt so relieved in his life. Now he could go home and get into a hot bath and forget his gastrointestinal difficulties.

Dumbfounded, Waterman glared as Dorf shuffled to the door and beyond.

The tally within the bank had dwindled to three in addition to Waterman: Dalton Fisk, Britni Rice and Gina Feltrop.

And where were the police anyway? Waterman was seriously considering a call to the mayor, who had been at least smart enough to understand the way the game is played. Not terribly bright but he knew how to take orders from a well-meaning businessmen like Waterman.

Before he could make the decision, Dalton Fisk surprised them with a bloodcurdling scream.

# Chapter 27

## 5:10 P.M.

Grinning like kids who had successfully ditched school, Brian, Todd and Max sat around Evvie's kitchen table and planned the split.

"Okay, here's what we should do," Brian started.

"Shut up," Max said. "You have got to be the stupidest person I've ever met."

"What are you trying to say?"

Max rolled his eyes, looking to Todd for help in explaining the obvious.

"It's just that we know more about money, okay?" Todd said soothingly, feeling guilty at the way he was talking to his best friend.

"Okay," Brian said sullenly. "But I want my share."

"You'll get it buddy," said Max, who had decided early on that his would be the lion's share. Even if he felt they deserved an equal part, they wouldn't understand how he'd conned them.

Dipping into the bag, he pulled out all the money except four stacks; those he would keep for himself.

Max laid out the stacks of money and then counted one. The fifty crisp bills meant each stack was a total of $1,000. There were nine stacks on the table.

"Okay, here's what we'll do," Max said, taking five stacks and putting them into one pile, while he gave the four remaining stacks to the two on the other side of the table. "This is yours to split."

Neither had seen that much money in one place before, and were thrilled beyond measure to have it. And they didn't have to pay it back, that was the best part.

"I'm glad you guys ran me down," said Max, smiling benevolently as he stuffed the $5,000 back into the bag to join the other $4,000. "It's been a good day."

Rising, he bid the two a good evening and turned to leave.

Nick Crawford was standing in the doorway, his weapon drawn.

## 5:12 P.M.

Evvie pulled out of the bank parking lot and headed for home, unaware that a confrontation was in progress that might very well destroy her abode.

Dorf was traveling the other direction, hoping his TiVo was working properly. Getting out of the bath to view today's episode of Dr. Phil with a big bowl of popcorn would be a perfect ending to his day.

Waterman had the phone to his ear, demanding to speak to the mayor at his home. The little girl was crying, which only incensed him further. "Just put your dad on the phone right now!"

"Hello?"

"It's Waterman. What kind of city are you running?"

"What's wrong? I just sat down to dinner."

"I don't give a damn about your dinner. My bank has been robbed! And no one has shown up from the police department to talk to me. I'm telling you Keller, get someone over here now or I'll bury you."

"Okay, just calm down. I'll look into it."

*But not right now,* Keller thought as he replaced the receiver. *I'll get hold of Kocke after dinner.*

With that, he left his sobbing daughter on the couch and returned to the table.

Dalton Fisk was tired of lying on the cold floor. He was convinced the man who had chased him was not coming back, and it was time he started acting like a man. A strange memory of him screaming tried to intrude but he wasn't sure it actually happened; shrugging it off, he arose and approached the teller.

"Can you cash my check please?" he asked Gina,

pointing to the document lying orphaned on the counter.

She looked to Waterman for permission. Despite the late hour, the bank was still open, and this man had been in line before the robbers made their play, so by all rights he should get his money.

Waterman shook his head. "No more transactions. We're waiting for the police and then we're closing it up. He can come back tomorrow."

Dalton Fisk was starting to get angry.

### 5:13 P.M.

Jerry Fillabag entered the gym and headed straight for his office, wondering where his amigos had disappeared to. Surely they would check in.

Waiting in his private sanctum was a man he was unfamiliar with, and one whose eyes glinted with a sheen of instability.

While Jerry was getting acquainted with Crazy Willy, Phillip Andrew Thomas was wolfing down his second greasy chicken meal of the day, despite the episode in the chief's Subaru, while trying very hard to get the images of disgusting impulsive behavior out of his head.

He wasn't doing very well, and he constantly had to resist the urge to check his mashed potatoes for toenail clippings.

### 5:14 P.M.

Back at Evvie's place, the trio of robbers beheld Nick Crawford and his blue-steel Beretta 9-millimeter.

"Put the money on the table and your hands on your head," Nick said.

"The bank gave us the money," said Brian. "They said we didn't have to give it back."

"They said we didn't have to *pay* it back," Todd corrected.

"Whatever," Nick replied. "It's going back to the bank and you three are under arrest."

"This was all their idea," Max said.

"It was not!" None of the robbers knew the word *indignant*, but it would have applied to Todd at that moment.

"They told me I had to help them," Max added, his eyes calculating distances.

Nick was getting another headache. "I was there. I saw all of you working together, so you can save it."

"You saw them run me down," Max said, edging around the table with his bag still in hand. "I was just trying to . . ."

He voice quit instantly as he dodged the table and fled for the hallway leading to the back of the trailer, where Evvie's nylon trunk rested.

### 5:15 P.M.

Outside, Danielle was reduced to biting her fingernails and wishing desperately for something to eat. Now that the petrified granola bars had run their course, she was famished. In the other vehicle, the rundown Silverado that appeared one oil change shy of a blown motor, Danielle could see a skinny woman sliding in behind the wheel and wondered what she was doing.

The daughter of a construction worker and part-time farmer, Danielle had been raised in a pragmatic household, at least as far as her father went. Her mother, however, was an idealist, and she could afford to be with a husband that earned enough she could stay home and watch her soaps.

Danielle respected her mother, knew she had taken the role of housewife seriously, but there were elements of her personality that made it difficult.

Where her father would look at a situation and determine the most efficient way to accomplish a goal; her mother, on the other hand, would look at the same situation and pretend it didn't exist.

Danielle had taken after her father, which is why she went into banking. Numbers were solid; they didn't lie.

And if there was a miscalculation, it would eventually be corrected with a little thought.

The situation before her now was outside her experience.

*What am I doing here while my future husband takes on three armed men?* she wondered. *This isn't a game; someone could get hurt.*

As if in answer to her silent query, a gunshot rang out, launching her into hysterics as she imagined Nick trying to hold his guts in after taking a shot from one of those huge guns.

Allen Frye had followed Nick toward the trailer but did not enter through the same door. Instead, he had traveled around to the back, where she presumed a door needed to be covered. She could see neither man now, and wondered where the shot had come from.

The back of the trailer, where Allen had gone? Or was it inside, still smoking over Nick's bleeding form?

Danielle gripped the handle and pushed the door open, determined to at least be at his side if indeed Nick was about to take his last breath.

Roseanne, meanwhile, started the Silverado and waited.

### 5:15.30 P.M.

Nick didn't want to shoot his pistol, but in the mad dash for the hallway, Max had started a melee among his former partners. Brian and Todd were not bright, but survival instinct was at least on a par with rodents, which will scatter when something large is approaching.

Demanding they halt did no perceivable good so he put a slug through Evvie's sagging ceiling and that did the trick, at least for Brian and Todd. "Don't make me shoot you," he added to further control the duo.

Max, meanwhile, continued to barrel down the narrow hallway, caroming off each wall like a huge pinball, to where he believed he would find a door, or at least a window. His large frame would be difficult to squeeze through a window, but he didn't want to go to jail.

He had managed to steer clear of the authorities, except for the summer he turned 15 and been caught with a beer. He couldn't help but think of that experience.

*Max had no home life to speak of, though his parents were not mean to him. They just didn't notice him, which was one of the driving forces behind his desire to become a hulk of a man.*

*When the deputy pulled up to his house, neither parent answered the door. Max was finally allowed to open the door and he and the skinny man with a badge walked in.*

*"Mom? Dad?"*

*"What are you doing home?"*

*"I'm in trouble."*

*"That's just great. Well figure it out."*

*With that, his mother returned to her crossword puzzle and his father went back to Family Feud.*

*The deputy was at a loss. "Excuse me folks, but we have a problem here," the man, whose name was Ernie, said into the stale silence.*

*"He's fifteen," Max's father said. "He can work it out."*

*". . . survey says!"*

*"Stupid answer."*

*Ernie looked down at Max and then at his parents, dumbfounded. Silently he turned to the door and beckoned Max to follow him.*

*"Guess you're gonna have to work this out," Ernie said, embarrassed.*

*"What do I have to do?"*

*"I guess I'll put you to work picking up trash on the highway," Ernie said. "A week ought to do it."*

*Many small-town deputies might have been inclined either to take advantage of the situation or throw it aside as a worthless effort. But Ernie was a good-natured man who truly believed in what he did for a living.*

*Max felt the tears starting to sting his eyes, knew they would fall. He didn't want to cry in front of this man because he wouldn't understand. He would think it was because a 220-pound 15-year old was scared.*

*In truth, though he was afraid, he was moved to tears at the attention given him by a complete stranger.*

"It's okay, son," Ernie said, graciously turning to the side, pretending to take in the flowers in the waning evening light. A moment later, he turned back. "I'll pick you up in the morning and you can pick up trash for a couple hours."

"Yes, sir."

"Who knows? Maybe it won't go a whole week."

Max smiled at the thought, coming to admire this man tremendously in a very short period of time.

"See you in the morning," Ernie said with a wink, leaving the porch for his cruiser.

Max had learned his lesson about alcohol from the three days he spent picking up trash.

He had respected Ernie and appreciated the effort, but the man chasing him was not Ernie, and Max didn't believe he'd escape *official* punishment this time.

The cop had gotten the jump on them, which in and of itself was something of a surprise to the large man, since Nick was supposed to be locked in the bank vault.

Now he was standing there with stacks of cash and two suspects; if Max could get away clean, maybe they would roll over, but first he had to get out of the trailer.

He felt a twinge of guilt over his role in today's activities, but he was between a rock and a hard place so he pushed onward.

No back door revealed itself, leading Max, oddly enough, to thoughts of fire safety. Ducking into a room on the right, he discovered what must be Evvie's bedroom.

A queen-sized bed filled the room, leaving only a half a foot between the end of the bed and the wall.

*How does she get to the closet?* Max could see an open alcove that served as a closet, full of dresses on hangers and shoes in one plastic bag and nylons in another, both suspended from a nail in the wall. To the left of the "closet" was a window, which would be a tight fit but one he believed he could negotiate. If it came to that, Max was pretty sure he could force the issue and just break out the wall.

Ignoring the narrow path, Max launched himself toward the bed, overlooking Evvie's trunk on the floor. He hit the old steamer with his shin and went sprawling, landing on the bed with a grunt of pain before scrambling to the far side as quickly as possible. When he reached the wall, he pushed on the window only to discover it was attached to wires which prevented it from opening fully.

"Arrrgh!" Venting his frustration and putting his considerable mass behind the shove, Max needed the work of mere seconds to snap the wires and shove the window, frame and all, out into the yard.

"Stop!" Nick trained his weapon on the large mass of flesh trying to wiggle out the window, but again, did not really want to shoot. "Come on, Max, don't do this."

Max might have replied but Nick didn't understand it if he did; either way he did not stop his frantic escape attempt.

## 5:19 P.M.

Allen Frye was in the right place at the right time. He had developed a thought on his way to Brian's trailer, but it had been Roseanne who had encouraged it.

"Why *don't* we take the money?" Her eyes glittered mischievously as she made her suggestion. "That other cop's going to be busy. It shouldn't take much to get some of it when he's not looking."

Allen had agreed, more so that she would look at him like that than in his ultimate belief in his ability to put anything past Nick Crawford.

And now, here he was, on the back side of the trailer, about 60 feet from the pond that had claimed Brian's dad, and the biggest man he'd ever seen was squirming through a hole in the house. Clutched in a meaty hand was a bag with The Newburn Bank stamped across it.

Allen knew he'd hit the jackpot.

"Hold it right there," he said, putting the muzzle of his gun under the large man's protruding jaw as he grabbed the sack of money with the other. "I'll take that for you."

"Get back little man," Max said without much menace. How could one bare his fangs with a gun under his chin?

"Thanks," Allen said, opening the bag to inspect his take, which appeared to be at least $400. Not a bad haul for an easy task. "See you around."

"You better hope not."

## 5:19 P.M.

"Hold it right there," was followed shortly by "I'll take that for you."

Nick assumed his reluctant backup was thwarting Max's escape, but when the bear threatened Allen, he understood the truth, and his heart sank.

It wasn't so much that he was afraid of any repercussions inherent with having to track down a second robbery suspect, this one using a police-issue gun to force the result; it was that Danielle was still in the car, right next to where Allen had parked. The last thing he wanted was for this to turn ugly and find her in the middle of a firefight.

Suddenly he could hear the engine in the big Silverado roar, coupled with a shower of gravel as the vehicle sped out of the drive.

*Shit!* Nick thought. On the heels of that was a prayer that Danielle was okay.

He had cuffed Brian and Todd to each other around a central beam in the living room, confident they would not escape. Now he was torn between chasing after Allen and helping Max free himself from the window.

He wished he had a radio so he could call the chief for help.

# Chapter 28

### 5:23 P.M.

"How do you feel?"

"Better," Chief Kocke admitted, surprised. He had never realized how liberating it was to confide in others his heretofore secret impulses.

Others had guessed, and he imagined a lot of people thought they knew the extent to which his perversion ran, but it wasn't until Phillip Andrew Thomas threatened him with exposure had he understood how much he feared the impulse.

"I'm glad you stopped by tonight," GiGi said. "That couldn't have been easy for you."

"I just went with my gut," Kocke replied. "I've been trying to stop doing it on a casual basis, but when I get mad, I just seem to need that release."

GiGi watched the other with eyes that promised more than detached interest, though she was afraid to say anything to the man. Brad rubbed his torn ear, wincing at the painful reminder.

Ron continued to lick his hands and the others in the group contemplated their own desires.

### 5:26 P.M.

The Orc awoke with a start as something was slobbering on his ear. Feeling suddenly apprehensive, his primitive mind flashed to what he had done earlier to the bad man, wishing he still had the piece of ear he had wrenched free of his head.

He opened his eyes and everything flooded back.

"Uggh!" he muttered, noticing the cows that had come to investigate. He tried to shoo them away but his arms still would not work. One was nibbling on his leg though he could not feel it.

The Orc had never felt helpless before and didn't like it at all.

### 5:29 P.M.

Jerry Fillabag was pleased. For the first time in his career as a kingpin, he'd finally met someone who thought big like he did. Crazy Willy was not all there, that was certain. But he had a good eye for making money and a few inroads that should prove quite beneficial to both as he maneuvered into the high-school market.

The two had discussed trivialities for a few minutes before Crazy Willy announced his intention to thrash a couple of cops.

"They tried to rip me off," he said. "No one does that and gets away with it."

"I know what you mean," Jerry replied sympathetically. "I've had my share of problems with cops but only recently were they local. I'm also missing a couple amigos who split with my money. How about we pool our resources, maybe work together on this thing?"

Jerry leaned forward to impart his needs as Crazy Willy met him half way.

Yes, Jerry was happy. With Crazy Willy doing the legwork, the Newburn Police Department would be demoralized, he would recover his amigos and cash, and he could resume his sale of Pakistani tea.

### 5:30 P.M.

In the end, Nick just couldn't leave Brian and Todd to the mercy of Max. Enraged, his ear hair quivering like dandelions before heavy wind, Max would probably tear the two apart where they'd been shackled.

No, he simply couldn't abandon them to that fate, and he had a pretty good idea where to find Allen Frye and his bony mistress.

He'd helped Max withdraw from the window and then held his weapon squarely in the other's face, making no overt moves but underlining the seriousness of the situation.

"I don't want any trouble out of you," he'd told Max. "I know you're pissed and so am I, but I can't have you tearing up this trailer or going after the other two."

He nodded in the direction of his two idiot charges and wondered again how Max had gotten mixed up with them. Nick decided to come right out and ask.

"I needed money," Max replied. "I've had a rough time lately and I got in over my head. It's time to pay for that mistake."

"By robbing a bank? There are plenty of other ways to fix your problem besides pointing a gun at a helpless victim," Nick said, acutely aware of his own pointed gun.

Max related his tale of misery to the officer and waited for a reply. Before Nick could offer one, he heard Danielle asking for him.

"He's in back," Brian told her.

"Nick? Are you okay?"

"I'm fine, come on back."

A cursory introduction seemed in order, though the two had already met at the bank when Britni's plan had nearly ended the whole fiasco.

"I'm sorry about earlier," Max said, and he actually meant it. "I was angry and those two told me no one would try to stop us, you know? I guess it was a pretty stupid thing to do."

"Yeah," was all Danielle could say. She wanted to be angry at this man, but he looked so forlorn; even his ear hair seemed wilted with his circumstance.

Max felt very ashamed, and his unhappy life threatened to overwhelm him as it had that day on his front porch. He took a deep breath and told the two about his trouble and the discipline he'd received.

Danielle and Nick had recognized the same emptiness Ernie had seen that warm summer day, and on hearing his story, they responded to it.

Brian and Todd were straining to hear the conversation but could only catch murmurs.

"What do you think they're talking about?"

"That woman was at the bank," Brian replied. "I think she recognized me."

"She couldn't have," Todd said, rolling his eyes. "We all had our masks on, remember?"

"She still looked at me like she knew me."

"You're retarded."

"You are."

"Oh that's clever." Todd was viewing Brian in a new light, one less admiring than previously.

"You are."

"Enough you two," Nick said, squatting on his haunches to look them both in the face. "Danielle and I are engaged, that's how she knew you."

"You ask her to marry you back there? Is that what y'all were talking about?"

Now it was Nick who rolled his eyes. Like Danielle, he had a little trouble staying angry with Max, and these two deserved nothing more than pity.

"Something like that," he said. "Now we need to talk about how we're going to fix this situation."

Nick and Danielle had discussed some options in Evvie's room and the only one that might actually work depended a lot on how these two morons responded.

"How would you like to walk away from this without going to jail?"

Nick's question hung in the air like stale cigarette smoke as the pair looked at each other for a way to answer, like this was some kind of trick.

"I guess that'd be okay," said Todd. "What do we have to do?"

"First, you have to give up the money you took, can you handle that?"

"That's not fair, we earned that money," Brian said sullenly.

"No you didn't. You took it at gunpoint, there's a

difference."

*Try telling that to Jerry Fillabag,* Max thought but did not say.

"Okay. Then what?" At least Todd's mind was focused enough for conversation.

"Then you spend the next five years paying it back," Danielle said.

"What!?" Now Todd's mind was fully engaged. Having to pay back money he would never get the use of suddenly clicked as he took in the implications.

"You heard her," said Max. "I'll be doing the same thing. We'll have to square this with the bank, but the lady here thinks that should work. We have to pick up the trash."

"What?" Brian, as always, was mystified. "I don't understand."

"Remember those forms you filled out at the bank?"

"Yeah," Todd said uneasily. "That girl said it was so we didn't have to pay it back."

"She was lying to you," Danielle said as gently as she could. "She was trying to stall for time."

Nick nodded at the two. "The truth is that was an actual loan application," he said. "That means you're legally obligated to pay the money back. The bank won't care what you did with it, as long as they get it back."

This was a calculated lie, since the bank had not actually approved the application, but Nick was correct in believing these dolts didn't know any better.

"She said we didn't have to pay it back," Brian repeated.

"I know, but that was then and this is now," Danielle said. "All three of you were in on this and all three of you will have to pay it back."

"How much?"

"Max said the total amount was $13,000, so with interest over five years, you're probably looking at paying back about $17,000, give or take," the loan officer replied. "Call it six thousand apiece."

Todd's suddenly understood that Max had been ripping them off. "You asshole! You were holding out on us."

Both he and Brian began thrashing, pulling at their bonds in an effort to get to Max, though what they expected to do was beyond Nick.

"Stop it!" he shouted.

"There's another consideration," Danielle said into the sudden silence. "If you don't clear this up, the Guardians are going to put the hurt on you."

The room grew heavy as the quintet considered the situation.

## 5:45 P.M.

Allen Frye pulled into the employee's lot behind Esther's Warehouse of Drugs and Teabag Emporium, killing the engine and smiling at Roseanne, who positively beamed with pride at what they'd accomplished.

She'd been ready when he raced to the SUV, peeling out the second he was safely within, and they switched positions at the blinker. Roseanne insisted she could drive, but after trading places, the emotions of the brief escape flooded through her, bringing with it images of *Law & Order* car chases.

"Did anyone see you?"

"Only the big guy, but he was stuck."

"That's good. Let's go to the store. I've got to have a hit."

Todd pulled out with the proper signal despite being alone on Route A and headed for town and the drugstore beyond. As they passed the police station, he noticed what appeared to be the same five cows congregated around the chief's Subaru and a man lying on the ground, but put it out of his mind as he considerately drove the speed limit to their destination.

His days as a police officer were over, and he hoped that was the chief himself being mauled by a herd of bovine.

Now, as they listened to the engine ticking as it cooled, Roseanne opened the bag to inspect its contents.

She was much better at counting money, even at a

glance, than her erstwhile lover, and knew right away it was a lot more than the $400 estimate Allen had supplied.

"Wow," she said. "They got a big score."

"How much?"

"Looks like around $10,000," Roseanne replied.

"That's some serious dough," Allen said with a whistle. "Think of all the shit we can get for that."

The two hurried into the haven that was the backroom of Esther's place, where they consummated their newfound love once more and then furthered their bliss with a helping from Roseanne's cigar box.

They were saving the rescued grass clippings as a treat to accompany tonight's episodes of *Law & Order*.

Neither considered anything beyond immediate gratification. Certainly thoughts of the Guardians coming to mete out justice never entered the equation.

# Chapter 29

Newburn Mayor Ted Keller was starting to panic.

When it came to administration, he was very comfortable. Checks for employees needed to be signed and he did it with relish. He really enjoyed knowing how little each employee made; it made him smile.

Running council meetings was something he could do in his sleep since he had practically memorized Robert's Rules Of Order during his first days in office. Even handling pissing contests between any of the four aldermen was child's play to him. All it took was the right amount of understanding in the root cause of the problem, coupled with knowing what everyone stood to gain or lose from the deal. With that little packet of info, he was a world-class problem solver, at least in his own mind.

But the scenario before him was unheard of in this town. For the first time since, well, ever, there was not a police officer to be found. Until 30 years ago, Newburn had been policed by the Sheriff's Department, and they always had a deputy close to town, if not actually within the city limits.

Chief Kocke had disappeared and his radio was off, nor would he answer his cell phone. The little dipshit Allen Frye had left a note about a drug lead at Esther's and had not been seen since, and *Super-Cop* had last been seen at The Newburn Bank, according to its owner and president, Edward Von Waterman III, who had torn a pretty good chunk out of Ted's backside the last time they spoke.

Ted Keller was a politician, which meant most of the time he was kissing ass, but he was a fervent family man. He might say things to his wife and daughter that good men should not say, but never would he appreciate having the likes of Waterman do it.

The old bastard had made his daughter cry, for the love of God. For that alone he wanted the bank president to suffer a little bit, which is why he waited until after dinner to place his first phone call to an empty station.

When he couldn't track down anyone through normal channels, he got into his Explorer and drove to the department's headquarters, where he found the note from Allen Frye still taped to the front door.

The Subaru was present, but the cows had since departed, leaving the man on the other side invisible in the gathering gloom of dusk. Neither could Bartie be seen in the shadows of the car.

Keller thought of Brian and Todd for the first time in several months, wondering if they at least would be available until this mess could be sorted out. He knew they were suspended, but what else could he do?

He drove to Esther's, which was trying to serve last-minute shoppers before the doors closed at 6:00.

Inside, he hoped to speak with Esther herself, but she had retired for the day and the young girl running the counter was of no help.

"Do you know if Allen Frye is here?"

"Who?"

"Allen Frye, he's a police officer," Keller replied. "He left a note saying he would be out here today and I need to find him."

"I didn't see a note," Stacey said, peering down the man from her druggist platform on high and wondering what kind of con he was running.

"The note wasn't here," Keller said tersely. "Why would it be here if he was coming here?"

"You tell me." Now she was becoming defiant. He hadn't shown the honorary badge all mayors carried (at least that's what he claimed when he demanded one) and if he thought he could push her around by mentioning some cop he was wrong.

"Jesus Christ," he muttered. "Let's start over, okay? My name is Mayor Ted Keller and I'm looking for one of the city's police officers, Allen Frye. He left a note at the station saying he would be here to investigate something. Does any of this ring a bell?"

"Nope."

Keller wanted to rip his rug right off his head and slap her in the face with it, but that would not be politically savvy. "Thanks anyway," he said, handing her his business card. "If he shows up, have him call me."

Stacey looked at the card as though it was covered in slime, wondering how she was supposed to know this Albert guy. Ted Keller placed the card on the counter and made his way through the few stragglers he'd interrupted with his queries.

His call to Waterman was not pleasant.

## 6:00 P.M.

With a final round of promises to work very hard on curbing their personal compulsions, the Newburn Society For Compulsive Disorders officially closed its meeting and the well-appointed room once more became a part of GiGi's home. The mood shifted from clinical to personal, at least to Chief Brad Kocke.

Most felt better for having shared their fears and behaviors with semi-strangers, though Buford knew his weekly attendance would not likely stifle his urges. He secretly enjoyed making others uncomfortable and he also held a private hope that someone would join who appreciated his condition.

Ron wasn't sure what to expect after just one meeting, but his need had seemed to diminish over the course of the last hour and he decided to return the following week.

As for Sheila Fowler, the meeting was a waste of time. In her opinion, if she wanted to be ridiculed for what she did, all she had to do was go to The Newburn Fitness & Weight Training Center, where people were constantly making faces at her after she finished with a machine.

Brad sat with a feeling of ease that he'd not felt since

before losing the election of '84, and didn't spare a glance at Sheila Fowler as she left.

Back then, he had been a nobody, although a good cop and conscientious citizen. Then he'd been accosted while off duty by a fruit who offered to do things to him for free the first time, some sort of trial basis, Brad guessed.

Instead of reacting to his benefactor with gratitude, Brad promptly beat him into a coma with his nightstick. Although he felt at the time his actions were justified by the attempted violation of his person, he could not help feeling guilty about what he'd done.

Telling himself it was self-defense did not ring true, since the fruit hadn't raised a menacing finger; another part of his anatomy, perhaps, but Kocke did not consider that a weapon.

Amazing, he reflected now, how quickly a man's life can change.

With guilt driving him, he found ways to justify his actions. The problem was that he had enjoyed the release of emotion that accompanied each thrashing.

Soon he found himself cruising the park, where the first occurrence had occurred, finding all manner of men and teens hanging out, waiting for the opportunity to commingle with members of the same sex.

Had they been there waiting for pretty girls, his duty under the law would have mandated a series of raids to rid the community of sexual predators. But no one really cared how homosexuals abased themselves and apparently, no one really cared about their demise.

It soon became a hobby and then a game to see if he could whip more than one in a single night.

His reputation as a source of terror to the gay community grew with each bloodied man found lying in the park, and several representatives of the collective had appealed to Kocke at the station under the guise of enlisting the police to intervene. Not one of them even suspected his involvement.

But all that was past him now.

The meeting had done wonders for his soul, as it were,

and now he felt something akin to affection beginning to infuse him as GiGi locked eyes with him.

"What are you thinking about?"

"The past and the future."

"What about the present?"

"What do you have in mind?" Brad Kocke the man had always enjoyed a good conversation with a woman, but being married to an inane chatterbox had ruined it for him.

"Dinner, perhaps. A night with a handsome man to follow. We'll cross the bridge about sleeping arrangements when we get to it."

*Damn,* Brad thought. *This woman is really coming on to me.*

But how did he play it? It had been a long time since he had a pleasant, informal dinner with a woman, and a night out did appeal to him.

His ear still stung like crazy, and he knew Doc Hemphill needed to look at it.

"Can I borrow your car? I need to make a stop first," he said. "I'll pick you up and we'll go to Jan's."

"Sounds fine to me. I'd like to change into something more revealing anyway."

"I'll just bring something back," Brad said.

### 6:05 P.M.

Brian and Todd rubbed their wrists once the cuffs had been removed, thankful to be free of their bindings. Each had subdued a few suspects in their brief stint as policemen, but neither until today had known what wearing the bracelets felt like.

Brian had sometimes fantasized about being chained up during a sexual encounter, but that had lost its appeal.

"What now?" Todd asked.

Nick eyed Todd, then took in Brian and Max as well before replying.

"We're going back to the bank," he said at last. "Danielle is going to calm down Mr. Waterman, explain everything and then you guys will be free to go."

"I'll get the paperwork done tomorrow and you should have your payment books by Friday," Danielle added.

"What about me? I don't have a home anymore. Since Jerry fired me I can't stay at the gym anymore, so I'm not sure what I'm going to do."

Nick and Danielle exchanged a glance, one usually reserved for married people but applicable in this case anyway. "I guess you can stay with me for a while until you get something figured out," Nick said. "You'll have to get a job so you can pay this money back, but I might have an idea or two about that."

With that, the group headed for the door and nearly ran down Evvie Fennigan, who had arrived a few minutes earlier but was wary about entering her trailer. She could see shapes outlined against the curtains but not who they belonged to.

Her shows had offered plenty of scenes in which a burglar or two waited inside to accost a tired woman as she entered her home, but the stories had always been just that.

Seeing the policeman who had been at the bank and Danielle, Evvie wasn't sure what to think. With the added sight of her son and the two others who had robbed the bank, she was suddenly terrified.

"What are are you people doing in my house?"

"Brian?" Nick's prompt was lost on the young man, who had the look of a man knowing he was about to bite into a worm.

"What's going on Brian?"

When he still held his silence, Danielle took over smoothly. "I'm sorry we startled you, Mrs. Fennigan," she said. "Nick came here and talked to these boys about the robbery, and we worked everything out."

"Well I'll be," Evvie exclaimed, dropping her purse and rushing to her son. "Thank the Good Lord. You repented your evil ways. I'm so proud of you."

"Mom," Brian said with a blush.

"Mrs. Fennigan," Nick said. "We have unfinished business at the bank and we really need to go now."

"Oh, okay. Is everything going to be all right?"

"I think so," Nick said, relating the events that had happened in her trailer and explaining the gaping hole in her bedroom wall.

Visibly relieved, Evvie caught Danielle's eyes and the two shared a moment of perfect clarity.

"Thank you," the elder said. "I appreciate what you're trying to do."

As soon as they left, Evvie Fennigan picked up the phone.

"There's work to do," she said, after which she relayed the information Nick and Danielle had provided, along with the supposed whereabouts of the remaining robber.

Satisfied she'd done her part, Evvie turned on the television and settled in for the news before Wheel came on.

### 6:10 P.M.

For the first time all day, Dorf Walkenhorst felt good. His cramping had ceased and he was clean. Even his cats maneuvered close to him, thankful his odor had been expunged.

The timer on the microwave signaled his popcorn was ready and took the large bowl and a shaker of seasoned salt to the living room. His TiVo was cued and ready to unleash Dr. Phil, which put him squarely at Heaven's doorstep.

### 6:12 P.M.

Sheila Fowler decided on a light workout before going home to her microwaved dinner. Usually a homebody, she considered herself grotesque, a characterization many Newburnians would agree with wholeheartedly.

Still, she liked the feeling engendered by a flexing of muscles and the strain of resistance, be it on the stationary bike or the treadmill. Doing a circuit on the machines also took her mind off her troubles, chief among them being how to rid herself of the hideous affliction she'd always suffered.

*I am Job incarnate*, she thought as she entered The Newburn Fitness & Weight Training Center.

A light crowd today, she noticed, with many of the machines unused. Even the bikes and mills were relatively open for use. Sheila found herself not questioning too much as she entered the ladies' locker room and changed into her sweatsuit.

A few minutes later she emerged and headed for the elliptical cycle for a warm-up ride. Seated at the unit next to her was a woman she'd noticed before but had never actually spoken with.

Ignoring her, Sheila put her feet in the stirrups and began a steady rhythm, wishing for the umpteenth time she had purchased a Walkman radio for her workouts.

"How's it going?"

Feeling like a turtle caught without its shell, Sheila froze for a second. "Are you talking to me?"

"Sure, why not? We have this part of the gym to ourselves. I was just being sociable."

"Oh. Sorry, I'm not used to people being sociable with me. It's going okay, I guess. How about you?"

"I could just about kill my neighbor, but otherwise I'm okay."

She could barely contain the surge of emotion. Another human had actually engaged her in CONVERSATION, and not because she was in a group of people who couldn't control themselves. Sheila felt lightheaded.

"Why?"

"Why what?"

"Why do you want to kill your neighbor?"

"She's seeing this new guy, okay? And I don't have anything against her but she's up all night long screaming and moaning. I can't get any sleep."

Sheila mulled this over as she considered how she was supposed to respond. How was she to know what to say? This was a first in the annals of life as Sheila Fowler knew it.

"Do you live in an apartment? Is that how you hear everything?" She believed this was a safe line of questioning to pursue.

"No, she lives next door to my house," the other replied.

"They leave all the windows open and carry on with loud music and then last night they got really kinky."

"What do you mean?"

"They were doing something in the garage, which is on my side of the house," she said. "Sounded like they were out there revving up the motor or something. I couldn't tell, but it really pissed me off."

"I heard about that," Sheila said. "You're talking about Brenda and Dalton."

"You know them?"

"I know Brenda. She said some guy attacked them last night and chased Dalton with a chainsaw."

"That sounds about right," the woman said. "I'm Marcia."

Sheila replied with her name and the two lapsed into comfortable silence, the only sound that of the fanwheels turning in time.

Sheila was surprised to find the conversation had completely removed her from the reality of pedaling the bike and that time had passed without notice. Further, she found herself flush with an excitement she's not experienced before as she peered into this woman's face.

Wrapped in her budding thoughts, Sheila failed to notice Jerry Fillabag watching from his office, a look of pure disgust marring his features.

### 6:18 P.M.

Turning from his window, Jerry picked up the phone and dialed the number scrawled on a piece of paper.

"You find anything yet?"

"Nothing yet. But I will."

"Keep me posted."

Jerry Fillabag was growing anxious. The amigos had probably fled Newburn as quickly as their illegal little feet could take them, and he knew that once they were far afield, he would have a hard time recovering the $75 they had collected from Lionel Leanman, and since it was his load lost, old Triple-L would have to cover it.

## 6:20 P.M.

Lionel Leanman had owned and operated the Double-L for almost 20 years, and in that time, he had made a lot of friends and a few enemies. Jerry, he knew, had never really been in the former category, but now he feared the gym owner would become an enemy.

The creepy little guy that had come around asking about the amigos sent a chill up his spine. In his own way, this guy was worse than the Orc, who was not smart enough to appear contemplative.

Crazy Willy, however, was not a completely unknown quantity. While Lionel had never secured his services, he was aware of them and of the reputation that surrounded the man like a swarm of flies in an outhouse.

"Jerry wants his money," Willy said after sampling the stale peanuts. "He wants the amigos."

"I already told him all I know," Lionel replied warily, not wanting to cross the loon. "They took off and I haven't seen them."

Like Jerry before him, Crazy Willy found himself believing the man. Crossing Jerry was a hazard to your health, especially now that he had brought another enforcer into the fold. Willy did not know the Orc except by reputation, but from what he'd heard he was a bad man.

Gnawing on body parts aside, he was by all accounts feral in virtually every other aspect as well, and that created a whole set of intangibles. Crazy Willy wanted people to fear him, if not respect him, and had cultivated his own "instability" to meet those ends. Beneath the veneer, he was cunning and intelligent, but softer than anyone could imagine.

"Give me a beer," he told Lionel, who obliged the other without recompense. "I'll keep tracking the amigos and if you hear anything or see anything, you better tell someone."

Lionel simply nodded and then turned to other duties behind the bar. This was getting to be a huge headache.

# Chapter 30

**6:30 P.M.**

"It's about time you showed up," said a visibly agitated Edward Von Waterman III, who had been ogling Britni as a way to pass the time. "What the hell is going on?"

Ted Keller lowered his gaze to the floor, the call he'd made a little while ago fresh in his mind. To be called a panty-waisted weasel was never a good time, but coming from Waterman, who controlled many things through his bank, it stung.

He tried to get along with the man but Waterman's acerbic nature was as finely tuned as a Corvette engine straight out of the factory. Most times he avoided contact, except on those occasions when it was politically necessary, and then he would laugh at every joke, appear to hang on every word, all the while wishing he was anywhere else in the world.

Like the phone call, in which Waterman had not only called the mayor a weasel but suggested he better get used to making sub sandwiches and living on food stamps, this encounter was unpleasant.

"Well? What the hell is going on in my town?"

"*Your* town, Mr. Waterman?"

"Yes. Everything that's done goes through *my* bank. No building is constructed, no business gets a foothold without *my* approval. *My* town. Now tell me what is going on."

If the others in the bank lobby were embarrassed by the dressing down of the town's chief politician, they tactfully hid it.

"The truth is I don't know," Ted finally managed. "I can't find the chief or either of the officers. I've called, tried the radio and went looking for them. They've disappeared."

"And left our peaceful town at the mercy of any

hoodlums who wish to stroll through?"

It was rhetorical, Ted knew, and wisely held his tongue hard against a sarcastic reply.

"What are we going to do?" he asked instead.

Waterman was about to deliver another piercing rant when a voice spoke up from near the door.

"We'll handle it," the newcomer said, his presence unnoticed by those inside as they were busy watching the painful exchange between mayor and bank owner.

"Who's we and who are you?" Ted Keller only knew demographics; individual faces did not apply.

"My name is not important," the tall, thirty-something man said quietly, confirming by their reaction that Evvie's message had been accurate. "What *is* important is that we have always kept an eye on our town, and we've been ready to step in when we're needed. We'll take care of this problem."

"I have to ask you again who 'we' are," said Ted.

"We're the Guardians," the man said, and with that, turned his back to the small group and exited The Newburn Bank.

### 6:40 P.M.

Phillip Andrew Thomas sat in his car and watched. It was all he had left to him, since Chief Kockebreath had ditched him in favor of listening to a bunch of grown people talk about the nasty things they did behind closed doors. *And sometimes in the open,* he thought, shivering.

His calls to the chief had gone unanswered and his messages unreturned, which left Phillip feeling quite perturbed. *Ignoring me is a big mistake,* he thought.

Perhaps he would draft a story about the botched drug bust, complete with pictures, and let the chainsaw thing go. He could easily depict a befuddled chief of police being caught up in a scam, and then drop the hammer with the Fruit-Smacker stuff.

If Chief Kockeknocker didn't call him back by 7:30, he

was going to do it.

Pulling out his laptop, Phillip began writing his most damning story to date.

### 6:51 P.M.

Dalton Fisk was furious. Being cooped up in a bank, albeit for some time unconscious, was a very difficult chore for the 41-year old truck driver.

Being on the road five days a week, his life was filled with a variety of sights and people, each more interesting than the last. Diners all over the country might seem isolated to the occasional traveler, but in the dead of night, a familiar neon light advertising diesel and a good buffet were always welcome to his kind.

Dalton knew several caretakers of the road, often tired and sometimes bitter women who were good at their craft but not much else. Their life was as dependent on drivers like Dalton as his was upon making it through to his final destination, where he would trade one load for another and retrace his tracks.

Conversation was a natural enough aspect for a trucker who usually traveled the highways crooning along with Waylon Jennings and Willie Nelson hits two decades old. From eight-tracks to cassettes and then CDs, and now MP3 players, he had never lost his taste for the old country music.

Much of what was wrong with the world, in Dalton's opinion, came from the abandonment of music as a way of relating to life.

But when he wasn't cruising along with his brights picking out litter and wildlife on the side of the road, he enjoyed his time at home. Newburn had been his place of birth and nowhere else did he feel as comfortable.

His enforced stay at The Newburn Bank had threatened him almost physically, first when he saw the man from the night before who had mercilessly chased him with a saw, and then when he was informed his stay would be indefinite. Not being able to cash his check was the icing on the cake.

He was due to leave for a run to New Orleans first thing in the morning, and at the rate he was going, he might not even get to sleep before his appointed departure, much less spend any time with Brenda.

Dalton had been mystified when the man had announced his affiliation with the Guardians. Brenda's uncle had once claimed to belong to that loose collection of vigilantes, but he had never heard of anyone else, and he was pushing 80 when he'd said it.

They were a mysterious group, walking in plain sight among their fellow Newburnians and holding their membership close to the vest.

To his knowledge, there was no secret sign or handshake with which each acknowledged others, and if they met, it must be in the most secret of locations.

Dalton watched the bank president speaking with the mayor and wondered if they had any idea what they were doing. The cops were apparently missing, which was not surprising to Dalton, who had finally outrun his attacker and had never heard a siren in the still night.

Why didn't they call the sheriff? Or even the state police? Surely there was some form of law enforcement that could respond in this situation.

But of course, that was what the man had meant when he said the Guardians would take care of it.

Silently wishing them luck, he still longed for a uniformed officer to relieve them of their imprisonment, even as his eyes scanned the front door, waiting for a chance to make a break for it.

## 6:55 P.M.

Chief Brad Kocke had a serious case of the butterflies. Blame it on his insightful meeting with the compulsive-disorder group or his fortuitous brush with the lovely GiGi. Whatever the cause, his heart was beating about twice as fast as it did when he was really into a smacking, and his bowels felt loose with nervous anticipation of the dinner and what might lie beyond.

His mind had returned to junior high, when he had met a girl at a movie for the first time. As a result, his adult responsibilities, such as looking after the town and making sure he had someone in a position to respond to an emergency, had abandoned him.

Despite his career and proven abilities as an officer and later chief of police, he was losing it. His interest in serving the public had been dulled by his confession and subsequent amorous feelings for GiGi. Even if it proved to be a one-night stand, which very well might be the case, he could not put his mind into any gear except lustful wanting.

Had his cell phone been set for loud tones instead of soft vibrate, perhaps his career could have been salvaged. He was, after all, technically looking for leads in the chainsaw case, though even he would be hard-pressed to justify his actions to this point. Especially since he didn't even think to talk to Sheila Fowler.

Doc Hemphill had met him at the clinic and did the best he could to disinfect the wound and put a bandage on it. The ear was mangled, unsurprising, considering the way the Orc had gone after it, but even had the missing piece been in hand when Doc Hemphill met the chief, little could have been done to reattach it. Not in Newburn.

Now, despite the fact his ear was afire with the medicinal spray used to ward off infection, he was feeling the crunch of actually sitting down to dinner with a woman.

The radio in the Subaru continued to call for him, but neither the Orc nor old Bartie were in a position to answer. And despite the message left for the coroner, there had been no response due to a three-car accident elsewhere in the county. Brad hadn't even thought to mention it to Doc Hemphill.

When Brad decided to stay at the meeting, his bulky counterpart had left him to pursue less revolting entertainment.

Brad opened his phone to call in a take-out order from Jan's and noticed he had missed 14 calls. Though he didn't have a name to go with the number in his phone for nine of them, he was well aware of who it was that had been trying to reach him.

Ted Keller, mayor and the MIC of police affairs to whom Chief Brad Kocke ultimately answered.

The other five belonged to Phillip Andrew Thomas, and a the voicemail inbox indicated four messages, two from each caller.

Now his anxiety shifted from lust to worry as he began to contemplate his potentially damaging position.

# Chapter 31

## 7:00 P.M.

**It may surprise the citizens of Newburn to realize their chief of police has been accused of stalking and beating men in the Riverfront Park because of their sexual orientation. A survivor of one such encounter, who agreed to speak to *The Newburn News* on the condition of anonymity, described the event as barbaric sport, done for no other reason than to give pleasure to the man wielding his police-issue baton.**

Phillip Andrew Thomas paused in his review of the story he planned to run if Chief Kockebreath did not get back to him. So far his story was solid, albeit quite editorial in nature, even after four readings. With each review, it became more cemented in his mind and yet each time through, he found something he could improve. It was his gift.

Presently, he changed the word *agreed* to *begged* and called it good. The anonymous tipster was of course fictitious, but no one else knew that; his editor would not press him too hard for an identity, especially with the sensational aspect of the story. With one more change, he would practically guarantee the indifference of Blowhard Bruce.

**A survivor of one such encounter, who agreed to speak out against the chief despite a fear of retaliation, described the event as "barbaric sport," done for no other reason than to give pleasure to the man wielding his police-issue baton.**

That ought to do it, Phillip thought, scanning over the remainder of the story.

**According to this terrified witness, who relates having seen Chief Brad Kocke administer frequent beatings, almost on a nightly basis, it was just a matter of time before the demented lawman's gaze picked him out of the crowd. Whether or not the man was homosexual is irrelevant; what matters is that a man sworn to uphold the law has allegedly taken out his whims on helpless victims. This reporter was told the chief never went on his hunts while in uniform, though the witness admitted to avoiding the park at various times and therefore could not say with certainty that Chief Kocke had contained his adventures to his off time.**

**Who will police the police? Mayor Ted Keller could not be reached for comment, but his record as political leader of this town would indicate a harsh reaction to news of this magnitude.**

**The witness, who suffered two broken ribs, a shattered ulna (the smaller of two bones in the forearm) and numerous bruises to the face, back and legs, said he was afraid to leave his home, calling it an "injustice" to be forced to constantly look over his shoulder for signs of an attacker. Further, he said several calls to his home were placed by someone threatening "to put him in the morgue" if he continued his "homosexual activities."**

**He believes the calls were made by the chief but cannot prove anything, and this leaves him filled with despair and terror.**

**The publisher and editor of *The Newburn News* call on our civic leaders to investigate these horrendous crimes and ask anyone who has suffered abuse of this nature to report it.**

Phillip decided he could lead off with the chainsaw incident, provided anything came of it; if not, he had enough background to concoct a fairly good account of what happened. What mattered was that after the front end of the story, he would drop the bomb on Kockelicker and that would be that. Sure there was a chance the paper could be sued for libel, but seeing how he had Kocke by the short hairs, Phillip didn't believe that eventuality would come to pass.

*Teach him to blow me off,* Phillip thought, pressing the Save button before closing his computer.

### 7:05 P.M.

Nick Crawford felt pretty good. His fiancee sat comfortably close to him in the car as they pulled up to the bank with the three apprehended bank robbers crammed into the back.

He had avoided shooting anyone, recovered some of the cash and made arrangements for the last, and for the first time all day, his head was not threatening to split open like a ripe melon dropped on the floor.

Additionally, he was reasonably certain he could arrest Allen Frye, recover the rest of the money and call it good. How he was going to write all this up he wasn't sure. Technically, Allen was still a police officer as his letter of resignation had yet to be accepted by the city council.

Dollars to donuts that group would want his balls, and Nick couldn't really blame them. To put a gun under the jaw of a civilian, no matter what he had done, was not what being a cop was all about.

And if he thought he could get away with it, he really didn't understand life in Newburn.

Nick's main concern was finding the wayward pothead first, before anyone else got wind of the situation.

The devil you know and all that.

His plan to deliver Danielle and the others to The Newburn Bank for their part of the operation was coming to fruition. He just didn't know how his presence before Allen Frye would be received, and if things went bad . . .

He stopped himself from completing the thought with a force of will. It wouldn't do him any good to worry until there was something to worry about.

"Are you okay?" Danielle's silky voice was a bare whisper, all that was necessary with their proximity.

"I'm fine," Nick replied. "I'm just tired and I want this day to end."

"I know what you mean." Raising her voice she asked, "You boys understand what we're going to do?"

"Yeah," Max said for the trio. He looked up from his cramped quarters and caught Nick's eyes in the rearview mirror. "I do. I don't know about these two."

Brian Fennigan continued to gaze out the window as acres of cropland crept past the car with the sun fading behind it. Todd Brown, while a little more attuned to the conversation, likewise remained silent.

"You don't have to go after him," Danielle whispered. "It could be dangerous."

Nick frowned. "It's my job. I know it's scary sometimes, but I have to do this."

"That's what I mean. You don't have to do this. The Guardians will take care of it."

"The Guardians?" Like everyone else in town, Nick knew the unofficial history of the vigilante group, but had never actually heard of one beyond the legend.

"Trust me. They don't play around."

"I was at the bank, so were you, and this is still my town," he said a bit defensively. "I didn't see anyone else standing up to them."

"That's not how they work. A Guardian must witness the act with his own eyes and then call in the group. No one else can get them to respond."

"Well who called them?"

"I think Evvie did after we left," Danielle replied. "We shared a look when she thanked me. There was something about that look . . ."

"What?"

"Maybe I'm wrong, but I think Evvie is a Guardian and she called in the others," Danielle said.

"How do you know all this?"

"I met a guy who claimed he was a Guardian," Danielle said. "He told me some things."

Nick turned into the bank's parking lot and was about to ask who this mysterious person was when he suddenly caught movement and slammed on the brakes.

Dalton Fisk stood before the car, his eyes alive with fury.

### 7:16 P.M.

It was *him*. The bastard who had twice scared the living crap out of him, something Dorf Walkenhorst would completely understand.

He'd barely caught a full glance at his antagonist the night before, but got enough detail to have recognized him inside the bank during the robbery. And now he was back, returning to the scene of the crime.

Dalton feared the cop had somehow known he was on the loose and had come to return him to the clutches of the bank president. Well he was not about to go along with that program.

Raising his arms in what he hoped was a threatening gesture, Dalton brought his hands down on the hood of the car, which was sitting still before him.

"Why can't you leave me alone?" He saw Nick and Danielle exchange a glance, the confusion on their face all part of a clever ploy to distract him.

Dalton's hands flared with pain as he hit the hood of the car again and again. No one had shouted at him to stop as he walked out the front door of The Newburn Bank, but they would likely notice his departure before long.

He really didn't have time to stand here. He managed one more chop with all the strength he could muster, which had absolutely no effect.

"How do you like that? I'll teach you to chase me around

you bastard!" Dalton was slipping, his enforced stay at the bank having worn on him worse than a two-day drive with the same eight-track.

Nick opened his door and stepped out, noticing Max do the same on the other side.

"What's the problem, sir? Can I help you?"

"You stink! I know your type. You think you can bully people around but not me. I'm not afraid of you."

Nick, his occasional flashes of memory from last night notwithstanding, had no idea who this man was or why he was attacking Danielle's car.

"Step away from the car, sir," Nick said in his "Officer In Charge" voice. "I don't want to arrest you but I will."

Dalton snickered like a teenage girl getting tickled in gym class. "You can't arrest me."

Nick sighed, pulling his badge away from his blue shirt, which should have been the first clue to his identity, and tilted it before the man.

"This gives me the power to arrest you, sir, and I will do it if you don't move away from the car right now," Nick said.

For the first time, uncertainty replaced the anger in Dalton's eyes and his hands quivered. In his frenzy, he never saw Max approach him from his left side, and before Dalton could decide, the choice was taken from him with a well-executed bear-hug.

"Owww! Put me down!"

Max looked at Nick, who shook his head and sighed anew. Turning to Danielle, he instructed her and the two goobers in the car to go into the bank with the berserk man. "I've got to get to Esther's and find Allen," he said. "I don't know why this guy is freaking out, but get him inside and I'll call you later."

"Are we going in now?" Brian was confused, which was pretty normal for him. "I have to pee."

This time it was Danielle who rolled her eyes before turning back to Nick. "Be careful," she said, resigning herself to the inevitable. "I love you."

Nick returned the sentiment and resumed his place behind the wheel, leaving three bank robbers, a loan officer and a paranoid man standing in front of the car.

He had no time to worry about this guy's problem, though had he known its root was due to last night's activity, Nick might have been willing to discuss it.

For now, he was late for a date with Allen Frye.

### 7:22 P.M.

*Better get it over with,* Chief Brad Kocke thought with a twitter. He was traveling to Jan's for takeout as part of his night with GiGi, but thought he'd better check in with those who had left him messages.

The first call was to Mayor Ted Keller, who was by far the one who could break him easier, though to be fair, he had no idea of the timeline imposed by Phillip Andrew Thomas.

"About time you called back. Where the hell are you?"

"I'm on a case," Kocke said.

"Where are you?" Keller repeated each word slowly, as if speaking to a dimwitted child.

"I'm on my way to the station," he lied.

"I'm here at the bank with Mr. Waterman," Keller said. "There was a robbery this afternoon and I still have witnesses here who need to make a statement. I'd suggest you get down here yesterday and do your job, or I'll find someone who will."

Click.

Brad didn't realize he was shaking until he flipped the phone closed. Part of his anxiety was worry about his job, much like it was in the old days of his nightlife; the other part was anger at being talked to like some kind of rent-a-cop. The thought of forcing Mr. Asshole Mayor to visit the park so he could see his colleague performing ritualistic acts of his true nature was overwhelming; beating the mayor himself was equally enticing.

But he didn't have any options when it came to either scenario.

Counting to ten slowed his breathing; another ten-spot and he felt confident enough to visit the bank, take some statements and then resume his plans with GiGi.

He opened the phone and dialed Phillip Andrew Thomas while en route.

## 7:28 P.M.

"Secret Agent Man . . . Secret Agent Man . . .," the phone chirped in a nasal tone that didn't capture the original song. Phillip had purchased the ringtone on a whim and most of the time let the phone ring for a while so he could listen to the song.

In this case, however, the number belonged to Chief Brad Kockeknocker, and it came in just before the deadline. Not that *The Newburn News* VIP was ready to trash his story.

"Talk to me," he said in a haughty tone.

"I have a new deal for you," Brad said, the sounds of the road coming through clearly with the windows down. "A new story, a better story."

"I'm listening," Phillip said, unconsciously imitating Kelsey Grammar's role as *Dr. Frasier Crane.*

"There was a robbery today at The Newburn Bank," Brad said. "I'm heading there now to take statements. I didn't tell you any of this, but if you stop by you can probably get a picture or two. The mayor is there right now."

Mayor Ted Keller was a prick, in Phillip's humble opinion, his distant blood ties notwithstanding, but he was the mayor, which carried with it all the political pull the title included. And that could be very useful.

"Okay, I'll be there," he said into the phone.

"And we keep everything we talked about earlier between us, right?"

"Depends on the story," Phillip hedged.

"Don't mess with me," Brad replied. "I'm in no mood for this shit. Just make the deal and we'll both come out on top."

"Okay, okay. Just remember that I'll have the story ready to go at a moment's notice, so don't ever try to double-cross me." Phillip was proud of his position, felt he had painted the lawman into a corner and that would be even more useful down the road than any attention he could get from the mayor.

"Not me. I'm done with that."

"How's that?"

"I've come to understand myself a little better and I realize why I was doing it," Brad said. "Let's just say I've found something else to ease my frustration."

Whether that was true or not had yet to be seen, but Brad's instincts were telling him a fruitful relationship awaited him at GiGi's.

"As long as you're not eating toenails or licking body parts, it's none of my concern," Phillip said. "See you at the bank."

# Chapter 32

"About time," Jerry Fillabag muttered as he flipped open his cell phone. "Tell me you found something."

"Yeah. The amigos are gone, no trace. But I found out where my guy is hiding and I'm going there now."

"That doesn't help me at all," Jerry said. "What about our deal?"

"I agreed to look for your amigos and I did that. They're gone," Crazy Willy paused. "You might have to get your money from that guy at the bar."

"And the chief? The newspaper guy? What about them?"

Crazy Willy drew in a breath and Jerry realized he was hitting a joint. "I don't know, man, but I think there's something going on at the bank," he said finally.

"Son of a bitch, which bank?" Jerry said, his thoughts churning.

"The old one."

*What am I supposed to do now? Go to the bank and attack the two? What if they're not there? Crazy Willy was supposed to take them out, that was the deal.*

He said as much to Crazy Willy and got a chuckle in response. "I'm taking out Allen Frye," he said. "That's all I care about. You're on your own with the others."

Click. No one hung up on Jerry Fillabag.

Fuming, he stalked out of his office. He didn't know where the Orc was, presuming he had fled the Subaru. Nor did he have his amigos; his replacement muscle had abandoned him and on top of everything, he didn't have his favorite pistol, unsure of where it had wound up in the earlier scuffle in front of the Double-L.

Someone was going to pay for this. He thought fleetingly of bringing Max Irons back into the fold, but then realized that bridge had been burned beyond repair.

His gaze locked on otherworldly plans of revenge, he didn't notice Sheila Fowler and Marcia Gladstone heading for the shower, hand in hand.

### 7:40 P.M.

Discretion being the bettor part of valor, it is sufficient to say that Sheila and Marcia were in the mood to explore the feelings that crept over them during their conversation.

Marcia was tired of dealing with cavemen, while Sheila had dealt with only one man, and that had been a very scary experience. Both believed they could do better and strived to prove that theory true, starting in the Newburn Fitness & Weight Training Center.

### 7:41 P.M.

The Guardian and his eager colleague were silent as they traveled to Esther's Warehouse of Drugs & Teabag Emporium. Kyle Grantz had to reel in his emotions. He was running high on adrenaline; this was his big chance after all.

Since he was a child he'd wanted to be a Guardian, like his great-great-great-grandfather, who was one of the two who had thwarted the first attempt. Every time he tried to engage in organizing a unified group, he was met with resistance.

"That's not how the Guardians work," Grandpa G, Bartie to his friends, had told him countless times. "This town isn't ready for that kind of thing."

The protection afforded the banking community had begun and ended with The Newburn Bank, despite the man who now ran things. Grandpa G couldn't stand the man, and had been lucky his services had never been called into question or he might have looked the other way.

Kyle glanced over at Dorf Walkenhorst, who was nearly as excited as his younger counterpart. Dorf was a good guy, in his own way, Kyle decided. He just had to learn to control his urge to shoot someone.

*It was okay to think it and during discreet conversation, voice it, but you don't come right out and tell the police that your primary goal is to shoot someone in the line of duty.*

He shook his head. Dorf was special all right, from his thinning wisps of hair to his Always-Glo security guard shoes.

Kyle had met him a few times while in the bank on business and spoken to him once. His knowledge of Dorf's views had come from a friend, whose position in town was such that Kyle couldn't very well speak to him about being a Guardian.

Nick was a real Guardian, and not just because his uniform proclaimed it. He was as honest as the day was long, and devoted. Why he had chosen to stay in Newburn and work for the inept department Kyle would never understand.

Surely his friend would do better in every way by leaving this little hamlet in search of a real career in law enforcement. But again, their friendship was what might be termed casual, and not such that Kyle felt comfortable telling him that to his face.

Friends or not, Kyle knew he was technically a vigilante, hoping to deliver street justice to someone who deserved it; his friendship would not likely prevent Nick from arresting him should he be caught. But this was what the original Guardians had done and the legend of that day's actions survived to inspire a few like Kyle.

But while the legend had inspired him, the truth had led Kyle down a different road.

Allen Frye was supposed to be a Guardian in all but name, his role as an officer of the peace ostensibly making him a brother in the effort to protect Newburn from bank robberies.

And yet this man, while not in the initial role as bank robber, had thrown away his duty in favor of a bag of cash, and had fled the scene. To the Guardians, it was unforgivable. At least the three robbers had repented, accepted their responsibility and were set to make reparations.

Kyle Grantz turned his Caravan into the dark parking lot and slowly cruised to the back of the building, where he'd been told a door into the Teabag Emporium would be found.

Time to go to work.

## 7:45 P.M.

Dorf Walkenhorst couldn't believe his fortune. He'd had without a doubt the single worst day of his life, but he'd survived to watch about half of Dr. Phil and his cats were purring contentedly when he'd left.

When he had hauled himself into the passenger seat of Kyle's Dodge Caravan, Dorf had hoped he would really get the chance to deliver justice the old-fashioned way. He wanted to be a part of it, even if it cost him the back half of Dr. Phil for today.

The episode had featured domestic abuse, a subject near and dear to Dorf's heart.

A woman had come on the show to cry about how her husband beat her with an extension cord every time he got mad, and how she was scared of living with him.

Dorf wondered how she had managed to get away long enough to visit the show, considering the woman claimed he never let her out of the house without supervision. *Jesus Christ,* he thought. *Someone needs to show that man the business end of a blunt instrument.*

His questions had been answered when the man sauntered from the green room to sit on the stage opposite her. The crowd instantly hated him, sending catcalls and hissing boos his way as he made it to his chair, all part of the carefully choreographed atmosphere taken from the Jerry Springer playbook.

The difference, Dorf believed, was that it didn't *look* like it was planned the way Jerry Springer and his goons performed. But it *was* a performance, the security guard knew.

By the time Dr. Phil had calmed the crowd and picked up a few loose items that had been hurled at the stage, the man's gaze was fixed on his wife and there was murder in them.

"*So tell me what's going on,*" *Dr. Phil urged the man.*
"*Why do you feel the need to hurt your wife?*"

"*It's discipline,*" *he said.* "*I'm not doing it to hurt her. It hurts me more to have to do it.*"

The crowd voiced its disbelief at this statement and Dorf leaned forward, hoping to see a replay of the Geraldo Rivera show in which a chair had broken his nose.

"*You think it's your place to mete out discipline to a grown woman?*"

"*What do you mean?*"

"*I mean, sir, that you're not her father, are you?*"

Dorf grinned, recalling a Jerry Springer show covering exactly that topic not long before.

"*No, but she needs to understand respect,*" *the man said with a wink.* "*I'm the man of the house and she's 'sposed to submit to my authority.*"

"*Says who?*" *The woman threw in this bit, speaking for the first time since her wayward husband had joined the show.*

"*Says the Bible,*" *her other half replied, unruffled.*

Dorf cursed as the phone rang, interrupting the commentary Dr. Phil was about to launch. He pressed the pause button and answered.

After a moment, his blood pumping with excitement, Dorf asked what was needed of him.

"I'll pick you up in ten minutes," Kyle had told him.

Thankful he was beyond the problem that had plagued him all day, Dorf blanked Dr. Phil's image and then clicked off the television.

Nick Crawford hadn't understood Dorf's desire to get involved and stop the robbery while it was fresh, but Kyle did, and had assured him his place among the Guardians was well-earned.

Dorf climbed out of his side of the van to see Nick Crawford approaching. He blinked with some surprise upon hearing that Nick was trying to forestall the rightful punishment for robbing The Newburn Bank.

Edward Von Waterman III was not a man easily surprised, his earlier discovery in the vault notwithstanding. That encounter was burned into his brain and would likely linger.

But aside from that, he was a man accustomed to controlling his environment, and surprises were few and far between.

Walking through the front door were the three robbers who had relieved him of his hard-earned money and Miss Collarbones herself, along with the man who had threatened to kill them all before fleeing the bank.

He and Mayor Ted Keller shared a look before the loan officer spoke.

"Mr. Waterman, these men are here to apologize," Danielle said. "They don't have the money but they've agreed to take responsibility for it."

"What does that mean?"

"It means they've agreed to repay it, regardless of what else happens," she answered. "Britni, do you have the form these gentlemen filled out earlier?"

"It's on your desk."

"Just a minute here," Waterman said, his mind still trying to unravel Danielle's comment. "What do you mean, no matter what else happens? Where's the money?"

"Max?"

The large mammal looked at Waterman without blinking. "We're sorry for scaring all of you and for taking the money," he said, feeling like a contrite boy in Sunday School, and resisting the urge to add "it won't happen again."

"That's it?" Waterman was stupefied. "You think you can come in here and apologize and that's it? I'll see you all in jail before the night's out."

"Mr. Waterman," Danielle began. "Technically these men borrowed the money."

"At gunpoint?" Ted Keller was equally curious as to how

this situation was unfolding. "That doesn't fit with what I understand of lending."

"It is unusual, I admit, but during the robbery, they completed a loan application," Danielle said. "As such, they have agreed to complete the transaction and pay back the money they took."

"Which they don't have?"

"Correct."

"I'd never approve a loan to these baffoons," Waterman said. "They came in here with shotguns and the big one threatened to shoot me in the face."

No one spoke for a moment as Danielle trotted to her desk, found the application and returned to stand by the trio of men, of whom only Max had shown the nerve to speak.

"This loan application will be approved," Danielle said, resisting the urge to remind the despicable man of the reason his facial pattern had been threatened.

"Why should I?" Waterman began to get angry. This was *his* bank, founded by *his* great-grandfather in a time when everyone and their brother was robbing banks. Just because his bank had not been robbed in, well, forever, did not mean Waterman was unfamiliar with the practice.

"Because if you do I will overlook the events in your office and later in the vault," Danielle said. "I don't think your investors would appreciate the more delicate ways in which you run your business."

"What kind of events?"

The voice was new to the conversation, as its owner had slipped in just ahead of Chief Brad Kocke. Phillip Andrew Thomas could smell scandal the way a camel smells water in the desert.

"Uh, that's not for public consumption," Waterman said quickly, scolding himself for firing Dorf, who could have at least guarded the door against intruders like the jerk from the newspaper.

Waterman looked first to Keller and then to Kocke, who was eyeing the room with obvious confusion. No help from either quarter, the bank president decided.

"Do we have a deal then?"

Waterman pinched the bridge of his nose and thought fiercely about his situation. There was no way he could conceive of to get out of this box. If he balked, Danielle would turn a casual afternoon in private into a horrid sex thing. There were several witnesses who would back her up; they all saw his disheveled form standing in the vault and none would hesitate to roll him over. After all, it was every sheep's private desire to hurt the shepherd. And besides all that, in this day and age it was virtually impossible to defend one's self against a sexual charge of any kind, especially harassment.

Sighing, he raised his eyes to his loan officer. "All right, but nothing more," he said. "And my 'private' business is just that, private."

Danielle smiled and turned to the three men with her, nodding to Phillip and Brad. "Just sign here, gentlemen," she said.

Phillip snapped a photo of the three men signing the paperwork much like children at a daycare would scribble on a picture they'd drawn for mommy.

"Do you still want statements?" Chief Kocke decided it better to err on the side of caution.

Waterman shook his head and Keller rolled his eyes. "A little late for that, don't you think?" the latter said caustically.

"What's going on here? I thought you had witnesses to a bank robbery."

"We do, and we have the robbers right there," Keller said with a grin, pleased at the way Danielle had knocked Waterman down a notch. "But they've just been reclassified as customers."

Phillip Andrew Thomas was in agony. He knew Waterman was guilty of something delicious, perhaps even a mid-afternoon grope, but unless the pretty brunette chose to speak to him, he was SOL. Same with the bank robbery, though he supposed he could turn this into a positive, which just about turned his stomach.

"We have a deal, Kocke," Phillip said. "A better story or your story."

"I know, but I don't know how to handle this," Brad replied.

Their signatures affixed, the three men looked about as relieved as a patient with full-blown GI blockage. They had just signed away the next five years of their lives to repay money they didn't even have.

The only consolation was that they were free, and if what Danielle had told them, freedom from the hospital or worse was another consideration.

"Chief can we come back to work?"

Brad looked at Todd as if he'd just swallowed a lump of something tart. "You're kidding, right?"

"We need a job," Todd replied. "We have to pay back this money."

"That's not my problem," Brad said. "You should have thought about that before you came in here with shotguns and robbed the place. You're damn lucky I don't run you in on theft."

"Chief, they're clear of the robbery," said Danielle.

"I'm talking about the marijuana they helped themselves to from evidence," Kocke said, his gaze never wavering from the two suspended part-timers. "Not to mention the shotguns they used."

"We didn't steal those guns," Brian said.

"So you admit stealing the dope?"

"We borrowed it," Brian said hopelessly.

"Shut up, man," Todd said as he nudged him. "Chief, there wasn't no evidence we took the marijuana. And we borrowed the guns. Nick has them."

"Where is Nick?"

Danielle supplied the details as to how the money came to disappear and where Nick had gone in the hopes of recovering it. "But the Guardians know where Allen is," she finished.

"Great, that's just great!" Chief Brad Kocke didn't particularly care for the vigilante group, his own brand of self-administered justice something he didn't compare.

"The Guardians? A group of octogenarians roaming about with walking sticks?" Phillip Andrew Thomas for the first time all day voiced a genuine chuckle. He'd heard rumors but unlike most, he did not really believe their continued existence outside of those few old fogies hopped up on various medications and Judge Wapner, trading stories about events that probably never happened.

"The ones who will likely beat Allen Frye to death before they take the money back," Danielle said, her stern voice cutting off Phillip's chuckle at the larynx. "I just hope Nick doesn't get hurt."

"I do," Dalton Fisk said. "I hope they break every bone in his body."

"Why?" Phillip felt like he was following a tennis match, with words being lobbed all over the place.

"Because the son of a bitch chased me with a chainsaw last night," Dalton replied defiantly. "He deserves whatever he gets."

Brad thought back to how this day began, which seemed like a week ago, and brought up the conversation with Allen Frye. "You're the guy," he said. "I'm screwed."

Phillip was suddenly very interested in Dalton Fisk. He might not be able to crack Waterman's exterior and get the nasty truth from him, and he was pretty sure Danielle would remain silent in accordance with her unusual deal. But this man was practically foaming at the mouth over Nick Crawford.

And Phillip had wanted to bring *Super-Cop* down for a very long time, since Nick had given him a ticket for double-parking a the post office. It was payback for the Kocke budget thing, Phillip was sure.

Danielle said nothing, her cheeks aflame with embarrassment and fear for what might happen next.

Keller watched the byplay with casual interest, wondering what kind of deal Chief Kocke had with his very distant relation from the paper, and why both he and Danielle reacted so harshly to the words of the other.

# Chapter 33

## 8:00 P.M.

A fringe benefit of having met and fallen for Roseanne was the fact she lived at the drugstore. Allen Frye thought it might be creepy, lying in the middle of the floor on a sleeping-bag pallet, but having Roseanne propped on his chest assuaged any uncertainties.

And with the TV tuned to TNT and the *Law & Order* theme music playing, things couldn't get much better.

Allen and Roseanne were enraptured by the Dick Wolfe creation, from the opening music to the scene in which cops and lawyers threw their coats over their shoulders and walked down the hall, announcing to the world that they were the *man*.

Tonight's episode was an older one, with both Chris Noth and Jill Hennessy, although with only a few scenes in which they were together. The pair curled up like teenagers about to watch a scary movie; they could have recited the lines with each other, but that was better left to the pros.

Instead, Allen applied his vast experience with rolling joints to craft a very large example with some of the grass clippings taken from the voracious bovines.

Though he didn't know it, his actions fulfilled Crazy Willy's assertion that Allen "could smoke teabags."

As he crafted the smoke, he kept an eye on the TV screen.

This was one of his favorite parts of the episode and one of the main reasons he loved Chris Noth.

*The detective gave the thug a shove into a brick wall. "You gonna talk now or do you want to do it at the station?"*

*"I ain't saying nothing, pig," the perp replied defiantly.*

*"Oh yes you are!" Chris rammed his knee into the guy's crotch and smiled at his partner, the guy who had been the dad in Dirty Dancing.*

Allen knew he (somebody Orb-something, he thought) had first appeared as a defense attorney and had done such a good job they offered him a leading role. Why tidbits of meaningless trivia such as this clung to his addled brain while the ability to count continuously slipped away was beyond him, but it his vast knowledge of L&O was a source of pride.

*The perp had acquiesced to the demands of the rough cop and spilled on where to find the pimp whose main hooker had been bludgeoned with a mop handle.*

As the show went to commercial, Allen lit up. The horrible smell and extremely harsh reaction of the smoke in his throat was enough to send him into a fit of gagging as Roseanne looked on in horror.

The door swung wide and a figure was silhouetted against the moonlight. He was not happy at what he discovered in the dim glow of the television.

### 8:07 P.M.

Crazy Willy was furious but despite his reputation, he was a coward. Oh, he could beat up people smaller and weaker than him with impunity, but put him in a fair fight and he was apt to run away.

He preferred to think of it as survival, but the truth was that he didn't much like anything resembling a fair fight. A reputation, like a rumor (*or a tumor,* he thought morbidly) grows in direct proportion to the environment in which it is created. A good rumor can thrive despite all indications it is untrue, and Crazy Willy had counted on ignorance for a long time in developing his image.

A few well-planned thrashings during high school had started the ball rolling. The fact that he was high most of the time and when so medicated, a pussycat, never seemed to register.

He was selling by the time he was 17 and no one in school ever ratted him out. He got caught when he was 19 and got a year's probation, which only added to the luster of his personality.

Suddenly he was a bonafide badass, with a record to prove it. Of course, no one knew that he was always 15 minutes early for his meetings with his probation officer, and that he didn't touch marijuana (for personal use) during his enforced time of good behavior.

Had the Orc been working with Jerry Fillabag when he decided to approach, Crazy Willy would have walked away. Making promises he had no intention of keeping had given him the information that led him to Esther's, where he would put the hurt on Allen Frye.

But now as he took in the heavy aroma of goats and licorice as smoke billowed about the floor like an apparition, Crazy Willy was ready to kill someone.

He spied Roseanne, his former best girl, who had cursed his name and broken things off, slapping Allen Frye on the back as the idiot tried to catch his breath. He obviously had tried to hit the giant joint that still gave off wisps of smoke, and it just as obviously was not a good experience.

In the bushes behind the drugstore, he had paused to reflect how much he really wanted to pursue his course of action. A cop and two guys with clubs were standing not 20 feet away and he could hear them talking about the dipshit inside.

*Maybe I should walk away,* he thought. *I could just go home and forget this whole thing, leave the stoner to these guys and be done with it.*

It was a very tempting thought, but despite his cowardice, he had a reputation to maintain, and dealing with Allen Frye shouldn't be too much trouble. Why the stoner was holed up in the drugstore was beyond him, but Crazy Willy didn't really care. All he wanted was to hurt the guy and then find the other two who presumed to cheat him.

As he watched his wayward woman administering a feeble attempt at helping Allen recover, Crazy Willy bristled at the concern he saw in her eyes. She'd never looked at him like that.

His earlier caution forgotten, Crazy Willy voiced his war cry and attacked.

# 8:10 P.M.

Unaware that Allen was choking and about to meet up with his former supplier, Nick Crawford was doing his duty in trying to thwart the two men from crossing the line, despite their reasoning.

"What I'm saying is that he has violated the trust of this community and as such, it is our responsibility to make sure he understands that mistake," Kyle said, quite eloquently in Dorf's opinion, though the aging security guard did not necessarily agree with everything he said.

"No. You can't have him."

"Dammit, Nick," Kyle said somewhat less eloquently, stroking the nine-iron in his hand. "Just walk away. Say you couldn't find him. It's not like we're going to kill him or anything."

"No, you're just going to beat him up," the officer said. "How noble."

"We're following the traditions set forth by the Guardians," Kyle tried again but without much conviction.

Like a neon light suddenly turned on in his brain, Nick connected Kyle with Bartie Grantz, whom he'd met earlier in the day; his preoccupation with this whole mess had not allowed him to put the two together. Now, as Kyle tried to engender support or at least ignorance of his activity, Nick wondered how Bartie's grandson had missed the boat.

"I met your grandpa earlier today," he told Kyle. "I doubt seriously he would approve of this."

"Grandpa Bartie is old and senile," the other replied. "He's been losing it for a long time. I'm surprised he hasn't croaked yet."

"He said this was his town and no two-bit drug dealer was going to come in here selling their crap," Nick said, paraphrasing a little since he had no desire to slip into the elder Grantz's vernacular. "He seemed like an honest man who didn't like people breaking the law.

"Breaking the law, yes," Kyle said. "But this is different. The Guardians have always stood up to bank robbers and followed a code for dealing with them. This asshole is no different and I'm sure Grandpa Bartie would tell you that to your face if you caught him early enough in the morning."

"It wouldn't matter to me if you have a note from God saying it's okay, I'm not going to let you do it."

"What if we split the money with you?"

Nick stared at Kyle as if he'd lost his mind. "You're going to take the money?"

"Not all of it," Kyle replied. "Just enough."

"Enough for what?" Nick's initial surprise was turning to anger.

"That's the way it's always been, Nick," Kyle said. "Just think of me as a modern-day Robin Hood."

"Would do you care? I mean, the bank is insured, right? And it's not like *we* robbed the bank," Dorf interjected.

"In the first place, Dorf, two wrongs don't make a right," Nick said, his hand swaying to the butt of his Beretta. "As for the Robin Hood reference, I doubt seriously Kyle is giving the money to the poor."

"I'm sorry you feel that way," Kyle said, lifting his club in a decidedly unfriendly fashion.

Like a scene out of a Clint Eastwood spaghetti western, Nick pulled his automatic in one smooth motion and had it aimed at Kyle's face before the other had begun his forward swing. Dorf was slow on the uptake and before he could act in concert with his partner, he realized the foolishness of the idea.

"Stop right there," Nick said, addressing both. "There's still a chance you can walk away from this in one piece."

Before either a furious Kyle or nervous Dorf could respond, a blood-curdling scream rent the still air.

## 8:11 P.M.

While Nick was thwarting a lynching for profit and Roseanne was trying to help her man recover his breath, Phillip Andrew Thomas had cornered Dalton Fisk outside The Newburn Bank, pumping him for information about the crazy events of the previous night.

Inside, Chief Brad Kocke was trying his best not to pull out Fruit-Smacker and rearrange Mayor Ted Keller's face. His civilian superior was still fuming, despite the sudden reversal in the classification of the idiots now talking to Britni as if they hadn't shoved large-caliber weapons in her face a few hours ago.

"You can't leave the station unattended like that," Keller said. "What if we'd had a real emergency?"

"I understand that, Ted," Kocke said evenly. "What I've been telling you is that all of us were on active duty. I was working on a lead in an assault case. Nick was apprehending those three and Allen was following up a drug case. If you expect us to just sit in that shitty little station and investigate by phone, you're in for a surprise."

"And I'm telling you, for the last time I might add, that if you cannot have someone in the station, at least keep your phone available and check in with me to let me know what's going on," Keller said.

His anger had abated somewhat, in direct proportion to the shaming of the bank president and the distance he'd gained from Edward Von Waterman III, who had retired to his office. "I called you nine times for Pete's sake! And no one would answer on the radio when I tried from the station. That's just sloppy, and if it happens again, I'll personally boot your ass out the door."

Technically, Kocke knew the mayor was bound by the decision of the council as a whole, but his threat was not all bluff either. Keller had support and knew how to wield what power he did possess.

It was an aggravation, but certainly not one worth being terminated over. "Okay, Ted, uh, Mayor, I apologize," he said. "It's been a long, strange day and we've been busting our asses to get some things figured out. No one intentionally blew you off, and we weren't out joyriding. But I understand where you're coming from and it won't happen again."

Mayor Ted Keller was suspicious of the appeasing words. He was fully aware of the chief's temper and how obstinate he could be when his fur was up. By the same token, he was a responsible man for the most part, and Keller decided he was content to let the matter drop, though not without a passing barb.

"Just make sure you don't let it happen again," he said, and without a glance to the rear of the bank, headed for home.

*Mister McGee, don't make me angry,* Brad thought. *You wouldn't like me when I'm angry.*

The thought of transforming into a giant green monster bent on dispensing pain, not with his hands but with his trusty baton, made the chief smile. *If you only knew, Keller . . .*

Waterman had watched the heated exchange in silence via a monitor on his desk; he didn't really care what was being said, but if his judge of physical movements was accurate, Keller had cowed the police chief somehow. "Good," the bank president said to himself, taking in the other views afforded by the four cameras mounted in the lobby.

He turned back to the computer, working the numbers in the most profitable way possible.

Gina and Britni were really chumming it up with the three idiots who robbed him, especially the big one who had threatened to shoot him in the face. In a way he was satisfied with the way things had turned out, since he'd be able to collect interest on the money, or fleece from the sheep. But on another level, he was furious with the upstart loan officer, who had presumed to make the deal in front of everyone. And she had threatened him to boot.

Nice collarbones or not, and regardless of the threat of sexual harassment, Waterman decided he would find a way to get rid of her. She was simply too much trouble to keep around.

As for Danielle, she was nowhere to be found in The Newburn Bank, having departed to find her fiancee. Whether she would be a help or a hindrance was not considered; she just knew she had to get to him.

Down the street, Lionel Leanman was pouring freely. He had not been to the track in Waterford for some time, but his spirits were soaring nonetheless. His decision to stand up to Jerry Fillabag had been a calculated risk, but he had won.

Patrons of the Double-L, who did not know the reason for his generosity (which was limited to one free beer), thanked him effusely and enjoyed the hospitality while it lasted.

Speaking of Jerry Fillabag, he had returned to the gym to lick his wounds. He was sitting in his extra large leather chair, which privately brought to mind images of the end of Conan the Destroyer, and contemplated his options.

His whole body hurt, from his still puffy cheek and jaw, down his chest and belly, where the bartender had sucker-punched him, and even into his knees, which had borne the brunt of his falls.

Mostly, though, his pride was hurt. He had been beaten in a public place by a man; taken down with a cheap shot to be sure, but the idiots who saw it wouldn't think of that. All they would remember (if they hadn't partaken of Mystery Shots, that was) was that Lionel Leanman had punched the guy from the gym and then told him off.

*He threatened to kill me,* Jerry thought with a flicker of fear. It wasn't every day that someone did that to him, and he had to treat it with respect. He couldn't let such behavior go unchallenged, but he was not in a position to retaliate, not before contracting some thugs.

That brought to mind the amigos and his best goon, the Orc, and musings of where they had gone.

The Orc had been introduced to physics, specifically the part that dealt with gravity and an object meeting an unyielding surface, when his neck crashed into the pavement and broke his fall.

The cows had left him to suffer in peace, deciding he wasn't a large blade of grass to be devoured. Their saliva-coated ministrations had left him aggravated but none the worse for wear.

Bartie was still unmoving in the car, but the Orc soon

began to feel something in his legs. Pins and needles soon throbbed, and his tiny brain was alight with joy. He was still unable to sit up, but his outlook improved dramatically with the sensation.

# Chapter 34

Nick was torn. The scream had sounded almost inhuman, but given his knowledge of the situation, it could only belong to Roseanne. Whatever was happening inside was serious enough to warrant a severe response, but at the same time, his gun pointed at Kyle's face was only thing keeping the vigilante from smashing open his head.

"Put it down, Kyle," said Nick. "I don't have time for this."

The officer turned his eyes toward the drugstore, wondering what would make the woman scream, knowing he had an obligation to find out. Kyle appeared to be seriously thinking about following through with the obvious threat implied when he pulled his club.

Dorf, however, was suddenly having second thoughts. It was one thing to shoot someone in the line of duty, and had that happened at the bank earlier in the day, Dorf would have considered himself a hero.

Even taking the stoner cop to task for his role in this mess was within his ability to accept, but taking out a police officer was not part of the deal. At a deep level, he knew that was wrong, and not just because he had wanted to join the team. His profession was similar to Nick's, just without the mobility.

Guarding against the threat of violence had more meaning for the cop, to be sure, but that didn't mean Dorf felt himself any less an officer of the peace.

He laid a hand gently on Kyle's arm, feeling the muscles bunched and ready to spring. "This isn't right," he said softly. "We can't do it like this."

Kyle did not speak or take his eyes from Nick Crawford, whose gaze was sweeping between the immediate threat and that inside the building. After a moment's consideration, the younger man lowered his weapon and drew a deep sigh.

"Okay, Nick, you win," Kyle said. "Let's go help the woman."

"No," the other replied. "This is official business and I don't want to drag you into it. Just stay out here and call the chief."

Nick rattled off the number of the chief's cell phone and turned to enter the drugstore, unsure what to expect.

## 8:15 P.M.

Brian Fennigan and Todd Brown were stymied. Both really wanted a smoke and neither had access to any. The whole reason they headed to town was to get money to buy dope from Crazy Willy, and that had ended horribly. Neither still truly understood why they had to pay back the money they stole, since they didn't even get to keep it. That damn Allen Frye had ruined everything.

Well, Nick had been the one to crash their party at Evvie's place, but Allen had taken the money they were supposed to have had. And what about Max? He was trying to take most of it for himself.

Todd had pieced together most of this and shared it with his partner, though not easily. Brian was befuddled as usual and after a couple of attempts, Todd gave up.

Now they were sitting in Todd's living room, in exactly the same pose they had achieved last night when they heard the chainsaw. The only difference was the lack of smoke.

"What are we going to do?"

"I dunno," Brian replied, looking bleakly at the turkey sandwich he'd sloppily put together from Todd's dwindling stock. "Guess we'll have to get a job."

"Where? Who's going to hire us?" Todd snorted in disgust, knowing his friend had a place to go, should he swallow his pride and beg Evvie for shelter.

The pair slipped into melancholy silence, wondering in their limited way what tomorrow would bring.

*****

Max, meanwhile, had gone to Jan's Country Griddle & Bait Shop, where he squeezed his bulk into a corner booth. After ordering the special, with extra thighs, he sat back and tried to think.

Like his erstwhile partners in crime, he was almost dizzy trying to figure out why he had thrown in with them.

Not only did he commit a crime, he had nothing to show for it. Further, the little dipshit cop had stuck a gun in his face and humiliated him.

On top of it all, he had no job, no place to go, and was reliant upon the pity of Nick Crawford. In all, it made for a cheerless meal.

If only there was some way to go back in time, back before he started taking the cowroids and got into this mess. When he thought of Jerry Fillabag, he was still angry but not desperately so, since it was his mistake.

He chewed fat and gristle, a particular specialty of Jan's, who spent all her time in the kitchen frying chicken in cast-iron skillets. She and Esther were long-time friends and shared the occasional meal and vitamins.

Max felt a twinge in his calf, both from where he'd overused it during workouts and then from being slammed to the ground by Brian's errant car door.

Absently, he rubbed it with greasy fingers, willing the pain away with gentle massage.

Suddenly the pain gave way to illumination, and he stumbled onto a way to at least exact revenge on his former employer.

So great was the excitement at this prospect, Max nearly choked on a bone, but the smile on his face belied any sense of urgency wrought by the impediment.

Regaining his airway, he silently finished his meal, his smile never dimming.

Allen Frye was seeing spots but his breath was coming back finally. He hacked a few more times, aware of the man's presence but only in a peripheral sense. Had he known it was Crazy Willy, he might have wished the joint had killed him. It might be less painful by half.

"Let go of me," Roseanne screamed, her tone caught between a yelp of pain and shriek of fury.

"Shut up," Crazy Willy said coldly, his high-school level emotions running through a variety of shades, all of them on the anger side of the equation. "You have got to be kidding me. Allen Frye?"

Willy's hold on her hair did not increase, but it did not slacken either.

"He's a good man," Roseanne said. "You leave him alone."

"Oh, I'll leave him alone to die," Crazy Willy snarled. "This bastard is going to pay."

Allen drew himself up, still winded but not fighting for breath. His throat hurt and he was a little dizzy, but he still had his gun and if he could reach it in time, all would be well.

Crazy Willy seemed to read his thoughts, for he yanked Roseanne to him and flung her into Allen's rising form, knocking them both to the floor.

"Just stay right there," he said. "We're going to have a little talk."

Allen caught movement behind Crazy Willy and hoped it was not the giant man whose jaw he'd jammed with his gun. Nick strode up behind the drug dealer, putting his finger to his lips in the universal pantomime for "quiet."

"Did you think you could get away with it?" Crazy Willy spoke to both, each understanding the question posed.

Allen wasn't sure what Willy wanted, while Roseanne's crime ran to the esoteric, although it was probably more painful to a man of his character.

"Willy, please, it wasn't working, you know that,"

Roseanne said. "It's nobody's fault."

"C'mon man, I didn't hurt him," Allen said.

"What the hell are you talking about?"

"The guy at Brian's mom's place," Allen said. "I didn't hurt him. I just wanted the money."

"I don't know anything about that," Crazy Willy said, mystified. "I was talking about why you thought you could rip me off."

The accusation hung in the air like the smoke from his ill-fated blunt. All he could figure was that Crazy Willy had been in on the robbery.

"I didn't know you were there, man," Allen said. "I mean, I thought it was just Brian and Todd."

"I know they were in on it, but so were you," Willy said.

"They didn't tell me about it before they did it," Allen said defensively. "And I wouldn't have done anything if I'd known you were there."

"Where?"

"At Evvie's."

Nick Crawford at first thought this line was meant to confuse Crazy Willy, who looked every bit the capable thug, dressed in all black leather and chains, despite the weather. Now, however, he realized it was no clever ploy; Allen was just being his typical idiotic self.

Enough was enough.

Besides, the room smelled like licorice and burned goat hair, and he was ready to get out of here.

"Everybody stand still," he said, his Beretta trained on Crazy Willy's bulk. "You, move over there next to the TV and keep your hands out."

Willy took in the cop before him, knew it was the man who'd been outside. The gun in his hand was meant to put people down hard, and he had no desire to find out just how hard.

Compliance was not in his nature, unless of course someone had the jump on him. He wordlessly moved to the TV, where *Law & Order* was still playing, unnoticed to this point.

*"Don't try to con me, punk,"* a voice said harshly.

*"I'm not. I'm telling you the truth,"* the perp said, staring wide-eyed at the detective played by Chris Noth.

*"You don't know the meaning of the word,"* Noth answered. *"I'm about two seconds from rearranging your face, meathead."*

Crazy Willy turned from the set in disgust, taking in the pair of lovers sitting on the floor, their arms wrapped in a warm embrace. He seethed, knowing if he'd shared an obsession for *Law & Order*, Roseanne would still be his girl.

"Now," Nick said. "Here's what's going to happen. Allen, you're under arrest for assault with a deadly weapon and larceny. Roseanne, I know you helped so you're facing accomplice charges. And Willy, I don't know what you want here, but you're going to be a nice boy and walk away, or I'll bust you for obstructing justice."

Crazy Willy grunted but said nothing. He turned a murderous glare on Allen and Roseanne, one which promised all kinds of misery.

### 8:20 P.M.

Chief Brad Kocke pushed GiGi's car for all it was worth, hoping his timing was good enough to help Nick Crawford.

The call from the drugstore had been alarming, to say the least. The man on the other end had told him Nick had been injured trying to arrest Allen Frye and that a guy named Crazy Willy was threatening to kill him.

That was all it took to get the chief moving, and he didn't waste time calling Mr. Mayor, knowing he would find out soon enough.

*Let him stew on that for a while,* he thought.

Phillip Andrew Thomas had completed his interview with Dalton Fisk, if you could call it that; Phillip considered it a close second to the wasted effort with the deaf team. Dalton fled the scene, leaving the acerbic reporter writing a weak story on his trusty laptop in his car. He saw Chief Kockebreath come rushing out and wondered where the fire was, so to speak. Instead of trying to hail him, Phillip just closed the computer and prepared to follow.

Brad was genuinely worried, as he was any time one of his officers was in trouble. Not the "I'm an idiot and tried to steal dope" kind of trouble, but the type of situation in which doing your duty brought about consequences from bad people.

Nick Crawford had been as green a rookie as ever put on a badge, but he'd learned quickly and applied himself feverishly to the task of being a good cop. In a town like Newburn, it wasn't often that cops were called upon to deal with dangerous situations; mostly they wrote speeding tickets, ran the crosswalk for the kids in the morning and made sure drunks didn't tear up the Double-L.

Crazy Willy was mean and tough, but he didn't operate heavily in Newburn. Brad knew most of his trade was plied in Waterford, where the track promised more losers than could be found in his small town.

But open operator or not, hurting a cop was over the line, and Brad was anxious to get there.

Glancing up, he caught the headlights behind him, moving closer as he continued through town toward Esther's Drug Warehouse & Teabag Emporium.

Phillip Andrew Thomas.

That could complicate things, but better to have him at his side than out of sight with his camera.

Sighing, wishing this day could end, Brad drove on, hoping he wasn't too late.

### 8:23 P.M.

Kyle Grantz was pleased with himself. He had guaranteed a quick response from the chief and sketched out a plan to get his hands on the money. Whether Dorf would cooperate was another question. The younger man hadn't much appreciated the way his partner had touched him and told him to back off.

*This is my show*, he thought. *I'm the one whose ancestor*

*was a Guardian. I have an obligation to continue that tradition.*

The truth was much less substantive, but Kyle refused to dwell on it. Besides, it was the truth according to Grandpa Bartie, and who knew if what he claimed was reality? Kyle was willing to bet on the legend and let Grandpa Bartie's ramblings fade away as unimportant.

"Do you have any questions?"

"Let me see," Dorf said sarcastically. "It's pretty complicated. We go busting in the door as the chief pulls into the lot, make a lot of noise and grab the money when everyone's distracted. That about the size of it?"

Kyle rolled his eyes. He was really getting tired of Dorf, even if he shared many of the old man's views on crime and punishment.

"I just need to know you're gonna go through with it," Kyle said, watching the other intently.

"I'll do it," Dorf said, hiding his intentions.

A squall of tires sounded in the night, followed by the rumble of an engine. It was time to go.

## 8:24 P.M.

As Danielle paced the bank floor, wondering why Waterman had yet to clear it out, Mayor Ted Keller drove toward home. He was pretty much used up, tired of dealing with the bank president and planning how best to rid himself of Chief Brad Kocke.

Waterman had finished manipulating the figures and headed out of his office with a predator's smile on his face. He was fairly confident what he'd done would go unnoticed even under severe scrutiny by the feds. This was the first time his bank had been robbed, after all, and the paperwork turned in by Miss Collarbones was shredded. His plan was coming together, though there was still the wildcard out there named Nick Crawford, who had looked rather more intelligent than the average sheep Waterman encountered.

If he actually managed to recover the money, there might

be some questions as to where the rest of it was, but that should be easily shunted, considering the number of morons involved already. It was only $15,000; Britni would understand.

The bank president stepped out into the lobby and told everyone to go home.

Danielle's relief was palpable and she wasted no time in hitting the door. She wanted desperately to go to Nick but knew it would be dangerous. *He has a job to do*, she thought. *Let him do it.*

As the bank emptied and each returned to their lives, GiGi sat chewing her lip thoughtfully.

No word from Brad, but that could mean any number of things. She really had warmed to him immediately and believed he shared her feelings. He was a cop, and no telling what might have come up.

She moved from the living room to the kitchen, where she put water on to boil. A cup of decaf, even instant, would help settle her fluttering nerves. It was all she could do to keep her shoes on, for her toes were itching for attention.

Dalton Fisk, meanwhile, had given Brenda a hasty account of what happened, and told her he was leaving.

His demeanor was much different that when he'd left earlier in the day, but his wanderings were a normal part of the picture, and she hadn't really concerned herself with where he'd been all day.

Hearing about the cop and learning of his identity was alarming, but she was ready to move on. After all, it wasn't her that had been chased with a chainsaw. She could sympathize with Dalton's reaction, but he was still acting like a terrified kitten.

Her cool reaction to the story prompted Dalton to fly from her little home in a snit; he climbed into his truck and headed for New Orleans. Brenda had only occasional regrets that he never returned.

Sheila Fowler and Marcia Browning had left the gym, heading for the latter's home, where the duo passed Dalton as he revved the motor in his tractor.

Back at the Newburn Fitness & Weight Training Center, Jerry continued to fume about his lot in life. He was no closer to making a decision on how to proceed. He itemized what he knew: his thugs were still gone, his body still ached with uncounted pains, and he was still furious about his encounter with Lionel Leanman.

Evvie Fennigan was cleaning up the mess left behind by her visitors when she found something under the table. It was certainly unexpected and was a welcome addition to her pursuit of nylons.

And at the police station, Chipper McGraw approached the chief's Subaru, wary of what he would find, considering the time that had passed since Brad's message.

The Orc was not in sight, which was a good thing for the coroner, though he didn't know it.

Inside the car, Bartie Grantz still reposed unmoving, but he was not dead, as had initially been feared.

His body had simply shut down with all the excitement and he was just now beginning to stir as the door opened.

Chipper had played the message twice, as was his custom to avoid mistakes, and both times it was the same Chief Brad Kocke said the old man was dead, sitting in his Subaru in the police station parking lot.

The old man struggling to draw in breath was not dead. He was sure of it. Chipper's training had been expensive, and he chose to deal with the dead because he didn't like treating the living. They complained too much.

But instead of dragging a corpse out of the car, Chipper now faced a living man who would no doubt find something to bitch about.

He supposed he should be happy the man was alive, considering his oath and all, but it had been a long day, and he'd already had to sort out bodies in a wreck near Waterford. This was just too much.

# Chapter 35

An uneasy truce had settled over the group inside the drug store a few minutes before, though Nick Crawford didn't believe it would last. He was, after all, there to bring back two of the three before him, which made him about as popular as jock itch.

Nick had already ascertained that Roseanne's scream was a response to being startled, though he could see a red mark on her face where Crazy Willy had grazed her on the way to the stringy black hair atop her head.

The television continued to play in the background, as the cops presented their information to the DA's office, who would take it to the courtroom. Nick didn't really care for *Law & Order*; he was more of a CSI man, and not one of the 14 copies either. Soon they would have CSI: Your Town.

After a few moments of listening to threats of more time tempered with promises of leniency, Nick turned off the TV and cut off *L&O* mid-sentence.

"All right," he said. "Willy, I want you to move back behind the counter and turn around. I'm going to cuff these two together and we're walking out. I don't want to see you again any time soon."

Crazy Willy did not deign to respond because he was more frightened than he'd ever admit. Staring down the barrel of a gun did that to him.

He climbed to his feet and walked to the back wall, where he spied the large bag of grass clippings, which he deduced had been the origin of the foul smoke Allen had tried.

Roseanne eyed him distrustfully the whole way, sure he would turn like a snake and strike at her. Allen was trembling beside her, though more from his encounter with the grass than anything else.

Once Crazy Willy was settled, and apparently complying, Nick squatted before the couple, handcuffs in his hand. He reached forward to slip the bracelet around Allen's wrist when he heard the sound of a heavy motor and the screeching brakes.

*What the hell?* Nick thought.

"Don't let him take that grass," Allen whispered to Nick, his eyes narrowing in thought.

He still couldn't figure out how Crazy Willy got involved with the bank thing, and where he was hanging out while the other three were at Evvie's. Maybe he was what they called a silent partner, he mused.

Allen also sat wondering why Willy had attacked Roseanne. She had nothing to do with the robbery, except for driving the SUV, but how did Willy know that?

Something was off here, Allen was sure of it, though for the life of him he couldn't figure it out.

Presently, he heard the snick of steel teeth racheting into the bracelet and felt the pressure of being cuffed. The second sound was Roseanne being bound to him, and he looked up at Nick for the first time.

"What's going to happen to us?"

"You should know, *officer*," Nick said with disgust.

Allen looked up, his eyes going wide. Nick reacted without thinking, swinging his gun around in a smooth movement honed by years of practice, though he'd only fired his weapon a handful of times.

The golf club swinging toward his head instead grazed his shoulder and upper arm. Nick refrained from firing as he dove to safety but came up with the gun aimed. "Dammit Kyle!"

Dorf pulled up short as the violence played itself out. Kyle raised the club threateningly but suddenly felt very vulnerable. The idea was to take Nick out with one swing and then deal with Allen Frye. The wannabe Guardian had not counted on his quarry slipping away from the blow.

Now Nick Crawford had a bead on him, and his club was

209

just about worthless. The couple joined at the wrists were scrambling backward like a pair of lobsters trying to escape the pot, while the leather-clad man behind the counter made no move at all.

Crazy Willy wasn't sure what to do, quite frankly. He figured this guy was here for the same reason, and maybe they could work together. First thing was to get rid of the cop.

Before he could think about a plan, the old security guard surprised everyone.

### 8:30 P.M.

Chief Brad Kocke, whose life had been changed by a simple meeting of people like him, now approached the back of the drugstore with mixed emotions. On the one hand, he was sworn to uphold the law and protect the innocent, especially one of his officers. By the same token, however, he was tired of dealing with it.

He wanted nothing more than to return to GiGi and let nature take its course.

No sooner than he'd opened his door, Brad noticed the car that had followed him screech to a stop beside him, Phillip Andrew Thomas behind the wheel.

The chief sighed, knowing it would happen and wondering if this day would ever end.

"Stay out of the way," he told the reporter through an open window. "Don't make me arrest you."

Phillip ignored the threat, gathering his camera, flash and notepad. He didn't know what was going down, but he was prepared for it. *It's been too long a day and I'm sick of getting half-stories*, he thought. *This better be good or old Kockebreath is going to pay for it.*

He allowed Brad a few steps toward the store and then fell in behind him.

As Chief Kocke put his hand on the door, a shot rang out, loud in its proximity.

"Son of a . . ." Brad yelled, his gut telling him he was

too late. Nick Crawford was probably dead.

Fury infused his blood and he yanked the door open with such force the "Employees Only" sign slammed into the window.

Pulling his sidearm, Brad rushed into the drugstore, raring to shoot someone. Phillip proceeded at a more cautious pace, hoping to avoid being caught in a hail of return fire.

The first thing he saw was Nick kneeling on the floor, not far from where he and Phillip had discovered Allen and his new girlfriend. The next thing to register in his mind was that Nick was unhurt, though he was favoring his left arm slightly. *Funny the little things you notice in times of stress,* he thought.

"Everybody stand still! I'm going to shoot anything that twitches."

Roseanne stared in disbelief while Allen had naturally covered his face to avoid any ricochet. Crazy Willy's heart was hammering away in unrestrained terror and he gripped the counter for support.

Dorf stood with his back to the door, partially blocking the chief's view of the man on the floor, his body curled into a fetal position and blood smearing the floor. In his hand was a .357 magnum, made famous by one of Dorf's idols, Dirty Harry. The barrel was still smoking though only a tiny wisp here and there indicated the recent firing. The rank smell of cordite, however, was even more telling.

"Dorf, drop the weapon," he said.

The security guard, recently divorced from employment at The Newburn Bank, wasted no time in following the chief's command.

"Thank you," Brad said, his voice tight. "Move over by Nick. Is he dead?"

A strobe of light filled the room, which was dimly lit to begin with, startling everyone and nearly earning the self-important writer a bullet from Chief Kocke.

"Don't do that again," Brad warned him. "Not until we're done here."

Phillip nodded his acquiescence; he had a picture of the

guy on the floor, and he was sure the blood would show up nicely and if not, he had PhotoJob. He really was a ghoul.

Brad turned his attention back to the morbid setting before him, wondering what could possibly happen now to make this worse.

The man groaned and began to thrash. *Guess that question's answered*, Brad thought.

"Nick, get a call to Waterford and get an ambulance over here," the chief said. "The rest of you stay put."

Kneeling, he put a hand on the man's shoulder and rolled him over. While the blood made it appear to be a critical wound, it was immediately evident his was just a flesh wound. Probably hurt like a bastard, Brad knew, but hardly life-threatening.

"I'm dying," Kyle said.

"You're not dying," the chief assured him. "It's just a graze."

"Feels like I'm dying," Kyle argued through gritted teeth.

Brad looked around, saw the sheet Allen and Roseanne had used for a pallet, and brought it to the wound, staunching the bleeding. Kyle screamed as though the chief had shoved a hot poker into the raw skin.

"Owww! That hurts so much," Kyle squealed, writhing on the floor.

"Jesus Christ," Brad said, turning to Dorf. "Tell me what happened here."

"Kyle here was planning to beat up Allen and take the money from the bank robbery," the aged security guard replied. "He hit Nick so I shot him."

Chief Kocke rubbed the bridge of his nose, feeling a bone-deep weariness trying to settle over him. "Okay," he said. "I'll talk to Nick. Keep an eye on this guy."

He left Dorf mumbling to himself about doing his duty, whatever that meant, and found Nick placing the phone in the cradle. "Ambulance in twenty or so," the younger officer said.

"What a mess," Brad said with a snort. "This whole day has been screwed up."

"Tell me about it," Nick replied, wincing as his arm began to throb, which reminded him in turn of what Danielle had revealed about Dalton Fisk. "Chief, about last night . . ."

Brad waved it off. "Don't worry about it," he said. "We have bigger fish to fry."

Nick absorbed the forgiveness in silence, inwardly relieved he wouldn't be called to task for his drunken activities.

Glancing around the room, he noted that Allen and Roseanne were flush against the counter, behind which Crazy Willy remained unmoved. Apparently the dog wasn't as big as his bark.

"Dorf said he was defending you," Brad said. "That true?"

"I guess, though I did have Kyle dead to rights."

"Did Dorf see that, or could he have thought you really needed help?"

"Hard to say," Nick responded carefully. "We both know he's always wanted to shoot someone in the line of duty, and I guess this was his chance. Good thing he brought his gun with him, huh?"

"Does seem to be a stroke of good luck," Brad admitted. "What do you think?"

"I think we let it slide," Nick said, surprising himself with the answer, though in hindsight, he would realize he was paying forward the leniency shown him.

Brad nodded and turned back to the room full of people. Phillip was on the floor, sitting cross-legged beside Kyle, who was rambling. Allen and Roseanne eyed the chief worriedly while Crazy Willy crept around the counter, his initial fright replaced with opportunism. As long as the loser and his ex were just sitting there, he might as well do something.

Chief Kocke shouted for Nick and headed for the drama unfolding across the room.

Crazy Willy grabbed Allen by the hair and slammed his head into the counter. "I'll teach you," Willy whispered, unaware of the chief's impending intervention. "No one rips me off."

"I swear I didn't know you were in on the bank thing," Allen screamed.

"What the hell are you talking about?"

Before Allen could answer, Brad slammed into the man in black, dumping him to the floor and gaining a position atop him. "Enough!"

Crazy Willy stopped thrashing and sank to the floor in defeat.

"Where's the money?" Nick asked, remembering part of what he came here to retrieve.

"What money?" Crazy Willy asked from his position beneath the chief.

"Not you," Nick replied. "Allen, where is it?"

Still dazed from having his head pounded into the counter, Allen could not answer coherently.

"It's in the bag of grass behind the counter," Roseanne supplied with a glance at Willy, who found yet another reason to seethe.

Nick looked at Dorf and nodded toward the counter. The security specialist sauntered to the counter and rooted through the clippings until he found the bag with The Newburn Bank stamp upon it, pulling it free but not opening it.

Silently he handed it to Nick, who then pulled Allen and Roseanne to their feet and herded them toward the door. A siren sounded in the night and announced the ambulance en route to the scene.

Dorf stood watching the scene, his earlier adrenaline rush worn off, a greasy fear taking its place. What if the chief charged him? He was too old to go to jail, and he knew full well how convicts treated dirty cops.

But then, Nick had just trusted him to get the loot, didn't he? Dorf was confused. Where was Dr. Phil when he needed him?

Chief Kocke knew the fight was over by the look in Crazy Willy's eyes, but he still felt an urge to throttle the man doing his best to impersonate the Road Warrior.

Perhaps now the day could end, Brad thought without much hope. There was still a ton of paperwork to muddle through before he could lay this to rest.

"Who is that guy?" he asked Dorf.

"Kyle Grantz," the elder replied. "He claimed to be a Guardian."

"Huh," Brad muttered, shoving Crazy Willy toward the door, his hands cuffed behind his back. "Let's go."

Phillip was unusually subdued, standing beside his car. Brad spared him a brief glance but decided not to inquire. Whatever it was could wait.

Leaving Nick to watch the scene until the ambulance arrived, Brad loaded the three prisoners into GiGi's car, sure to put Crazy Willy up front where he could reach him. He wasn't sure what to do when he got to the station, since there was only one cell, but Brad figured he would think of something.

His cell phone chirped and he thought of dismissing it. The number did not belong to the mayor, however, so he answered, and was glad he did.

GiGi's voice was like a breath of fresh air. They spoke briefly, the chief promising to get there as soon as possible and then she was gone.

His spirits soared as he entered the police-station lot, noting his Subaru was sitting in the same place.

*Crap!* he thought. *Bartie Grantz. And what about the Orc?*

"Stay here," he told his passengers, climbing out of the car to discover his personal vehicle devoid of anyone. "Guess old Chipper finally got here."

Brad took his charges into the station, put Allen and Roseanne into the cell and Crazy Willy in the bathroom, and collapsed into the MIC chair.

*What a day,* he thought. On the heels of that, his mind suddenly connected Kyle and Bartie.

### 8:45 P.M.

"Why did you shoot him?" Nick asked softly. "I had him in my sights."

Dorf shrugged then decided to answer. He had stayed behind, despite his confusion, because he needed to know where he stood. He feared going home to Dr. Phil, only to be interrupted by officers demanding his surrender.

"He was not right," Dorf said, pointing to his temple. "He really wanted to hurt you for interfering and I couldn't let him do that."

"But you didn't necessarily have to shoot him," Nick countered.

"Maybe, maybe not," Dorf replied tiredly. "I just know that I've always wanted to be a cop, and after what happened at the bank, I felt I needed to do something."

"Well, I'm glad you didn't shoot me by mistake," Nick said, recalling how furious he had been with Dorf for tackling him in the bank.

"Me too."

A few moments later, EMTs arrived and placed Kyle on a stretcher and loaded him into the waiting ambulance, firing up the lights as they headed for Waterford General.

Kyle hadn't uttered a sound after squealing like a stuck pig and for that, both Dorf and Nick were grateful.

The men sat in silence as they watched the flashing lights fade into the night. After a few minutes, Dorf asked sheepishly what would happen next.

"Allen and Roseanne are probably going to jail," the officer replied.

"I meant with me," Dorf said. "Am I going to be charged for shooting Kyle?"

"I don't think so. The chief and I talked about it and I told him to let it slide."

Dorf stared in shock. "You? I, uh, I mean, thanks."

Nick Crawford smiled easily for the first time today, realizing the older man was not accustomed to being treated with kindness.

"No problem."

# Chapter 36

## 8:50 P.M.

Danielle paced the kitchen in her home, worried about what had happened to Nick. Still no call to say he was all right; no call had come in saying he was dead, either, which counted for something.

But that didn't stop her from wearing a path in the linoleum.

At the Newburn Fitness & Weight Training Center, Jerry Fillabag was still stewing. His inaction was due in part to an inability to figure out a way to exact revenge. The rest was simple uncertainty.

He finally decided that keeping a low profile was the best option. The tea deal was probably gone, but he still had the cow-roid angle, and that would more than make up for the loss.

And then a tentative knock on his door changed everything. The Orc, covered in vomit except for the parts licked clean by Jeb Stuart's bovine, entered the room with all the grace of a boar hog on ice skates.

"Ughh!" he said, looking around the room.

"You came back," Jerry said, feeling a joy he'd not believed possible. Guess that's what happens when you think the whole world has abandoned you, he thought, but first things first.

Knowing a conversation would be worthless, Jerry Fillabag outlined instructions instead, which included a little payback on that jerk of a bar owner. Perhaps his venture was not yet stalled.

## 8:55 P.M.

The quintet of cows, long overdue for their nightly feed, wandered aimlessly through town.

Jeb Stuart lay sleeping after a hard day, unaware of his herd's escape.

<h2 style="text-align:center">9:05 P.M.</h2>

Granpa G sat in the community room of the Newburn Acres, which sounded more like a farm than a retirement center, he often thought. Freshly showered and feeling rested (a near-coma will do that to you, Chipper McGraw had said), he was still worrying about the drug deal he'd witnessed.

Did the cops ever check into it? He thought of calling the police station to find out, but then decided he would do it in the morning.

But he couldn't get the images of those men out of his head. Each carrying a bag of grass into the drugstore and then again to the bar. Chipper had told him he was lucky to be alive, considering the stress his old heart had borne, and to take it easy for a while.

"The best I can figure is your body decided it was too stressed out and shut down," Chipper told him on the drive to the center. "I won't say you were technically in a coma, but it looks like you pushed yourself to the point of exhaustion and your body had no other options. I don't even want to know how you wound up in the chief's car, but you need to lie down and get some sack time."

But for a true Guardian, rest came when the job was done, and his town was probably still in the midst of a drug epidemic.

Alone in the "rec room" as his caretakers called it, Bartie paid little attention to Stone Phillips rattling on about a childcare provider feeding children horse meat. He was restless, eager for action.

The only recourse available to him was to make sure the deal had soured, to ensure that his town was not in the grip of drugs.

And to do that, he would have to ignore Chipper's advice, which even he admitted was unusual.

"I'm not used to dealing with the living," he told Bartie

before the old man stepped from the car. "But if you want to avoid seeing me in the near future, I'd get to Doc Hemphill tomorrow and let him look you over. You took quite a shock today."

Standing slowly, allowing the blood to flow south at an easy rate to avoid dizziness, Bartie Grantz returned to his room for a moment to collect his gear before heading out into the moonlit night.

### 9:15 P.M.

Dalton Fisk pushed the Peterbilt about 12 miles over the limit in his haste to put Newburn behind him. He didn't care if he ever returned to that little town. True, he'd grown up there, spent his time there when he wasn't pushing loads across the country, but it wasn't comfortable anymore.

Brenda's reaction had left him feeling a little sick. He hadn't expected her to take him into her arms and treat him like his mother would have, had she been alive. All he'd wanted was a sympathetic ear, and she couldn't even give him that.

Between her lack of support and the cop, he was tired of dealing with Newburn. Maybe he'd just stay in New Orleans for a while. The truck was his, and his contracts were set up for the next three months.

Surely in that time he could find a place to settle down.

### 9:16 P.M.

While Dalton was pushing southeast, listening to *Calling Baton Rouge*, perhaps the best song Garth Brooks ever recorded, Phillip Andrew Thomas was doing his best to piece together seemingly incongruous information for a story.

The man on the floor, Kyle Grantz, according to his notes, had delivered a deathbed soliloquy, though according to everyone he wasn't dying. That didn't deter Phillip from taking notes and planning to run a story.

It was likely to produce a furor among the people of

Newburn, especially those drawing Social Security (what there was to be drawn, he mused).

Phillip wondered how far he could push it, and decided he would go to the very limit in presenting the truth of the Guardians.

### 9:17 P.M.

Nick and Dorf had parted ways amiably after the former had secured the scene with police tape.

Dorf headed for home, where for the first time since his grandson had taught him to record Dr. Phil, he was going to forego the second half of the show in favor of sleep. First thing tomorrow he would need to find a job.

It pained him to have been terminated, though working for Waterman had been difficult on the best days.

There were two other banks in town, and he might be able to get into one of them. Neither they nor Waterman liked one another, so he doubted they'd even check with the old man.

Perhaps this was a good thing, this change in his life. He turned in full of hope, and a sense of fulfillment knowing he'd attained one of his goals.

Being on the Dr. Phil show might be a near thing if he couldn't find work soon.

His cats welcomed him with disinterest, showing him their tails as they scooted out the door. Grunting, Dorf let them go without protest. They'd been cooped up all day as it was, and he was too tired to care.

### 9:20 P.M.

Chief Brad Kocke had completed the criminal report and counted the money. According to Nick, the total taken was $13,000, but he had only $8,990 in front of him. He supposed Allen and Roseanne had spent the rest of it, and noted that in his report. They were on the hook for larceny, though the initial robbery had been forgiven, an odd state of affairs in which Max, Todd and Brian would repay the money as a loan.

If, Brad amended silently, the cantankerous bank president didn't weasel out of it.

He heard a noise and swiveled in his MIC chair to look at the cell, which held Allen and Roseanne.

The two were making out like a couple of teenagers, which he supposed was not far from the truth.

Sighing, he thought of ordering them to stop, but as long as they kept their clothes on, he would let them find comfort where they could. After all, they were looking at enforced time apart in the near future for their actions.

Instead, Chief Kocke went to the bathroom, where he opened the door to check on Crazy Willy.

Brad's hand rested on the butt of his gun but he hoped not to need it. He did not.

To his surprise, Crazy Willy was huddled on the floor, his cheeks wet from recent weeping.

*Great*, the chief thought. *Now I get to play nursemaid to a tough that's lost it.*

"Don't look at me," Willy said, turning his face to the wall.

"I always heard you were a badass," the chief said. "I guess I heard wrong."

Crazy Willy, now dubbed Weeping Willy by the chief, said nothing as Brad closed the door.

"What a crazy day," he muttered to himself as he returned to his desk to call Nick.

### 9:22 P.M.

Max Irons had stayed until Jan herself had ushered everyone out, pointing to the sign which showed the closing time at nine. He was ready to go, but didn't like being shown the door. It reminded him too much of his departure from the Newburn Fitness & Weight Training Center.

Regardless, he stepped into the warm night with pleasure, his mood having improved throughout his meal as he thought of the possibilities.

His first stop would be the police station, where he would spill his guts about the cowroid operation. After that, he would find Nick Crawford and take him up on his offer of room and board.

Max knew he wasn't the brightest person, but he was living proof of the steroid's effects. He'd even submit to a test to prove his claim, if that was required, so long as he didn't have to pay for it.

At the least, perhaps Jerry Fillabag would be so wrapped up in defending himself he would forget about the debt he had imposed on Max.

The walk from Jan's had taken him a little longer than he expected, but he wasn't hurrying either, and as Max neared the station, he noted the lights were burning brightly. *Good,* he thought. *Someone can help me, maybe even Nick himself.*

But as he reached the door, he noted the high-riding headlights as they splashed over him, making him feel like King Kong atop that tower.

He caught a glimpse of the driver, noting Jerry sitting high in his Dodge, but the more alarming sight was the Orc, riding shotgun. His belief he could take on the Orc in a one-on-one fight held true, but Max knew there were others, and suddenly he felt exposed beneath the glare of high beams.

Turning to face the vehicle fully, Max stood still and dared them to notice him. The stratagem apparently failed for the big truck roared past without so much as a twitch of the brake lights.

Drawing a deep breath, Max decided to follow Jerry and the Orc instead of asking the police for help. Maybe he could find a way to corner the thug and exact his own payback. He was inexplicably furious at the sight of his former friend and employer, and increased his gait as he followed the diminishing tail lights with hate in his eyes.

### 9:25 P.M.

Bartie Grantz pulled his dinosaur of a vehicle into a parking space two doors up from the Double-L, killing the engine. He wondered at the near-perfect parking job, considering he was legally blind. The drive from the center should have taken a handful of moments at most, but the other danger of having Bartie behind the wheel was his inability to read road signs, and as such, he took the scenic route, barely making his way to the bar.

No matter, he told himself. I'm here to stop this drug deal.

Still convinced he was the only thing standing in the path of strung-out kids and evil drug lords, Bartie fondled the worn oak staff lovingly. He'd never actually used it, though it had been passed down to him and he revered its singular purpose, much like a wizard would his staff.

Nor did he want to use it, but he would if it came to that. All Bartie Grantz wanted was to stop the druggies and preserve his town. That was his duty as a Guardian.

Bartie walked to the door of the Double-L, hearing the noise generated by a crowd of drunken fools willingly parting with their paychecks for a few hours of oblivion.

Steeling himself, he pushed the door open and went inside, unaware that pulling up behind him were Jerry Fillabag and the Orc.

## 9:30 P.M.

"You understand what we're doing?"

"Uhnuh," the Orc grunted.

"Okay." Jerry Fillabag climbed out of his Dodge 2500 and waited for his enforcer to join him.

The plan was simple, suited to the needs of his brawny counterpart, who lacked the basic skills required for planning. They would walk in like they owned the place, the Orc would beat up Lionel Leanman, they would take the money he owed, and leave.

*Slick*, Jerry thought. Before anyone could react, he and his ogre would be gone.

Much like Bartie during his entrance, the duo did not realize they too had been followed. Max approached the

Double-L apace, but not so quick to overtake them. He was searching the shadows for evidence of the amigos before making a move.

The Orc and Jerry entered the tavern and approached the bar, only to find Lionel chatting amiably with a dead man.

What the Orc lacked in intelligence, however, was more than made up for in imagination, particularly where it met with superstition.

Max watched through the glass in the door as his quarry fell apart, the Orc reacting harshly to something he'd just seen.

*****

Meanwhile, Brenda heard a knock at her door and wondered if Dalton had returned. Not that she cared tremendously.

Her relationship with him had begun a bare three weeks ago, and he was already pushing to move in, though he spent several days on the road, so her involvement with him was intermittent at best.

She had feelings for him, but Brenda was not the sort to fall in love quickly. She'd been hurt too many times before to allow anyone very close.

Stifling an urge to let the visitor believe her asleep, Brenda opened the door and was surprised to see her neighbor Danielle standing there. She looked awful.

Her face was drawn and the circles under her eyes were so blue it appeared she had been beaten up. There were tracks on her face and her eyes were swollen, as if she'd been crying.

Wasting no time, Brenda ushered her into the house and led her to the kitchen table, where life revolved for most people.

"What's the matter?"

"I'm scared," Danielle said, chewing her lip. "I haven't heard from Nick and I know he's in a dangerous situation, and there's nothing I can do about it."

At the mention of Nick Crawford, Brenda couldn't help

but smile. He'd had a huge effect on Dalton, that was certain, though no one deserved to have his life threatened by a chainsaw-wielding maniac in the dark.

But she wouldn't say that to Danielle. The two had been neighbors and friends for a few years and had shared many a cup of coffee at one or the other's kitchen, and it would have been unkind to deflect her obvious torment over last night's events.

When Brenda had called Danielle this morning to ask if she'd heard the ruckus, the latter had expressed genuine surprise. Now, her neighbor was on the verge of breaking down, her worry and fatigue evident in the way her shoulders sagged.

"Let me make you some tea," Brenda said. "I got it today at Esther's and it's supposed to be the best for stress-relief."

As Brenda busied herself with the kettle, Danielle thought about the long day she'd had. Her stomach was beyond empty; she was nearly starved. Adrenaline and Mr. Pibb had kept her going, but even though her hunger was nagging, she was too agitated to eat. Instead, she sipped hot tea and told Brenda the whole story, from her phone call in which Dorf tried to explain his problems, all the way up to the late night at the bank.

"You really think your boss is going to stick to it?" Brenda asked, trying to balance all she'd heard about the old fool with what Danielle had told her. "I mean, it sounds like you had him over a barrel, and in front of witnesses, but what's to say he won't back out of it?"

Danielle hadn't given that much thought, but decided it was worth consideration. Waterman was a dirty, ogling old man but he was shrewd, and if he could find a way out, he would do it.

The hot tea before her was having an effect. Though it smelled a little odd, it had calmed her nerves and now she wanted to sleep. But the thought of walking next door was daunting.

Instead, she stopped speaking, looking at Brenda pleadingly. Like many times in the past, when Danielle had been home alone and in need of friendship, her neighbor's couch had always been comfortable.

And it was now, as Danielle slipped off her shoes and laid back.

Brenda watched her friend with concern, knowing she was very tired and hoping a night's sleep would calm her as the tea had.

*Wonderful stuff,* Brenda thought. *Who would have thought the Pakistanis could make such good tea?*

Brenda poured herself a second cup and settled in, waiting for Danielle to pass completely into sleep before heading for her own bed.

### 9:31 P.M.

Nick Crawford thought seriously about just going home. He was dog-tired and his body ached tremendously. The chief had called him as he headed toward the heart of town, telling him he had things under control, if you called having two of his prisoners two seconds from carnal activity and the other sobbing in the bathroom "under control."

Chief Brad Kocke was as tired as Nick, but leaving his prisoners unattended was not something he would do, and the only other option was to transport them to Waterford, where the sheriff would house them until morning, when they would be arraigned. But the city would have to pay for that, and Mayor Ted Keller would not look upon the expense with understanding, the chief knew.

So he was stuck. Fortunately, a cot had been put in the hall closet for those times when an officer was required overnight. Newburn was such a quiet little town, only in severe times (like today) was the station open.

911 calls were routed through the center in Waterford and officers in Newburn were dispatched as needed.

In the last four years, there had been only one call, that being when Evvie's husband flipped his tractor.

Everyone else was courteous enough to have a problem during the day, when the station was staffed.

Brad had tried to staff it with Brian and Todd but soon found that to be a joke, since they fell asleep or pushed each other around in the MIC chair, which is how the caster was broken.

Weary beyond measure, Brad hauled out the cot and set it up a few feet from the cell, between it and the bathroom door, which could not be locked.

The front door, however, could be locked and he did this before pulling out his phone for one more call.

Despite his strong desire to spend the night with her, Brad knew it was impossible. GiGi was disappointed, as he expected, but she was sympathetic, which he had not expected.

Now, climbing into the cot and pulling a blanket over his tired body, Brad smiled in the dimly lit station, hoping Crazy Willy's demeanor did not change in the middle of the night.

# Chapter 37

## 9:33 P.M.

Nick drove past the station, seeing the lights dimmed. He had to smile, thinking of the chief holding a slumber party inside. He'd told him he would relieve him first thing in the morning and to call if he needed help.

After trying Danielle at home for the third time to no avail, he finally gave up, figuring she was asleep.

Instead, despite his recollections of the night before, Nick decided he could do with a beer before heading home, where he hoped a few pain-relief tablets would push back his aches enough for sleep.

When he opened the door of the Double-L, he was assaulted by a shriek that sent his blood pumping. His weariness fell before a storm of chemicals and his hand immediately went to his gun.

Before him, Jerry Fillabag stood shouting at another man, who was screaming incoherently and pointing at Bartie Grantz, who looked like he'd rather be anywhere than here in the bar.

At this time of night, Nick had to wonder what he was doing here. Behind him, standing sentinel at the bar with a shotgun, was Lionel Leanman, who appeared ready to start shooting.

*Won't this day ever end?* Nick wondered as he pushed across the threshold.

Lionel had looked up briefly as the door opened, but he was not expecting to see a uniformed officer enter. Especially not *Super-Cop*, whose visit last night had been particularly rough. He'd already been startled with the appearance of the giant man, who had slipped in quietly after the Orc began screaming and now stood silently in the corner, watching events unfold.

"EEggh, hhhunhh," the Orc cried, his gaze roaming around the tavern for a sign of support.

When he and Jerry had entered the bar, the Orc saw Bartie Grantz and immediately his primitive brain called forth images of undead monsters seeking revenge.

Why such a monster might seek him out did not occur to the Orc, who began shrieking.

Though he did not share the superstitious fear which had enveloped his enforcer, Jerry Fillabag was taken aback at seeing the old man. He was dead! The memory of the messy interlude in the car was still fresh in his mind, and Jerry bitterly recalled screaming like the Orc was now.

Turning, he gripped the Orc's shoulders and began shouting at him to calm down. Jerry considered slapping him but wasn't sure how the feeble-minded thug would react.

His fury at Lionel Leanman was tempered by the fright the Orc felt, and he was further discouraged as the barman pulled out a shotgun.

The Orc continued to wail, a high-pitched keening that reminded Jerry of nails on a blackboard. As he stood trying to find a way to cope, the cop entered.

"What the hell is going on here?"

"I don't know," Lionel said, never taking his eyes off of Jerry. "He just started screaming."

Turning to the gym kingpin, Nick raised his eyebrows meaningfully.

"He's freaking out because we thought that man was dead," Jerry said. The Orc's eyes were bulging now, threatening to divorce themselves from their sockets. "I better get him out of here."

"Just a minute," Nick said in his Commanding Officer voice. "What's the story with this man?"

Bartie Grantz stepped forward, making the Orc cringe back so fearfully he slammed into a nearby table, disrupting the mugs of beer and toppling to the floor.

"I saw this man making drug deals all over town today," Bartie said, pointing to the cringing Orc, who chose to curl up in a fetal ball and whimper. "The chief looked into it but I don't know what happened. I guess I passed out for a while."

"What about it, Mister Fillabag?"

"I already told the chief it was tea, not drugs," Jerry replied. "And Lionel knows that's the truth."

Nick felt like he was at a tennis match, moving his head from one side to the other to follow the references.

"That true?"

The barrel of the shotgun wavered as Lionel Leanman considered his answer. "I'm not sure what he's dealing," he said finally. "He asked me to sell this stuff, looks like grass. Could be tea, I suppose, but I don't know what's in it."

"It's *Pakistani* tea," Jerry said forcefully. "There's nothing *in* it."

"Then why were you sneaking around?"

"I wasn't sneaking around." Jerry sounded defensive, even to his own ears.

"No, you just sent your amigos and that moron over here to threaten me into selling your stuff," Lionel said. "Then you tried to strong-arm me after *your* guys ran off with the money. I told you earlier not to come back."

"That's right officer," Jerry said. "He threatened to kill me."

"Only after you threatened me."

"Did not."

"Did too."

Nick was reminded forcefully of Brian and Todd, and wondered where they'd disappeared to; *and what about Max?* At that thought, he happened to turn around and saw Max standing there with a grin on his face.

"Max? What are you doing here?"

"I want to file a complaint," he said. "Jerry Fillabag is selling illegal steroids at his gym."

At the sound of his voice, Jerry spun to take in his former "best builder" as he laid out his claim.

Nick saw the brief twitch on the gym-owner's face before it settled back into a mask of barely contained fury.

"You have something to say, Mister Fillabag?"

"This is outrageous," Jerry replied, his fallen thug

temporarily forgotten. "I had to fire him for stealing from me just this morning!"

"So you're saying you're not selling steroids?" Nick's voice was smooth, his tone neutral, despite knowing the man was lying.

"I'm saying this man can't be trusted," Jerry said. "I fired him and now he's making up wild accusations."

"So you are selling steroids?"

"I'm not listening to this," Jerry said, forgetting the Orc completely as he took a step toward the door.

"Just a minute." Nick moved to block his way despite his fatigue, as Lionel tracked his enemy with the rifle. "We're going to talk about this whether you want to or not. But not tonight. I'm too tired to do much more, so I'll be by to see you tomorrow."

Jerry stared at the cop angrily; if he'd been a cartoon character, Nick believed steam would be pouring from both ears. "Fine," he said acidly, stalking out of the bar; a moment later tires squalling on the pavement could be heard.

The Orc had quieted at last but he was still staring wildly at Bartie Grantz.

Nick drew a breath that trembled in his chest, his body warning of imminent collapse. He never would have believed as he stared in the mirror this morning that he'd have this kind of day.

It was definitely one for the books.

Lionel Leanman relaxed his grip on the shotgun and stowed it behind the bar. He invited both Nick and Max to the bar, where he offered up a free beer. Not forgetting the old man, Lionel poured a glass of Sprite by way of thanks.

"Your timing is excellent," he told Nick. "I was just about ready to shoot him."

"I vote for shooting him too," Max added, taking a long draw of Bud Light.

Nick smiled but made no comment as he contemplated the brew. After last night, he was unsure whether he should have a drink but then took a sip and felt better.

"So what's the story?"

"Just like I said, he tried to push me around," Lionel said. "I didn't want anything to do with him or his tea, but Jerry can be persuasive."

Max knew exactly what he was talking about and sympathized with the Double-L's proprietor.

"And you, Mister Grantz?"

"That man is bad news," the Guardian replied, stroking his staff, which had survived the day so long ago when his great-grandfather had partaken in the only thwarted robbery attempt in Newburn's history. "He needs to be locked up."

Or worse, he didn't add.

"You know he's going to ditch any evidence tonight," Nick said. "I wish there was something I could do, but I'm about to collapse."

"I'll watch his place for you," Bartie offered. "I'm not tired and I can handle anything he might try."

Nick considered the proposal, wanting to say yes for Max's sake; without evidence his claim was worthless, despite the body language that indicated Jerry Fillabag was hiding something.

"I'm sorry Mister Grantz, but if something were to happen to you, I'd be responsible," said Nick. "I can't let you put yourself in danger like that."

"I'll go with him," Max said, a second before Lionel offered the same thing.

Arching his eyebrows at the bar owner, Nick gestured to the room, which held six or seven drinkers and one incapacitated thug.

"I'll just close up early, that's all," Lionel said, a defensive note in his voice. "They need to go home to their families anyway."

"What about the Orc?" Max interjected.

"Good question," Nick said. "I guess I'll have to take him to the station."

At the mention of his name, the muscle-bound ogre climbed to his feet. Seeming to sense what was going on, he dashed for the door and disappeared into the night.

"Guess that answers that," Lionel said. "Go home, Nick,

get some sleep. We'll keep an eye on the gym and make sure the bastard doesn't do anything."

Feeling a bit overcome by the gesture, Nick smiled and offered a two-finger salute before leaving the bar for home. "For the record, I didn't hear that," he said.

# Chapter 38

**10:00 P.M.**

Danielle awoke with a start, confused for a moment as to where she was, but soon remembering her visit with Brenda, whose compassionate shoulder had been welcome.

The living room was darkened but not completely, as Brenda had left a hall light on before retiring.

She thought of turning over and going back to sleep but Danielle had been strung out most of the day with concern for Nick, and her thoughts turned to him. Nothing would bring more comfort than lying next to him this night. Instead of allowing herself to drift back to slumber, she arose, found her purse and had to dig through several layers of junk before finding the cell phone within.

The Dooney & Burke knockoff had a special pocket for cell phones, but she was of the school that just threw everything in and sorted through it as needed. It drove Nick crazy whenever she asked him to retrieve something small, say nail-clippers.

His grousing as his masculine hands pulled out used tissue, several partial packs of gum and her wallet brought to mind the love she felt for him. She had drifted off to sleep because she was mentally and emotionally exhausted, despite her efforts to remain vigilant.

Now, thinking of him, her eyes were wide and the worry return, wiping the smile of remembered rummaging from her like chalk from a board.

*Please let him be all right,* she thought, opening the phone.

To her surprise, he answered on the first ring.

"Hi sweetheart," he said into the phone, sending her spirits soaring. You have to love caller-ID.

"How's everything?"

"It's been a long, weird day but it's finally over," Nick replied as he turned onto Oak Street. "I called your house a few times, where are you?"

"Brenda's, but I'm heading home in a minute," Danielle said.

"I'll see you soon."

A few moments later he turned into Danielle's driveway to find her standing there. The walk from Brenda's house next door was short and she was impatient though Nick pulled up just a minute after she arrived at her door.

Rushing to him, she spared nothing in her embrace, barely allowing him to step from the car before crushing him beneath a fierce hug.

"I'm so happy to see you're okay," she said, kissing his neck.

"Good to see you too."

Danielle's didn't ask about his encounter with Allen Frye. There would be time enough for that in the morning.

For now, all she wanted was to hold him tight. It wasn't a sexual situation. Both were tired and ready for sleep, and to enter that land together, their bodies imparting and taking warmth, was a far more satisfactory end to the day.

She looked at him as he stripped from his uniform, which had seen a lot of action that day, and knew for certain this was the man she wanted to be with for the rest of her life. During their two-week hiatus from the engagement, she'd gone through many different emotions, from confusion to bitter anger and finally chagrin as she realized what he'd thought. In the course of today's events, when she feared she'd lose him, Danielle resolved to never allow anything to fester ever again.

Arguments would occur, she knew, and might escalate, but never would she go to bed in anger. Life was too short, she knew.

Let us withdraw from this simply appointed bedroom in a small home on Oak Street, one in which Nick Crawford and Danielle Stone were the picture of rediscovered love.

*****

Newburn is a town that rolls up the streets sometime between 8:30 and 10:00, the outskirts retiring earlier and arising at dawn. Jan usually collapsed into her easy chair in the house next to her restaurant, watching TV until she fell asleep, and tonight was no different.

Phillip Andrew Thomas was sleeping fitfully on his couch, the VCR showing scenes unnoticed from his small collection of adult cinema. His laptop's screensaver rolled through 3D swirls, his stories saved beneath the veneer. He still had a day to work out some of the details, but he expected his final piece to sell plenty of papers, even in Waterford.

Brian Fennigan and Todd Brown had given up on their contemplation of the future, opting instead to play Street Fighter 2, which Todd always won easily. He had the special features down to an art, while Brian struggled to keep his fighter upright, let alone summon a super-punch or kick.

After an hour of getting killed, Brian called it quits and went to bed, a futon with a thin blanket in a filthy room. Todd played for a while thereafter and then moved to his dirty room, which was a reflection of the living room, and cleared off a spot for sleep, which came surprisingly easy.

Edward Von Waterman III, whose day had been as trying as anyone's, was fast asleep, his dream of sticking it to the "man" leaving a smile on his chubby face.

Chief Brad Kocke, alone and uncomfortable on a cot in the station, didn't really fall too deep into sleep for fear that Weeping Willy would ambush him. His pair of prisoners in the cell had contented themselves with a good old-fashioned make-out session before calling it a night, much to his relief. Brad had no desire to witness anything more of their relationship than that which was necessary.

Weeping Willy was not a threat; he had cried himself to sleep on the cold bathroom tile, vowing he would leave town as soon as possible to avoid having to see these people. Most of his business was in Waterford anyway, and he could always move to St. Louis. He wept because he allowed himself to consider his mother, and how much he missed her. Theirs had not been a good relationship, and the last parting words he had for her included, "I hope you die alone." Now that *he* was alone and tired, he wanted his mommy like any other human, and it grieved him - surprisingly - to realize that.

At Dorf's home, his labored breathing was unheard by four of his cats, who had left when he returned to chase rodents and try to breed. The fifth was curled up at his feet, her soft coat rising with breath that seemed to be in time with Dorf's. His face carried a smile, for his imagination had once more conjured his guest appearance on the set of Dr. Phil, where his exploits as a police officer would be shared with the world.

Jerry Fillabag sat behind his desk, his sore cheek firmly planted on the blotter and drool coursing from one side of his mouth. Of course he had thought of removing the evidence from his gym, but the reality was that any one of his customers could be compelled to present the enhancement vitamins he'd sold them. And that would leave him holding the bag. Removing cases of the cowroids would be just about useless.

He would just have to hope his lawyer was better than the city of Newburn.

Outside the Newburn Fitness & Weight Training Center, the trio of Lionel Leanman, Bartie Grantz and Max Irons had fallen down on the job, which wasn't really surprising. Bartie's old battery might have been recharged by his collapse, but it was still an old battery and didn't hold much.

Max and Lionel had tried to talk for a while, though they didn't have much in common. One was dedicated to building his body, the other to selling spirits which eventually would destroy it.

After a while they gave up, setting in to watch the gym in comfortable silence. Even that paled as nothing was happening, and soon their vigilance faltered, and not long after, they joined Bartie in a sleep that could not be comfortable, as any who fall asleep on a road trip will attest.

GiGi was accustomed to sleeping alone, though she had really hoped to share her bed with Brad Kocke tonight. But duty had required them to remain separate, and despite her disappointment, she understood. Normally, disappointment was a catalyst for her impulsive behavior, but she found the strength to avoid her curse by thinking of how much Brad wanted to beat his own affliction, no pun intended. She believed that together they might actually approach normalcy.

Sheila Fowler was likewise able to keep her impulses in check, as she found herself in a miraculous scenario. At Marcia's house, lying next to her, all was right with the world. She only hoped it would stay that way by the light of day. So thinking, she'd drifted off with her arm draped over Marcia's back.

The other members of the Newburn Society for Compulsive Disorders did not share newfound interests to help fight their urges.

Somewhere between Newburn and Waterford, the Orc was following the highway and not really caring where he wound up, as long as he didn't have to see dead men come back to life. His plan, such as it was, involved finding a way to St. Louis, where he understood his life.

At the Fill-Er-Up Truck Stop near St. Genevieve, Missouri, Dalton Fisk had stopped for a brief rest. His long night thrashing in fear and subsequent day spent dealing with the bank robbery and whatnot, had left him more exhausted than he realized. He would push on in a few hours, but in the meantime, he had drifted off in the cabin. A knock on his truck door roused him before he fell too deep, and when he looked out the window, he saw a woman.

Called a "lot-lizard" by those in the know, she was middle-aged, with stark red hair and too much make-up, but she had pretty hazel eyes, Dalton thought. He knew what she wanted and though he was interested, he really didn't have money to spare on this trip.

Yet he opened the door and spoke to her. After a few

238

minutes, she offered a trade: companionship for travel.

He willingly agreed and decided to spend the night.

The moon rose high above the plane of earth, giving its shine willingly, as the inhabitants of Newburn and beyond lie sleeping. The quiet and motionless landscape around the small Missouri town was peaceful, for most of those who called it home had no idea that the long, strange day had occurred.

Dawn would bring about several changes in town, but for now, the community rolled over, scratched themselves absently used the bathroom before returning to their slumber.

# Chapter 39

## TUESDAY MORNING

The sun rose with its eternal majestic glory, offering warmth and light to those whose lives depended on both. It would be a real scorcher of a day, if the forecasters from St. Louis were to be believed, but Missouri is the Show-Me State for a reason, and residents of Newburn faced the day with little in the way of expectation.

While not untouched by the outside world, what with DISH and DirecTV vying to place a satellite on every structure and even a few RVs, Newburn did enjoy a slower pace.

Arising in the morning was a process for most, the day officially starting as sunlight peeked through the blinds in the bedroom, usually accompanied by the aroma of coffee as the automatic drips performed their sole function.

In the outlying farm homes, most of the people had been up for a time, sipping coffee and eating a hearty breakfast, usually skimming the St. Louis Post-Dispatch (if they remembered to renew their subscriptions) or talking about the coming work in the fields.

This time of year was especially busy, and not one of the farmers would be caught indoors after 6:30 in the morning.

In town, things were a little slower to develop, as businessmen arose to the same smell of coffee but sat before the paper (they always remembered to keep their subscriptions up), catching up on the news that happened through the night or in the rest of the world before making the trek to work, mostly in the suburbs of St. Louis.

The 'tweeners, whose who lived in rural Newburn but did not belong to either community, people like Evvie Fennigan, arose not long after the sun but felt no great rush to move. Since her husband's untimely death, mornings had been a quiet time of reflection for her, and Evvie wasn't about to be rushed through her rituals.

Spouses kissed their loved ones and set them on their way, adults to their place of work, children to summer-school or to play or to daycare.

Life happened, it was that simple. It happens everywhere, every day, and all but a handful in Newburn had any reason to think the day before had been anything but ordinary.

But for the few who had been wrapped up in the bizarre day, arising this morning was filled with wondering whether or not the events had actually taken place or had been the product of a weird dream. Too much garlic at dinner, perhaps.

*****

Chief Brad Kocke was not among those who might have questioned anything regarding the most strange day in his life, and that's going some for a man who'd sat before the group investigating the beatings on Riverfront.

When he awoke, without the benefit of an automatic coffee-maker, his first sight was Allen Frye rubbing himself suggestively against Roseanne Jenkins, who was still asleep. Brad thought of his other prisoner and wondered what he'd find upon opening the bathroom door.

Rubbing sleep from his eyes, cursing the cot that had tortured him through the night, the chief walked to the bathroom and rapped twice. Hearing nothing, he opened the door and beheld Crazy Willy lying in the same spot he'd been last night.

Trying not to wake him, Chief Kocke relieved himself and withdrew, the drug dealer sleeping through the whole process, despite the occasional splash.

Roseanne had awakened in his absence and Brad found her returning her lover's embrace.

"Stop it right now," he barked harshly.

Allen looked abashed, Roseanne just looked sleepy.

"For Christ's sake, I haven't even had coffee yet."

Sparing another stern look at the pair, Brad went to table

beside the counter and started a pot.

A few moments later, the bathroom door opened and Crazy Willy peered out, finding the chief sitting in the MIC chair.

"Morning Sunshine," Brad said sarcastically. "Feeling better?"

"Don't call me that," Willy said sullenly, the weight of his breakdown bearing on him heavily.

"Okay, Crazy Willy," the other said.

"Don't call me that either," Willy said. "It's just Will."

"You don't say," Brad said. "You find Jesus last night?"

"Something like that," Will replied. "I realized I've been wasting my life."

"Seems like someone could have told you that a long time ago," Brad said, unsure whether to take this new persona at face value.

The two stared at each other for a moment before Willy's shoulders slumped. "You're right," he said softly. "I just want to go home, sir. To my mother's."

Brad was taken aback. He was rarely called "sir" but the young man looked sincere. He thought heavily about the situation.

On the one hand, all he'd been tagged for was assault, and that was hardly a great matter when compared to armed criminal action, larceny and assault with a deadly weapon, as Allen Frye faced. Hell, even Roseanne would probably walk for her role in driving the car, since no one could prove it (he didn't know Danielle had witnessed the hasty departure).

"Where does your mom live?"

"Waterford."

"I'll drop you off on the way," Brad said, turning to his other two charges, who sat watching the exchange distrustfully. "We're all going to Waterford in a little while."

Brad watched as Will walked over to the cell, considered stopping him, and then decided he wouldn't cause any trouble. Call it a leap of faith.

Will stopped before the cell with about two feet to spare, taking a deep breath as if willing himself to speak.

Brad turned to the phone and dialed Nick Crawford, while keeping an ear cocked for trouble.

"I just wanted to apologize," Will said, eyeing Roseanne squarely. "I'm sorry for being such a jerk."

"Wow," she muttered. "That's the first time I've ever heard you apologize."

Will grinned and it turned his ordinary face into something approaching nobility, or at least human, not that Roseanne had much experience in the former.

"I realized last night that I'm at rock-bottom," he said. "I wanted so bad to be somebody. I wanted someone to look at me the way you look at him."

Roseanne found Allen's hand and squeezed it warmly. "Do you mean that?"

"Yeah. I hope he makes you happy."

"As long as we have *Law & Order* and each other, we'll be fine," Roseanne said.

Will started to turn away when Allen spoke up. "Are we cool about the bank thing? I mean, I didn't know you were involved, I swear."

Rolling his eyes, Will stepped away from the cell without answering, leaving Allen Frye to continue wondering.

*****

Danielle answered Nick's cell phone, spoke for a moment and then handed it to Nick, who was still lying snugly in bed beside her. For them, the morning was in no rush to pass.

"Hello?"

"Nick, it's Brad," the chief said, a note of amusement in his voice. "I have to take these guys to the courthouse and arraign 'em. Can you cover things?"

"Sure. What time?" Nick glanced at the alarm clock, it's bright red numbers indicating 7:34.

"Take your time, get some breakfast with your lady, be here in about an hour," Brad said.

"Thanks Chief," Nick said, surrendering the phone to Danielle, who recognized the sly grin on his face.

"Do we have time?"

For an answer, Nick buried his face in the crook of her neck.

*****

Phillip Andrew Thomas, his arm asleep from lying crookedly on the couch all night, made his way gingerly to the bathroom, where he dry-swallowed a couple painkillers and hoped for the best.

His computer had long since shut down as the battery faded, and he plugged it in after returning to the living room.

A moment later, he began to review *The Story*. It was one of his better pieces, in his opinion, the only one that really counted. His readers had long since grown to adore him; Phillip believed he could print his grocery list and someone would read it.

But this was better than anything he'd ever composed, even the story about the deaf team beating the Newburn Crickets.

His approach had been stymied the first few times as he pondered which was the most important part of the story. The bank robbery? The chainsaw incident? The drug deal?

Of course, he planned all along to present the words of a dying man (in his own mind at least), revealing the truth of the Guardians, but how to reach it? One did not just start out with it; you built up to it, the way he imagined foreplay was supposed to lead up to the deed.

He had decided that his common denominator was Chief Kocke, and he decided to start at the beginning and work his way through to the end.

*****

Brian and Todd stumbled around the latter's apartment, feeling quite out of sorts. They had gone most of a day without their magic smoke, and it was starting to wear on them.

"Why don't you clean this place up?"

"Why don't you? You're living here too, you know."

"Your name's on the lease," Brian said, counting a point for himself.

"Then get the hell out of here," Todd countered.

"Fine!"

"Good luck moving in with your mom, loser," Todd said with a grin. "Shithead."

Brian, despite his nerves, realized dimly that fighting with Todd was counterproductive. And the grin, coupled with the word served to remind him of his situation. Todd was right. Moving back in with his mother was next to impossible; even if she would agree to it, he wasn't sure he could accept her hospitality.

"To hell with it," Brian said finally. "Let it stay where it lays, right?"

"Damn straight," Todd said, the storm passing over without damage.

With the problems awaiting them, it was just as well.

*****

Jerry Fillabag was feeling worse than he did when he sat down last night, though how that was possible he had no idea.

The drool had dried against his face and his neck was throbbing in time with the aches in his jaw and knees, and he had a bad case of cotton-mouth to top it off.

Remembering the previous day's activities, and the accusation laid at his feet, Jerry stood up and looked around the office. It was still early and his earlier resignation was replaced by sudden anxiety. Perhaps he could get rid of the stuff and still walk away from this. He decided he had to at least try.

He was not prepared, however, for the trio awaiting him with his first dolly-load of 'roids.

"Well, well," Max said. "Looks like Nick was right."

"What?" Bartie was polishing his glasses (much good it would do him) and had failed to note the arrival of Jerry from the gym.

"Jerry Fillabag is getting rid of evidence," Max replied.

Lionel Leanman, who sat rubbing a crick in his neck, grunted agreement and both he and Max got out of the car. The latter opened his cell phone and called Nick's number, which the cop had provided last night.

Just when he thought it would go to voicemail, a grumpy voice answered.

"Hello."

"Nick? It's Lionel," the bar man said. "Jerry's trying to dump his drugs."

Despite knowing his adventure was being cut short, Nick was at once filled with adrenaline.

"I'll be right there," he said.

Nick briefly explained the situation to Danielle while getting dressed, adding with a sly look, "We'll finish this later. Don't go anywhere."

Danielle purred but said nothing, her eyes conveying a request he hurry.

At the Newburn Fitness & Weight Training Center, Jerry pulled up short, nearly dumping the four cases of cowroids.

"Going somewhere?" Lionel took the lead, his dislike for the man just slightly more than the others, though Max was a very close second.

"Get out of my way, Lionel," Jerry said. "I don't want any trouble."

"You should have thought of that before you drug me into this mess," Triple-L replied coldly. "You bought this piece of trouble."

Max stared at his former friend and employer, wondering if Jerry ever worried about the people he stepped on. Probably not, the bodybuilder decided.

"Whatever," Jerry said, pulling the dolly back to move the boxes to his Dodge.

Max put one big foot on a wheel and prevented its movement.

"Not you too," Jerry said.

"What? I don't owe you nothing after what you did to me."

"I did what was best for everyone," Jerry replied, setting

the dolly level once more, deciding if the huge man wanted to stop him, there would be nothing he could do.

"You say that, but here you are with all these 'roids," Max said. "You fired me for using them because it was 'bad for the gym's image,' but I got to thinking about that. Why do you have so many boxes of steroids in the first place? You've been selling them to your members, haven't you?"

Jerry sighed, but before he could respond, a car pulled up behind Lionel's vehicle and Nick stepped out.

"Mornin' Mister Fillabag," he said in his Officer Friendly voice, squatting to examine the labels on the cases. "What's all this?"

Jerry looked around, taking in the four men before him. Max, with his understandable hatred, stared at him with daggers; Lionel's gaze held satisfaction; and Bartie's aged eyes didn't appear to be focused on him, but Jerry knew the old man was paying attention to what was happening. As for *Super-Cop*, he continued to read the fake labels Jerry had slapped on the boxes, which proclaimed the contents to be "enhancement vitamins," which was technically true and completely illegal.

His world was tipping, he knew that. *Where did I go wrong?* he wondered. *What forces collided to leave me in this situation?*

Jerry did the only thing he could think of he pleaded the fifth.

Nick promptly arrested him on a charge of distributing a controlled substance and called the chief.

*****

"What's up Nick?"

"I have a situation here," he said. "I arrested Jerry Fillabag for selling illegal drugs and I need to arraign him."

"What drugs? We already cleared him of that. It's tea."

"Tea? Looks like pills to me."

"What are you talking about?"

Nick filled him in on Max's complaint and the subsequent discovery as Jerry tried to get rid of four cases of the pills.

"You let three civilians do a stakeout?"

"Officially, no," Nick replied. "They volunteered and I turned them down. What happened after I left I can't say."

Chief Brad Kocke, who had spent the majority of Monday with not only an old man (who he thought had died in his Subaru) and the local newspaper writer, read between the lines and let it go. Not that he worried overly much about his own decision, but it really didn't matter. Citizen arrests were legal in Missouri, and he supposed if three men wanted to hang out in a car watching a building all night, that was their choice.

"I can't squeeze any more into my car," Brad said at last. "It'll be tight as it is with these three."

"Shit," he said, then had an inspiration. "Wait a minute. Dorf drove Kyle's van home last night. Let's have him drive you all to Waterford in that. Kyle's in the hospital so he won't mind."

On hearing this, Bartie came to life. "What happened to Kyle?"

"Dorf Walkenhorst shot him," Nick said.

"Why would Dorf shoot my grandson?"

"Because he was trying to take off my head with a golf club."

"I'm confused."

"I'll tell you about it later."

"Nick, you there?" Brad detested three-way conversations more than anything but cross-dressers.

"Yeah, Chief, right here," Nick said. "Sorry about that. What do you think?"

The two agreed the idea sounded reasonable, and Bartie decided to accompany the growing group so he could visit Kyle.

*****

Dorf found the idea quite agreeable, since he didn't have to lace up his Always-Glo security guard shoes for the foreseeable future, and arrived at the station a few minutes after Nick had entered with Jerry Fillabag in cuffs.

The Caravan would seat eight adults comfortably and it seemed to Brad the only person missing from the jaunt was Phillip Andrew Thomas.

Dorf rode in the middle seat next to Bartie Grantz, while Will rode shotgun and the *L&O* lovers sat side-by-side in the rear of the van.

Chief Kocke waved to Nick as he pulled onto the highway and headed for Waterford, where one lost man would find his life again, hopefully, provided his mother would take him in.

Allen Frye was so wrapped up in emotion for Roseanne, what he faced in the courthouse had not registered. While Roseanne might have concerned herself, she did not. To her mind, sitting next to Allen was the only thought worth consideration.

Dorf, meanwhile, stood up pretty well to the barrage of questions put forth by the ancient Bartie. He sounds like a damn lawyer, the ex-security guard thought.

Halfway to the county seat, Bartie seemed to accept the situation and became pensive.

The old man wished his son had taken the responsibilities inherent with being a Guardian, for it was obvious Kyle's approach to Guardianship was improper. Bartie felt chagrin that he had not done a better job.

# Chapter 40

The following appeared on the front page of the *Newburn News* on June 25, 2004.

## *Guardians A Hoax?*

### By Phillip Andrew Thomas
### Senior Staff Writer

Most people in Newburn have heard of the Guardians, a group of vigilantes who have ostensibly protected the town since their inception on a hot summer day at The Newburn Bank.

But what many do not know is that most of what happened that day was exaggerated and details of the story were incorporated for the sake of building a legend.

According to Kyle Grantz, who was wounded during an altercation with police following a robbery at The Newburn Bank, the legend of the Guardians is nothing more than a long-lived game of "telephone."

How does he know? His grandfather's great-grandfather was one of two men involved in the thwarted bank robbery.

"They're full of crap and always have been," Grantz said. "The old guy got lucky. He and his friend sucker-punched those guys from behind with their walking sticks and they went down cold. They took the money and gave it back to the bank, and when they got back outside, the two were gone. They were hot and tired and just wanted to go home, but the people of this town treated them like soldiers just come back from the war."

Grantz went on to say that he had been interested in Guardian lore since he was a child, when his grandfather, Bartholomew, told him of the legend.

It was Kyle's father, Russell, who told him the truth of his heritage.

"Dad told me all about how grandpa was always trying to make it seem like the old man was a hero, but I don't believe it," Kyle said. "My dad told me they did attack the robbers, but not until after they had left the bank. The legend is that both of them were allowed to leave after they came around, and they were told to spread the word of the fate that would befall anyone who tried to rob The Newburn Bank. But they were gone before anyone talked to them. Supposedly, the mayor set aside the day for them and was going to name a street after them but he lost the election before he could do it."

When Bartie Grantz was asked about his grandson's assertions, he replied, "It doesn't matter what started it. Everyone lived in fear of bandits back then. Folks today can just call 911 and get help. Back then, the only help would have to come from Waterford and the sheriff didn't really like Newburn. But I'll tell you this: they believed what they did was right, and they never had regrets."

Unfortunately, the Newburn News was not established at the time of this incident, and the Waterford Courier did not have any record of it.

For all anyone knows, the events could have been completely fabricated.

Bartie Grantz vehemently dismisses that speculation. "The story was still being told when I was a kid and that was a long time ago," he said. "I don't believe my father and grandfather would have lied about something like that."

Kyle is not convinced. "I'm not going to say they made the whole thing up, but there's a lot less to it than people say."

What is known is that Kyle Grantz is facing assault charges for his alleged attack on Sgt. Nick Crawford, once he is released from Waterford Community Hospital.

Law enforcement officials refused to comment on the details of the attack.

Also charged in connection with the bank robbery . . .

*****

Brad Kocke was interested in spite of himself. He knew what much of the story was going to entail, and he'd heard quite a story from Bartie Grantz on the way to Waterford and back, with even more from Kyle at the hospital, and he still didn't know what to believe.

The main thing he cared about, however, was the fact that his own nightly ambitions (which he had sworn off) were not mentioned. Phillip had kept his word, which surprised the chief somewhat.

The chief sat alone in the office, settling into his MIC chair as the dull afternoon crawled past.

# Epilogue

As Chief Brad Kocke could have told him, Jerry Fillabag was doomed from the start. His arrogance undid him as he refused to deal with the district attorney, which drove her to push for the maximum; after two days of testimony, including star witness Max Irons, Jerry was found guilty on all counts and sentenced to three years in the Missouri Department of Corrections. His dreams of manufacturing a basketball championship fell apart faster than a Yugo.

A stroke of luck, if you believe in such things, befell Max Irons during the course of the trial, as Jerry Fillabag tried to shift responsibility by telling the judge that Max owned half the gym and was therefore guilty by association.

The judge was unmoved by the stratagem, but Max decided to investigate the claim and found that he was, on paper, half-owner of the gym. What had been an attempt to evade taxation turned into a nightmare for Jerry, as Max moved back into his place above the fitness center. He sought advice from Danielle Stone, who helped him reorganize the financial structure so he could draw a salary and keep it running.

Allen Frye, meanwhile, had reduced his charges via plea bargain, accepting a sentence of 30 days in the county jail for assault with a deadly weapon.

Roseanne came to see him every day and after a week of longing and worrying about her waiting for him, Allen made a special request. To his surprise, it was granted.

Nine days into his sentence, with Brian Fennigan and Todd Brown witnessing the events, along with the chief deputy and jailer, Allen Frye was married by the Reverend Pete Mitchell. In the make-shift chapel (the reception area of the county jail), Roseanne walked down the "aisle" humming the theme song from *Law & Order*.

Will was invited to the small ceremony but declined for a

couple reasons. The main reason was that he and his mom were traveling for a day of antiquing; besides, while he wished them no ill-will, he just wasn't ready to see her. His one goal in life at the moment was rebuilding the relationship with the only woman who had ever loved him, and he was looking forward to it.

*****

On the other side of the legal fence, Chief Brad Kocke let the events of that Monday roll off his back. Mayor Ted Keller blew some hot air over it but found no support among the council for much more than a tantrum. They had all heard about his encounter at the drugstore and found it to be very amusing; his ranting now was simply a way to save face.

Brad went to a special council meeting, abased himself in front of the mayor and that was that.

He returned to his MIC chair none the worse for wear.

His personal life improved immensely as he began seeing GiGi during every moment he wasn't on duty and even some when he was in uniform. Attending the weekly meeting of the Newburn Society for Compulsive Disorders was helping him as much as his time with GiGi, and the urge to inflict pain faded easier than he believed possible.

Sgt. Nick Crawford and Danielle Stone moved forward with their wedding plans, though they wouldn't be nearly as romantic as that held by Allen and Roseanne.

Danielle's mother was making a nuisance of herself trying to help, which nearly drove Nick to drink.

Instead he bit his tongue when forced to deal with her, and otherwise left them to their own vision for the nuptials.

With the termination of Allen Frye and the resignations of Brian and Todd, neither of whom knew they resigned, the department was in need of a third officer.

Despite the slow nature of the business in town, it was prudent to have another qualified officer on hand.

Over a beer a few nights after *the* day, Nick suggested bringing in Dorf Walkenhorst.

"Are you kidding?"

"Not at all," said Nick with a grin. "We know he can shoot and when it counted, he came down on the right side of the situation."

Nothing was decided that night but Dorf was hired four days later. Brad's logic was that nothing could be worse than the trio he was replacing.

*****

Lionel Leanman gained a new element in terms of business. Drunks love a good story, he knew, and the tale of how he stood up to Jerry Fillabag was often requested during happy hour.

Like the legend of the Guardians, however, it was likely to grow well out of proportion.

Evvie Fennigan, who had called Bartie but talked to Kyle and set about the chain of events, luxuriated every day in a new pair of nylons, compliments of the bundle of cash found beneath her kitchen table the night her home had been invaded. To her way of thinking, it was just reward for having her window ripped out of the wall, which had cost $92 to repair.

Edward Von Waterman III was sweating, and not in the presence of delicate collarbones. The state's bank examiners and a representative of the FDIC were in his office, asking him to explain the events of the robbery for the fifth time. His manipulation of the numbers was unraveling and by the end of the day, he would be facing federal fraud charges.

*****

Jeb Stuart finally realized his bovines had escaped, and with the help of his son, the five escapees were herded back through the broken fence, which continued to be broken for some time.

The grass, otherwise known as Pakistani tea, continued to sit in the back room of Esther's Warehouse of Drugs & Tea Emporium, which had been closed until further notice.

Not a great loss, since the only people who ever went in that room were Allen, Roseanne and the amigos.

*****

Despite his dismay and personal turmoil regarding his grandson, Bartie was adamant about protecting the role of the Guardians.

His own take on what happened may have been dismissed but he knew that he alone stood sentinel.

Kyle made a mockery of the responsibility and tried to use it for his own gain, and that could not be forgiven. His assault on a police officer was likewise reprehensible, but he was being punished for that crime, and Bartie did not wish to add insult to injury.

But in his heart, he knew that Kyle was a grandson in name only. His wounds would heal, but the gap between him and Bartie would remain like a missing tooth.

Wiping a tear absently, he grieved for the losses he'd encountered. In the old days, men were men and you knew where you stood. Even if the events had taken on a life of their own after the fact, Bartie would always respect his great-grandfather for standing up to the oppressors.

Now, he was alone and was the only one left that held to the true way. Evvie Fennigan knew of the history and had called him because of her desire to be a part of it, but Bartie knew she never could. Despite her feelings, she simply was not a *believer*, and part of the tears that lined his weathered face were for that loss, the one in which the code he'd grown up living was now a joke, plastered in the paper like a scandal.

Bartie sat in the rec room's only recliner, listening to the banter of his fellow residents and wondered what tomorrow would bring.